DOUBLE (TERRORIST) CELLS

*To Eileen
the wonderful
gardener!

Olwin Church,

The "clean, bean mystery
machine!"*

DOUBLE (TERRORIST) CELLS

Olive Church

iUniverse, Inc.

New York Lincoln Shanghai

Double (Terrorist) Cells

iUniverse, Inc.

For information address:
iUniverse, Inc.
2021 Pine Lake Road, Suite 100
Lincoln, NE 68512
www.iuniverse.com

ISBN: 0-595-28215-6

Printed in the United States of America

IN MEMORY OF

All those lost through the Attacks on America.

May we never again face terrorism, from American or foreign fanatics.

Contents

▼

PROLOGUE

▼

TERRORIST CELL NUMBER ONE

Associated Press: *Jerica Davidson is a Tree Hugger!*

"I don't see why the loggers have to cut down the pretty trees," she said, a timely quote that flew around the globe. The networks and cable television news shows picked it up, the newspapers and tabloids printed it. Because anything Jerica said or did was big news. Everybody knew she was the President and First Lady's only daughter.

President Dominic Alexander Davidson and his wife, Julia, had met at the University of Wyoming as students. Dom called North Dakota home, but he chose UW because of the excellent rodeo program. Back then Dominic was determined to make good on the rodeo circuit. Their daughter Jerica chose her parents' alma mater, and had just completed her freshman year. She was as naïve now as Dom had been back then. There's a saying about my home state, Dom had told Alison, his friend and landlady.

"Some day somebody will try to bring North Dakota out of the Nineteenth Century, but it will only come screaming and dragging its feet."

That pretty much described Jerica Davidson—naïve, home-grown. Also, since her father had been elected President of the United States and was sworn into office a few months earlier, pretty bouncy blond Jerica was even more sheltered. The Secret Service had vetted her sorority roommate, Callie Jenkins; also Callie's friends. Attending UW on scholarship, Callie came from Medicine Bow, a small village to the north of Laramie. She seemed okay. But that was before she got hooked on drugs and stopped bathing.

Instead of turning up in Washington, D.C. to be with her parents for the summer, Jerica had begged to stay in Wyoming. "The Chi Omega House is closed, but we can get an apartment for a couple of months." That was Callie's idea, but Jerica didn't bother explaining. She did agree to spending August with her parents, although in truth she wasn't that crazy about the nation's capitol city. Too big and busy. Anyhow, it was time she started growing up, learning how to get by on her own, Jerica insisted. Reluctantly, the President and First Lady relented. When they had met Callie back in the fall, she was a sweet young thing. Besides, Jerica had four Secret Service people watching over her.

*   *   *   *

"You sure Jerica doesn't suspect what we're up to?" Butch said to Callie now.

Callie gazed at him through slitted eyes. "How many times I gotta tell ya? Jerica is as naive as a new born lamb. We'll get her committed to our cause before we give her the real scoop. Once we blow up a logging operation and then brag around that it was the tree huggers who did it, it'll be too late for Jerica to back out. The media will make sure of that." Callie shifted in the passenger seat. She couldn't care less about trees. Born and raised in Wyoming, she'd seen plenty in the forests. No big deal.

From west of West Yellowstone in Montana, the pair had traveled in Butch's van the ninety miles north to Bozeman to shop. For weapons.

Then they returned south to pick up the rest of their arsenal; in Pocatello, Idaho, and in Rock Springs, Wyoming. Their circuitous route would draw few suspicions. This was hunting territory, after all, though not yet hunting season.

"Bunch a hicks. They won't think nuthin'," Butch said from behind the steering wheel of his nondescript tan van. To travel into the various towns, he had washed and trimmed his long, dishwater-blond hair. The biggest concession he made, though, was in removing his nose earring.

The Secret Service knew that Butch Edwards was hanging around Callie and Jerica, but there was not much information to be gleaned about the rugged chap from Wisconsin. What nobody knew, neither Callie nor Jerica, was that no matter where Butch traveled and no matter what he did, he'd left little if any trail for anybody to follow, Secret Service or otherwise. He had no credit cards, no bank accounts, no record of military service nor any criminal offenses and thus no fingerprints on file. As far as the authorities knew, Butch was just some hick from the sticks, a former logger from out of state. The important thing about Butch, Butch figured, was that he knew how to blow up things. He'd been the one assigned to set the dynamite charges to blow out stumps the loggers didn't want left behind them when they pulled out of an area. What his former bosses didn't know was that Butch, like a pyrotechnic, was keen on the action. He moved from logging to creating bombs from Internet recipes and blowing up all kinds of things. Nobody knew about that either. It was just for fun.

Until he got caught. Not by the cops, not by his employer, but by *The Man*— a guy who stayed in the shadows, unseen. Butch didn't understand the guy's motivation or overall agenda and didn't care. He was hooked on bombs like Callie was hooked on marijuana, coke, and now heroin. Whatever the guy's agenda, it suited Butch just fine. Because *The Man* blackmailed Butch into organizing not one, but two ecoterrorist teams.

"I want you operating in two places simultaneously—Wisconsin and Wyoming," said *The Man*. "So you've got to recruit two cells. Whenever you blow up something in Wyoming, the other cell must blow up something else in Wisconsin. We're protesting the logging of timber. With double ecoterrorist cells, see, we can make the press and the authorities believe we've got a huge and powerful nation-wide organization. Got it?"

Butch got it. Made him no never mind why. But when the media labeled the First Miss a *tree hugger*, he supposed *The Man's* half-baked scheme made sense. There always seemed to be protesters coming out of the woodwork to demonstrate against something.

The money was good, damn good. Butch was so excited about the assignment, he'd nearly forgotten to ask about payment. Now his pockets were stuffed with greenbacks, plus he had another cash stashed in a coffee can on the top shelf of his closet.

"I got an idea," said Callie, beside him. She lit a joint and took a deep drag. "Let's blow up something. For practice."

"Like what?" Butch peered at the foul-smelling woman who hated baths. This was new. While Callie was at the Chi Omega House, she was clean and tidy. But then she'd got hooked on drugs and everything about her changed, from attending university classes to how she behaved and spoke. Lucky for her she'd checked out of the sorority. Had they kicked her out of the house, the Secret Service would have gotten suspicious for sure.

They were approaching Wamsutter, a small cluster of ramshackle buildings sitting beneath the glaring sun of the Red Desert, a flat wind-blown area featuring red sand between Rock Springs and Rawlins. Callie was right. Butch too was itching to wreak havoc. That was his mission, as passed on to him from *The Man*; the man with no name and no other identity, back in Milwaukee. The "practice"

Callie suggested didn't interest Butch; he had plenty of bomb experience behind him. For th'hell of it, that was different. "Sure, we can do that." He braked to take the exit off Interstate 80.

"How 'bout the post office? This berg surely has one."

"Naw. That's a federal offense. We'll do a gas station." He drove over the pot-holed graveled street and pulled up at the self-service pump. Nobody around. Shrugging, Butch climbed into the back of the van to emerge with a bunch of dynamite sticks tied together. "Crude, but they'll do. No time to build a proper bomb."

Callie sat placidly in the passenger seat, chain smoking weed. He reached through the driver's side window for her toke. "Gimme that."

"Huh? You said you weren't into any a this stuff."

"You dumb broad, I'm not. I wanna light the dynamite. Hurry, afore somebody shows up." He climbed back into the van, lit the fuse on one of the sticks, and tossed the bundle out the window. Then he gunned it.

He pulled away fast, but not far. Boom! The conflagration commenced. Butch's dynamite went off and the gasoline pumps exploded.

"Hey, man, this is better than Fourth of July fireworks," Callie said, delivering her statement in a flat, emotionless tone.

Butch parked a block away. He wanted a front-row seat to cover the aftermath. Then he had another thought—it wouldn't do to be caught sitting out in the open where he could be suspect. Better move it. A diner down the road on the other side would do. Truckers and locals poured out of the café to gawk. Pickup trucks paused on the dusty road. Nobody did anything but stare. Momentarily paralyzed, they could have been Lot's wife, turned to pillars of salt.

The pair of disheveled, road-weary ecoterrorists walked nonchalantly into the dimly lit combination bar and diner that reeked of stale beer and greasy fries. They took a seat next to the window at a Formica-topped table with chrome legs and old chairs with ripped plastic seats. The chairs and table wobbled. They were alone until the waitress returned, followed by the bartender.

"Too bad the sheriff's not around," Butch overheard the waitress say.

"At least nobody was kilt," replied the bartender.

Callie ordered coffee from the fat waitress with the big beehive hairdo straight out of the sixties, who avoided eye contact with the foul-smelling young woman. Another couple of booms, as the underground gas tanks exploded. Again the service people rushed out the door, to join the diners who hadn't as yet returned. This time the gathering buzzed like a beehive as truckers used their mobile phones and tourists jabbered into cellphones.

"Guess we're not gonna get no service here," Butch said, rising and hauling Callie after him out of the empty diner."Come on, Babe."

"But I wanted coffee."

"We gotta get home with this stuff." He meant their cache of ammunition.

Butch kept his mouth shut as he drove, staying well below the speed limit. He wished Callie would shut up. She rattled on, as usual, about how much she hated Joan Vicente, the University of Wyoming professor who had flunked her in communications.

When Callie Jenkins left campus as a result of the failing grade, and without checking out, Bud, her main squeeze at the time, followed suit. Later, when she dropped Bud for Butch, Bud didn't bat an eye or lift a finger. Quickly Butch came up with the cause. Their carrot-top buddy, Bud Andrews, was after bigger fish these days.

"Yeah?" suggested Callie, with no inflection at all in her voice.

"Sure. Your roommate."

"The President's daughter? Get real. What chance would Bud have with Jerica?"

"Right. The First Miss. Isn't that what you call the Davidson dame?"

Driving along in silence, the babe with the bad odor smoking pot beside him, Butch let his mind drift to the President's daughter and what he knew of her. Jerica Davidson, an attractive blonde, clone of the First Lady in the looks department, eighteen, vulnerable and innocent, a budding rose about to bloom. Easily influenced, too, looked like. Especially right now, with Callie laying their exciting adventures and temptations on the doorstep of the protected girl. Callie's role— keep hinting to Jerica that she could be part of it, if she would throw in with their bunch.

Butch Edwards, their leader, directed Callie and Bud how to do it—throw out the lines, reel in the pretty fish. "Keep it cool. Don't tell Jerica too much about our operations." Not that involving her was his idea. That came straight from his boss.

"Ah," Bud said back then, his eyes lighting up. "Tantalize her with tidbits."

Butch had correctly interpreted the gleam in Bud's eyes to mean he'd like to get in Jerica's pants. Some coup, lay the President's chickadee.

As for himself, he was bedding Callie, but he had no burning need, not like Bud. "Put that thing out, Babe," Butch barked now. "You're stinkin' up the whole van."

Butch Edwards, mid-thirties, dishwater blonde like Callie; never been to college, never wanted to. Bunch a nonsense, he figured, while strutting his stuff and bragging about his ecoterrorist experiences to Callie and Bud. Butch couldn't wait for the action to begin in earnest.

Passing by Rawlins and occasionally glancing in the rearview mirror for a tell-tale cop car, Butch continued traveling east on Interstate 80 toward Laramie and a reunion with the other pair. Of course they wouldn't tell Jerica about the havoc they'd wreaked in Wamsutter. That's what *The Man*, their boss, kept calling it: "wreaking havoc." Innocent Jerica knew nothing of their ecoterrorist plot, with their mediocre bombings serving as rehearsal to something really grand. *The Man* had yet to reveal their primary targets.

No sign of the highway patrol or any other cops. Butch relaxed. Dry, hot August, the grass turning golden. Some ranchers were harvesting, putting up hay to feed their critters over the winter. Elk Mountain loomed beyond the highway to the south. The ribbon of road unraveled beneath them. Butch thought it boring. Lost to the mid-western punk hailing from Milwaukee was the beauty of wind-swept vistas dotted with evergreen and the snowcapped peaks of the Snowy Range rising majestically to the south.

"So? Roll down the window. Why're you such a saint all of a sudden?"

Butch fumed, but he let out the smoke through his open window. He was anxious to see Bud's eyes pop when he saw their purchases and heard about their attack on the gas station. The dirty old van was stuffed with ammunition and guns and materials to construct crude bombs. The ecoterrorist team, bent on protesting the harvesting of trees, was well financed. Whatever *The Man's* connections, he sure came with big bucks.

Butch wasn't all that interested in what *The Man* called a worthy cause. His own brothers were the ones committed. Still, Butch liked to blow up things. He wished he'd been in on the Oklahoma City bombing, or got a chance to help execute the attacks on the World Trade Center and the Pentagon. As for flying any of those planes on some stupid suicide mission, forget that. The youngest Edwards brother was no zealous martyr. He did have a burning desire, though, to see his name in the news and his face on TV as the perpetrator. Butch silently crossed his fingers, while hoping he too would be assigned to hit a big-time target.

Man, right now Butch was feeling like a kid in a toy store with an unlimited budget. He glanced in the back of the van, making a mental inventory: AK47s, Uzis, automatics, sub-machine guns—the best he could lay hands on from Russia and Israel. The Uzi eagle pistol, the newly imported CZ-50, chambered for a .32 ACP. The Kel-Tec P-11 in 9 mm, Smith & Wesson's Model 686 revolvers in .357 Magnum. One of Butch's favorites was a 47-ounce Colt Python. He had flame throwers, too. Also fertilizer and kerosene, along with nails too numberless to count; nitroglycerine, TNT, and even black powder. Personally Butch liked the old Molotov cocktail. Pour gasoline in a bottle, stuff a rag in the neck, light it, throw it. Simple. And letter bombs.

"You want me t'make a letter bomb, Callie? You can send it to Professor Vicente."

Callie brightened, though her tone varied not one iota. "Hey, that's a thought. I'd sure like to see the bitch without her fingers and those long painted nails. Serve the dame right for flunking me."

"The professor's office is in Hoyt Hall, right?" Butch said. "That's a coincidence. Because, for some reason of his own, the boss has already made Hoyt Hall one of our early targets. Me, I'd like to get the small stuff over with. Move on somewheres else."

"Yeah, man. Cool," she mumbled, belching. Without another word, Callie Jenkins, former sorority sister to First Miss Jerica Davidson, dropped off to sleep.

CHAPTER 1

▼

ABOARD AIR FORCE ONE

Air Force One lifted off from F. E. Warren Air Base in Cheyenne, with Alison Morissey aboard—minus her own hair! Landlady to Dominic long before he was President, Alison had remained good friends all these years to both Dom and Julia.

"My hair will grow in some day," Ali told Julia, who peered at Alison from big round cerulean blue eyes. The First Lady knew about the forest fire that had taken Alison's hair, but fortunately not her life. "I've bought several wigs," Alison explained, inviting Julia's opinion of her present version, so much like her own short salt-and-pepper hair.

The two old friends talked fashions awhile before Julia excused herself, saying the President's Aide would be along with coffee shortly. Left alone in the lounge, Alison leaned back her head on the plush sofa and closed her eyes.

Her daughter had come over the hill from Laramie, home of the University of Wyoming, to see her mother off. Professor Joan Vicente traveled so often providing consulting services to corporations. Alison couldn't help worrying that something awful might happen to her only daughter. However, nowadays she'd hatched a whole new set of worries. Since the attacks on America, Ali also fretted over the safety of her "surrogate son," the U. S. President.

That's what the international press had dubbed Alison Morissey, and her, his *Surrogate Mother,* not understanding, perhaps, that she was no more than a decade older than Dom or that even at the tender age when they had met, she could take him under her wing. He'd roomed with her, called her a friend. She'd nurtured his ego, turned him in the direction of future success; meaning that first he needed self-confidence, to believe in himself. With Alison's help, Dom did. He scored big on the University of Wyoming's rodeo team, met and married the lovely Julia, returned to North Dakota and eventually ran for the U.S. Senate. But he and Julia never forgot Alison Morissey, nicknamed "Ali."

"Coffee, Ma'am?" mumbled a swarthy-skinned man with black hair and matching mustache. "I'm Mark Prescott." Unsmiling, he stared at Alison from piercing black beady eyes. He appeared ferocious.

Startled, Alison jumped up, knocking into the Aide's tray and sloshing coffee down the front of his navy blue blazer. "Oh, dear me, I'm so awful."

Grabbing handkerchief, dabbing at the young man's front, muttering half-formed apologies, Alison gazed again into Mark Prescott's eyes. They blazed with resentment, even hatred, she was certain. Jerking back, a small hand flying to her bosom, Alison dropped her glance. As the Aide whirled and left the lounge, she stared at his straight back, his stiff marching gait. Reminded her of Nazi Gestapo.

As far as Ali knew, she'd never been politically incorrect in her life. Yet with all she'd read and all she'd viewed about the Taliban and Islamic Jihad, "Holy War," against Christianity, the West, and Americans in particular, she'd been afraid. She was paranoid. Prescott could be an Arab sleeper, assigned to take out the President, her Dom!

She knew it! She'd stumbled onto a thug. Right here on the President's airplane, employed on Dom's own staff. No mistaking the venom in those piercing black eyes that seemed to race up her body and then down again. Prescott obviously resented her invitation to fly with the President. Possibly because she'd scoped him, could foil his plans.

Omigod, could the Aide actually mean to do harm to the President? What if she had inadvertently uncovered an assassin? A plot to murder both Dom and Julia. Though barely a few years older than the youngish president, Alison could have been a mother tigress hovering over her cub. With the terror she felt sending the blood to pump through her veins, she could see herself actually ripping out Mark Prescott's heart!

That the President had many protectors—many agencies and bureaus and Secret Service personnel to look after him—cut no ice. Irrational, paranoid, Alison could readily empathize with those mothers and sisters of men still missing in action. Sometimes, when nobody would listen, you had to jump into the fray all by yourself. Still, she wasn't alone, and there must be someone who would listen to her, even though her fears were based on nothing but gut-wrenching intuition. These conflicting and debilitating emotions roiled round inside Alison's head and heart.

Meanwhile, she already felt so guilty, for another reason—leaving home against her husband's wishes. With Randy out of town, Alison could have been pondering how to prop up her tortuous marriage, that without Divine intervention seemed destined to go straight down the toilet. Or she could have been baking bread and casseroles, ready for Hubby Randy's return.

Instead of hovering over the stove, of tending to home and hearth, here she was, flying off into the blue with the President of the United States. And that wasn't all. Now she was contemplating a terrorist attack or an assassination plot on her Dom. On the other hand, Alison could have reminded her cantankerous husband that this wouldn't be the first time she'd had a premonition of trouble. Call it a gut feeling, a woman's intuition.

Detective Walt Fletcher, out home in Cheyenne, could have spoken up for Alison. He knew that although she sometimes appeared the absentminded dingbat, it was only because her mind was often elsewhere. Her senses alert, she seemed able to pick up on the nuances signifying trouble that passed straight over other people's heads. Detective Fletcher and the Mayor concurred, but even the public ceremony honoring Alison for saving the banking community did nothing to jolt Randy from his belief that his wife was a nut. When her concentration focused on a single problem or threat, all consciousness of ordinary life, including her husband's personal needs, seemed to fly straight out the window. That's what Randy said to Peter, too; Colonel Peter Schwartzkopf, husband to Lisa, Ali's best friend and cousin. It was Peter who reminded Randy that it was Alison who'd jumped in to thwart a fraudulent art scheme and heist. Randy objected. "She could have been killed!" Didn't matter, Alison would do it again, because that time too she'd set her heart on saving a friend.

What a treat this trip with the President and Julia was; at first—before running into Prescott. The occasion, a formal state dinner with one of Kyrgyzstan's cabinet ministers and his wife, Magda. The latter was an old (but not necessarily good) friend to Alison Morissey. The President said that Magda refused to come to America unless Alison too was invited to the White House. No problem. She and the Davidsons were very good friends from way back.

Alison's husband had refused to come, another blight on her otherwise perfect tomato of a day. Randolph said he was heading to Canada for a long awaited fishing trip. No phones, no people other than his buddy, no civilization. Just Randolph and Ralph playing macho, pitting themselves against nature. Grizzlies, too, perhaps.

Ali had yet to admit her marriage was a failure. In May, daughter Joan had sent her off to a seminar on "Improving Relationships." Alison gritted her teeth. Might have helped, had Randy been with her. As it was, the cranky old fool continued playing thorn stuck in her side. Alison missed the closeness and passion they'd once felt for each other. What th'hell was she to do about him?

"I don't care about Eurasia or any of those little 'stan' countries any more. I'm retired," said short little Randy, former petroleum geologist, to his even shorter, itty-bitty wife in the wig, when she told him about the White House invitation. "Besides, Kyrgyzstan never did have enough oil to worry about."

A mineral-rich country squashed between China, Kazakhstan, Uzbekistan, and Tajikistan, Kyrgyzstan had hydroelectric but not petroleum power, the Morisseys had learned early on; back when they were in the area visiting countries that did have oil—Muslim dominated countries, some of which were under the Taliban thumb back then; the Taliban, who believed in keeping women down and, worse, in committing terrorist acts.

Long before the western world worried over or even knew much about the Taliban, Alison and her female cousins were chairing fund raisers on behalf of the beleagured women beneath the heel of the male-dominated Taliban regime. Then the terror they promulgated against women and captives came home to America.

At the Morisseys' first stop, Alison met Magda. Mrs. Oblasty fanaticized about another world, one in which she would be crowned empress. Meanwhile, she told Alison, she whiled away the hours plotting how to get her husband elected president in the tiny country that was smaller than Dominic Davidson's home state of North Dakota.

On the plane now, Ali mused. With her Randy beyond shouting distance, she could hardly confess to him her fears that the Davidsons were in mortal danger or prod him into taking action. Randy would ridicule her. Shivering with fear, Alison felt so alone, so isolated. She couldn't just sit here twiddling her thumbs. She must do something, tackle this challenge all by herself. In her imagined debate with her husband, a quotation popped to mind, the one Randy often quoted from Leavitt: *There is a time in the life of every problem when it is big enough to see, yet (still) small enough to solve.*

Warn the Davidsons? No, not yet. Like Randy, they would laugh at her. Distracted from her irrational fears by the arrival of the First Lady, Alison took a deep breath. Like many Americans following the attacks on America, she was paranoid, easily frightened, especially by dark-skinned people who might be foreign terrorists, even "sleepers" awaiting the call to wreak havoc and mass destruction on America and Americans. Another breath, so she could speak.

Seated on the long plush royal blue couch near the President's office and conference room, Julia and Alison chatted, like the old friends they were. Julia wore a vanilla voile dress by Rena Lange and Ali a cotton print dress with purple and lavender flowers by Chloe. The two ladies sat side by side on the deep, cushiony sofa. A faint aroma of mulberry and pine sweetened the air.

Mrs. Davidson spoke of her daughter. The tall, slender blonde with chignon missed Jerica so much, she admitted. Alison vacillated between making false assurances and sharing the qualms her own daughter Joan felt about the First Miss's friends.

Just then Prescott stuck his head in from next door. Alison caught him in a scowl that quickly switched to honey-soaked smile when Julia turned to him.

"Yes, Mark?"

"The President is on the phone with Jerica. I thought you'd want to talk to her." Again Julia left Alison alone. Again Ali's paranoia engulfed her.

Another cause for thinking the planet was shrinking—the more Alison thought about Mark Prescott, the more she thought she recognized him. She'd seen so many Arabs on television, the similarity must simply be coincidence. Oh, dear, she couldn't bear to falsely finger the chap simply because he looked like he called the Middle East home.

Think again, Ali, she chided self. Could he be Mediterranean, perhaps Mafioso? Her own family history came to mind to send her into a quandary of confusion. Yet some of the men on her clan's paternal side came with a similar look. It was Granddad Vicente, if she remembered right, who had arrived on American shores from Sicily. In searching the family history, Alison had learned that over the past fifteen hundred years or so, the Sicilians had been conquered by and their blood commingled with many Mediterranean and Middle Eastern people. Conclusion: some of her own uncles and male cousins also had Prescott's "look."

By the time Julia returned Alison was staring appreciatively at the vivid splashy wall paintings by recently discovered abstract artist, T. J. Jordan, out of Independence, Missouri. While in Vermont Ali had bought several, as gifts, and also for herself and Randy, though the paintings cost the earth. Now Ali and Julia admired the lovely abstracts together. It was Alison who had alerted the Davidsons to the artist's budding promise. Julia said she and Dom had commissioned another half-dozen for the White House.

Still standing, Julia changed the subject by suggesting a tour. Alison had toured Air Force One before, but now she agreed to take another peek around, mainly because she wanted to grab this opportunity to analyze Mark Prescott's actions. He, not a Secret Service man, would accompany them throughout the plane.

While Julia talked to members of the press corps, Ali watched Mark closely. She glared at him when his back was turned. She felt like a little girl, biting her tongue to keep from sticking it out at him. Suddenly she gasped, for she was absolutely certain she had spotted a blade, the light glinting off a dagger or a thin knife.

What on earth should she do? Tackle him? Another quick glance; nothing to see. A trick of lighting, perhaps? Gnawing at a fingernail, Ali nervously followed the pair.

Behind the President's work center was his private sleeping quarters with bath, which he shared with Julia. Separate twin beds, they were also used as couches. Dom's, though, stayed made up, in preparation for an impromptu nap.

Next to the President's office and conference room ranged the narrow lounge, hardly more than a walkway, where Alison expected to spend most of the trip. She spotted quarters for the Secret Service staff, the press, and for the sophisticated global communications center. They skipped touring the work areas of galley, flight deck, storage and operational systems.

Plenty of commotion, all manner of staff: Secret Service people scowling, conferring, plotting maneuvers and rotations, all designed to protect her Dom and his Julia. Communications people staffing the computers and phone systems; transmitting and receiving data from around the world via satellites; sifting, sorting, analyzing, summarizing. News the President could use.

Back in the lounge again and alone, Ali closed her eyes to think. Her mind mentally turned pages in her family history book, glommed onto this image and that statistic. And, just that fast, her brain switched tracks; from fingering Prescott as a Muslim terrorist to perceiving him as a Mafia hit man.

Either way, her Dom was in danger!

She must start somewhere. Little gray cells hopping about, they landed on Aunt Nasty, a wise old woman among the clan. Aunty might listen.

Randy claimed Alison was a will-o'-the-wisp, a flibberty-gibbet. He insisted his little wife was a victim of Attention Deficit Disorder, ADD. Instead of focusing on whatever he was ranting on about, her mind wandered. Instead of paying attention to her cooking, she burned herself, cut herself. She made messes, spilling stuff all over her clothes. With fright for Dom threatening to overwhelm her, this time was no different.

Instead of flying *off the handle*, Randy's phrase, to rush about the airplane, her mind spun nearly out of control. She had to do something.

The process of elimination her next step, Alison reached for the phone. She would call her aunt in Mexico. Old Aunty Nasturtium knew, and knew about, everybody in their extended clan. For one thing, Prescott might even be a distant relation. If Aunty didn't know Mark, if there was no way to prove he was Sicilian, then he could be an Arab.

She must learn the truth before she made a fool of herself. Before it was too late.

Just as the connection clicked through, an obvious fact shot to the surface of Alison's brain. No call made from or received into the Presidential plane would surely go unmonitored, not unless Dom himself decreed complete privacy. She'd better be careful what she said.

Banalties bursting from her lips and then quickly buried, Alison shot her putt quickly across the goal line. "Aunt Nasturtium, is cousin Nasty with you?"

Ali should have phrased her query differently because a long waterfall of chit-chat spilled over the dam of Nasty One's chatter before Alison could interrupt."Never mind, Aunty," she added hurriedly. "I don't want to talk to Nasty Two right now. Just keep her there." Suddenly she had another thought. Instead of pursuing this fruitless phone conversation, why not hop on down there? Of course. Great idea. Out of her mouth burst the seed of her next move. "Forget this call. We'll talk when I get there. Guess what, I'm coming down to visit you in a couple of days. If that's okay."

A big decision, made on impulse. She would travel to Mexico. No matter how much Randy objected, the upcoming trip made perfect sense to Alison. After all, her husband was the first to propose the notion.

Randy had suggested, albeit with a mouth full of sarcasm, that while she was out knocking around the country so irresponsibly, she might as well take in Mexico to visit kin. With this Mark Prescott business, Alison concluded that of course she must pursue her husband's sarcastic suggestion. Of course he would be furious. Later, though, he might understand. Especially if she managed to save the President from death!

That he could be murdered momentarily did not occur to her. Not aboard Air Force One, of course not. The terrorists, including Mark, would not try to take out Dom aboard the crowded plane. She had time to stop them, to find out more, to gather *intelligence*, just as if she were a CIA operative!

Next stop, San Miguel de Allende. Her fears for the President beating her head all out of whack, Alison could think of no other alternatives at the moment. She must get the word from the horse's mouth. Aunty knew all.

On the phone with Nasturtium, or *Nasty One* as she was nicknamed, Ali wanted so badly to ask about Prescott, uncover what the Nasties, mother and daughter, knew. But she dare not mention his name and especially her fears for the President over this line. Anybody could be listening—Mark, or a fellow thug. If Prescott was a plant, a hit man, he must surely be cooperating with others. One man alone could not accomplish the next to impossible—take out the President of the United States!

Alison politely asked how Nasturtium was getting on. Her Aunt replied caustically: "As Robert Frost put it, *In three words I can sum up everything I've learned about life. It goes on.*" Ali broke off when she saw Mark peer in. She closed her eyes, feigning sleep. The last thing she wanted to do was get bombarded with the Aide's conversation.

Alone, with nothing but the low hum of the flying plane, Alison thought Dom might be working or resting. If he wanted her company, he'd join her. She wanted so badly, though, to check on the President herself. Make sure he was okay.

Dominic Davidson, an Abe-Lincoln look-alike, had come to appear as haggard as the Civil War President. Tall, slender Dom with dark wavy hair, thick eyebrows, chiseled jaw and cheekbones and, nowadays, a lined face above a short, well-trimmed beard. So many problems the President faced, from ongoing hot spots in Eurasia to the drug war at home; from the continuing threats of international terrorism to the domestic issues of social and health programs, education, and, as always, balancing the budget.

Carl Crosby, one of the President's speechwriters, peered in and Alison motioned him to join her on the couch. They had met back in Vermont a few months earlier. With tea and scones arriving in his wake, they curled up to visit now. In Carl's hand he held a book, *From Freedom to Slavery*, by Gerry Spence, purportedly one of America's greatest trial lawyers and a Wyomingite.

Tall, skinny, strawberry blond, and pale, Crosby reminded Ali of a thermometer because every time he got nervous or upset the blood rushed to his neck and straight up over his face to the neckline that met cowlick. Then the blood, or his thermometer-look, would promptly drop away.

Ali asked Carl about Spence's book. Jerica had recommended it to him. Both the President's daughter and the author were into this business of tree hugging, Carl said.

"If you want to understand tree hugging, read Gerry Spence," Carl said, unsmiling. "Also, if you want beautiful writing, read Gerry Spence. He can produce such a rhythm with words, almost like a poet." He flipped open a page. "Listen to this, Alison: *We say, poetically, that only God can make a tree and then destroy whole forests to make toilet paper.* Spence also reminds us that it was Justice William O. Douglas of the United States Supreme Court who argued, vainly, that *trees have standing to bring* (their own) *lawsuit.*"

Ali liked Carl, or perhaps she pitied him. He reminded her of the gangly, acne-scarred Dom Davidson when he'd come as a youth to board with her during the summer between semesters while enrolled at the University of Wyoming. Ali was very young, herself, with a small daughter, Joan. Now Dom's daughter called UW her academic home.

Yes, Carl knew and liked Jerica. "Innocent, naïve kid, though. I'm afraid the Davidsons have protected her too much."

"Innocent, naïve?" Ali smiled. "Sounds familiar."

Carl blushed, turning into a thermometer. "You mean me, right? A guy can grow up fast nowadays."

"Girls, too."

Ali needed to talk to somebody. Carl? Why not. Apparently he was trustworthy. Leaning forward, sipping cold tea, she confessed her fears for the President's life.

At first Crosby looked aghast. Then his thermometer moved into full gear. Embarrassed, he meant to challenge her.

So she told him about the blade, the knife she had spotted in Mark's hand. Hidden beneath the edge of his jacket.

Although polite, an arched eyebrow suggested skepticism. Carl hesitantly suggested she could have been seeing things. "Probably just a letter opener. Nothing more deadly than that."

So this was what would happen if and when she shared her fears with anybody in authority. Pass it off with some excuse. Look at her like she was crazy. The White House must get so many threats, so many crank calls and even genuine concerns shoved at them. Easy to disbelieve. Oh, dear.

Just then Prescott came in, scowling and carrying a mug of coffee. Silent, snarling, he looked meaner than ever. Alison's heart took a nose dive. Could be paranoia, she chided herself. Yet her feelings for Dominic were typical of any mother, or even an older sister. Her determination to protect Dom, despite those officially assigned to do just that, sent her brain fleeing from any sense of reason. Perspiration burst from every pore.

How on earth could she convince the President's speechwriter, much less anybody else, that she had more reasons than a possible knife for suspecting Mark of plotting against the President? Hardly any time left, as they were due to land shortly. With Mark glued to her and Carl, her last chance was gone.

Just then through the open doorway, she spied Dom at his desk. Ali couldn't hear, but she lipread the President's one-sided conversation.

"Terrorists!" she whispered. To Carl, she added, "That's what the President said on the phone."

Mark smirked.

CHAPTER 2

▼

MAKING MISCHIEF IN WYOMING

Randy hadn't gone to Canada, as he'd told his wife. He was holed up in a log cabin in the Snowy Range Mountains above Centennial, forty or so miles west of Laramie. Pacing the wood-planked floor of the small cabin and pulling at his thinning hair, he wasn't worried about staring down the throat of an attacking grizzly bear or getting eaten by a mountain lion.

Randolph Morissey had more serious problems facing him. How could he ever admit to Alison that he had lost her fortune, her inheritance? The secret trip he had made to Billings to check into the big Montana medical center had revealed the truth of his suspicions. Cancer! Two months he had at most.

Trembling, Randy reached for the heavy pewter coffeepot simmering on the back of the potbelly stove. With shaking hands he poured himself a cup of the steaming brew, its fragrance tantalizing his taste buds. Lifting the scarred tin cup to his lips, he burned his mouth and tongue. "Damn it," he muttered, an excuse to refocus his ire and frustration.

Randy suspected that his little Ali would have preferred a more demonstrative lover. That wasn't his way. He went for more tangible evidence to show his enduring love. He had meant to double his wife's fortune and his own savings, by investing in some highly speculative stocks—the Russian and the Brazilian funds, among them. Instead, he had lost everything. He'd only wanted to take care of his little darling. Instead, when he died, soon, very soon, Alison would be destitute. He couldn't imagine how she would manage.

Granted, he'd been irritable lately. Everything and everybody made him crazy. He was ill, dammit. But he wasn't about to tell his wife. He couldn't take the pity, the hovering. Meanwhile, if he was extra critical and demanding, it was only because he wanted to teach her how to cope. She'd have to, soon enough.

*   *   *   *

In Laramie, Jerica managed to elude her tormentors. Caroline and Jose were assigned the protection duty, while the other Secret Service team was off duty. But Jerica had been so good lately, that the young woman with the cornrows, and the short, square-shaped man with the accent had both grown lax in their surveillance

"She ought to appreciate us more," complained Caroline to her partner. "We're only here to protect her."

Jose was less trusting. "Got to watch her. No telling what mischief that gal is dreaming up. If not Jerica, then Callie."

*   *   *   *

"I feel like I'm in prison," Jerica wailed to her roommate.

"Why put up with it?" Callie replied. Any excuse was good enough. She needed to get out of their small apartment, go find a fix. The four walls were closing in on her. Literally, Callie believed, as she lay on her back watching the ceiling descend, the walls waver. She lifted her head. "Let's split, kid."

"Take a bath, first, Callie, and I'm game."

Sticking out her tongue in disgust, Callie slopped through a careless sponge bath. No soap, though.

Past midnight. Callie said she figured the Secret Service pair should be asleep by now. The two girls crawled through a window and tiptoed down the metal fire escape. They hid in the alley behind the garbage cans to see if their escape was noted. Then, hunched low, they scampered out to the street.

Their tiny efficiency apartment perched over a store, it faced the railroad tracks off a back alley downtown. From there it wasn't far to Callie's destination. When they had traversed the viaduct leading into West Laramie, it was no more than a couple of blocks to Bud's Bar.

Callie didn't make a connection and Jerica didn't have any fun. The bar soon closed and they walked home again, silent and morose. Callie was especially irritable. She badly needed a fix.

CHAPTER 3

▼

ABOARD AIR FORCE ONE

Alison resisted making small talk with Prescott. She sipped her tea and stared down her front. She fidgeted, pleating and unpleating her skirt.

After listening to Mrs. Morissey's suspicions, Crosby didn't speak to Mark either. Carl wasn't that good at pretense or hiding his feelings. So the trio just sat there, staring at the floor, or nothing. Not talking. Fidgeting.

Carl Crosby said he needed to polish the President's latest speech. He left. To Prescott, Alison excused herself and reached for the phone. She wanted to call home, talk to cousin Lisa. Naturally Lisa, on the other end when the connection was made, fretted that something was wrong.

"Of course not, dear. I called to chat. How's everybody?"

If Lisa Schwartzkopf thought it odd for Ali to be calling Cheyenne from Air Force One, she didn't say. Instead she launched into an account of various clan members. Alison, Lisa, the Nasties and all their brothers were *double cousins* because their fathers, named for U.S. Presidents, were brothers who'd married their mothers, named for flowers, who were sisters. From their Irish-Welsh maternal side, there came the girls' short stature, the Nasties' red hair and balding crowns, Lisa's fair complexion and blond hair, and all the doubles' hearing impairment. At gatherings of the clan you heard a lot of shouting and queries of

"Huh?" "What?" "Speak up!" From their French-Sicilian paternal side, came Alison's olive-hued skin and brunette hair, and the men's round bellies.

Alison and Lisa were the same age, born within an hour of each other, which was another reason, Lisa claimed, they were also best friends and soul mates, like two ova in a fallopian tube. Alison wished Lisa and her husband, Colonel Peter, were with her now. They were such a comfort.

By taking sidelong glances at Prescott, Alison watched the Arab, or whatever he was. He appeared annoyed, probably with her gossiping over an official phone, or with her in general. Finally, he set down his mug and rose to leave. "Got work to do for the President," he harumped importantly.

"Lisa," Ali interrupted her cousin's lengthy story about Hepzibah Vicente, the family's centenarian-in-law, "the reason why I called…."

"You couldn't talk freely before? I suspected you had good reason for this call, but were unable to speak your mind…."

"Quick, Lisa, before he returns."

"Who?"

"Never mind. Lisa, dear, do you emember the family album we unearthed from our Sicilian side of the family? Somewhere in there was an old sepia photo. Taken in or near Taormina. One of our Vicente kin was standing with a group of strangers. Do you recall any of those people?"

"Of course." Lisa, efficient and organized as an old paper file cabinet, regurgitated the facts like a pregnant Vicente woman regularly upchucking with morning sickness. "Alberto Vicente, a third cousin on our grandfather's side. Still lives in Sicily. You and I will be traveling over there soon to meet him. Right? The trip's still on, isn't it?"

"Yes, but that's not why I'm calling. Who were the people with Alberto?"

"You mean that bunch of short, dark-complected, apple-shaped men with the slicked-back, black hair and beady eyes? They're members of the Pesci clan, Alison. The powerful New Jersey and Brooklyn-based 'family,' if you get my meaning."

"Ah, so that's it." Ali's voice dropped to a whisper. "Not Arab or Muslim?"

"Don't be silly. However, the Pescis could be Sicilian Mafia, Ali…."

"Hush! Don't say that word. Somebody could be listening."

Alison begged off before revealing her purpose. She broke the connection to sit quietly, while demurely smoothing her skirt and sipping the tea that had grown cold. Mark Prescott returned. Dark complected, slicked-back, black hair, apple shaped—Prescott. Or perhaps he really was a Pesci, a Pesci hit man!

"What was that about?" Mark asked sternly. "This is one of the President's telephones, reserved for official business. Not to be used for gossip."

"I owe you an apology, Mr. Pesci. Uh, Prescott."

His back turned, she nevertheless noticed him stiffen.

Julia arrived in time to hear the wording of Alison's so-called apology. The tall, elegant blonde with the fashionable chignon laughed.

"It's all right, Mark," she said, dismissing Prescott with a casual gesture.

He scowled at Mrs. Morissey, opening his mouth as if starting to respond. Then he smoothly whirled around on one heel and departed.

Ever the gracious First Lady, Julia chaired the National Conservation Council and sat on the history education committee as an ad hoc member. She and Dom would never forget Alison, they frequently reminded her. They rarely mentioned Randolph Morissey. Ali knew he could be a bitter pill to take. Although a geologist and consultant to the White House and also a member of Julia's environmentalist group, Randy was neither warm nor personable. (He also voted the other ticket.)

By themselves, now, the two old friends smiled at each other. Julia said: "You're up to something, Ali."

"How can you tell?"

"Whatever confrontation you've had with Mark, you're not really sorry. I know you too well, Ali, not to recognize your typical ruse: 'I *owe* you an apology,' indeed. Alison, have you ever in your life actually apologized to anybody about anything?"

"Julia, to me, being sorry is akin to repenting. Admitting that you've sinned and promising with all your heart—and hoping to die—that you'll never ever commit that particular sin again. I can say 'pardon me,' or 'excuse me,' after bumping people or spilling things—heaven only knows, I do those things often enough. But to apologize or to say I'm sorry to Mark Prescott because he almost caught me? Nosiree, Bob."

Julia laughed, a series of musical notes akin to a harp's delightful tones."Caught you doing what? What are you up to now, Ali, that the President's Aide shouldn't overhear?"

Alison peered suspiciously around the silent and apparently secure lounge on Air Force One. "Is this room bugged?"

This time the musical laughter was replaced with a loud guffaw, straight off the barnyard—her affluent grandfather's Minnesota dairy. "What on earth?"

Julia and Dom's expletive repertoire included a lot of the old sayings that Alison herself used: *Nosiree Bob, what on earth, pity sakes, heck, goll-ee.* The First Lady shook her head and told Ali she could speak freely.

Alison's initial trip along the Muslim track had switched quickly to the one labeled Sicilian. "Prescott's real name could be Pesci, Julia. Mark's the spitting image of his kin in Sicily. I've seen photos! He's very likely a Mafioso. And I think he's looking for an opportunity to assassinate the President!

CHAPTER 4

▼

TERRORIST CELL
NUMBER TWO

Butch was too bossy by far. When *The Man* in Milwaukee sent Butch to Wyoming, his older brother, Ellery, was elated. Meanwhile, like Butch, Ellery had permission to create whatever havoc he chose, providing he didn't get caught.

Butch reported to Ellery that he had blown up a gas station. Ellery reported to *The Man* that Butch had pulled it off, just for practice, with nobody catching him. Looked like lil Bro had proved he could get away clean.

Ellery could control their middle brother, Eden, but getting Butch to pay attention was an altogether different matter. Butch was so damn arrogant. Thought he knew everything. Just thinking about Butch made Ellery's heart race, his palms sweat. Man, felt like *Cain and Abel.* The Edwards boys knew their Bible stories, because mama, a zealously religious woman, could beat the preacher at both Bible quoting and pulpit pounding.

Besides Eden, Ellery's team included Todd and his girlfriend, Lily, plus the Castles, Charles and Bonnie; *Bonnie and Clyde,* Eden kept calling the retired doughboys. The Castles didn't know what was going down. They were too busy folding flyers and stuffing envelopes. The gullible Castles sincerely believed this mission involved saving trees.

Their Wisconsin mission, as *The Man* called it, was simple. Blow up the Federal Courthouse, an historic site in downtown Milwaukee. Big problem, though.

Butch was the bomb specialist, not Ellery. When they got ready to make their move, Ellery figured Butch would be recalled.

While watching the Castles scowl over their big important envelope-stuffing job, their little chests puffed out with importance, Ellery smirked. He wondered what they'd think when Butch arrived all ready to build a bunch of bombs. Ellery didn't like saying "Butch"; dumb handle. Little bro should stick with the name Pa gave him. The Edwards boys all had "E" names: Ellery, Eden, and Edward. Edward Edwards, Jr. Nuts, Butch got the brains <u>and</u> the "junior."

In a corner of the musty back room of a garage near Lake Michigan where the Edwards boys had set up shop, the blonde bookends, Todd and Lily, argued, their voices rising, their faces turning red. The operation, designed to "Save the Trees," was supposedly one of propaganda, of consciousness raising. That's what the Castles believed. Lily wanted to tell them the truth; Todd and Ellery resisted. Eden didn't give a damn.

When the blondes' squabbling got too loud, Ellery sent Eden to shut them up. "Tell 'em to stuff it, Eden. The Castles will overhear, and catch on."

Eden shrugged. He tore off a hunk of tobacco from a pouch, and stuck it in the corner of his mouth. Slouching on a rickety folding chair with a five-gallon coffee can nearby to use as a spittoon, he was slow in moving. "Who cares?"

"You'd better start caring. Charles and Bonnie could rat to the cops."

Eden rolled his eyes and changed the subject. Glancing over his shoulder at the blondes, he muttered, "Look at 'em, Todd and Lily are lovebirds again."

The young people resembled pretzels, with their skinny jean-clad legs entwined, their slobbering loud enough to hear.

Bonnie looked up from the card table, poked Charles, and they both grinned. "Young love. Ain't it sweet, darling." Statement, not question. He smiled back and patted her soft hand with the protruding veins and age spots.

"After the protest march comes off, we're headed for Arizona, Luv."

"You bet. You've earned your retirement."

Ellery's pager buzzed and he jumped. He wasn't used to this technology. Raised amidst the isolation of the deep woods in northern Wisconsin, the Edwards brothers had only recently got a frig, replacing the old icebox that required big chunks of ice to keep their beer cool.

Ellery glanced at the pager gadget, noting the number. He chortled.

"What's funny, Bro?" Eden asked, sending a long squirt of brown juice into the rusty coffee can. "The Man wants you, I s'pose."

"That's why I laughed, dummy. Nobody pages me but him."

Ellery skirted the cuddlers to make his call. Mustn't let the Castles overhear. He mostly listened, sometimes smirking, sometimes scowling. At last he squawked, sounding like an injured duck. "Yawk! That soon?"

Todd and Lily came unwound like a child's top whose battery suddenly gives out. "What? When?" Todd gasped, grabbing Ellery by the shirt collar.

"Shut th'hell up, Todd. You want the Castles to hear us?"

"Who cares," Lily protested. "'bout time they got in on the act."

Ellery snarled in reply and Todd clasped Lily around the shoulders. The young people pulled Edwards into a tight circle, a huddle before the big kickoff. "Come on, Ellery, give," whispered Todd.

"Okay. The Man says we're gonna do it, for sure. Blow up the Federal building. Only, here's the rub. He don't trust us. He wants to recall Butch."

The blonde clones looked puzzled. "So what?" Lily said.

Ellery bit his lip. He'd almost given away his jealousy. They needn't know the competition, the bitter envy, that drove him to resent Butch.

IN WASHINGTON, D. C.

On Air Force One, brunch consisted of grapefruit, cantaloupe and honeydew slices, brioches, eggs Benedict, a variety of juices, and plenty of hot steaming coffee. Prescott started to join them, but Dom sent his Aide off on errands, telling him he could eat with whomever else he chose—the speechwriter, the press, or any number of Secret Service and communications people.

But not with the Davidsons. Prescott (nee, Pesci?) pouted, like a tot denied his parents' company when grownup guests are present.

"First, though, Mark, please order a limousine to meet the plane for Mrs. Morissey," the President ordered.

"He doesn't like me, Dom," Alison said after Prescott had departed.

"Nonsense, Ali. He doesn't appreciate piddly errands. Mark thinks I should have brought Rose along." Rose Washington Lincoln was the President's private secretary. Rose and Ali got along fine. First of all, Rose was the name of her heroine, the double cousins' admirable great-great-grandmother. Also, though, Rose Washington Lincoln (she insisted on people using all three names) was most likeable. Totally unlike Prescott.

To Julia, Alison said, "I suppose you told Dom my suspicions."

"Of course she did, Ali," said Dom. He didn't laugh at her, but his gentle smile suggested ridicule.

"And you told Prescott?" Suddenly Alison didn't trust any of them.

"Uh, well, yes and no. We didn't plan to share your worries with Mark, but he came into the office before we noticed. He overheard us talking."

"So now he hates me."

"I wouldn't say that," Julia said, patting Ali's wrist with one hand and dabbing daintily at her lips with a linen napkin held in the other. "Mark's like a son to us, Alison. And, like a peevish child sometimes, he resents our closeness to you. That's all it is."

"But...."

"We know his background, Ali," Dom said. "Naturally all that was checked and double checked before he was allowed on board. Yes, we know his real name is Pesci; Mario Pesci. His family changed his name when he was a youngster. So he could have a chance at success somewhere besides in the land of the super underworld."

"Boy howdy, he sure got his wish. A job in the Super Overworld."

Dom ignored her outburst. "The whole Pesci family went legit at least two generations ago. No problem."

Alison sighed, while half-holding her breath. She had to ask. If she didn't ask, she'd have to wait until the rest of the world heard the news. "Dom," she said hesitantly. "I read your lips while you were on the phone." While her eyes apologized for eavesdropping, her mouth did not. "Are you going to tell us what's up? You said *terrorists*. Not again!"

This time it was the President who sighed, as if resigned to Alison's probing. "Could be international terrorists on our shores again. The FBI reported detaining a couple of suspicious characters at the Nogales, Mexico, border crossing."

"What about others coming in from Canada?"

"Maybe."

"Fanatics cloned from Osama bin Laden or Mullah Mohammed Omar?"

"Could be."

Obviously he would reveal no more, even if he knew. Alison shut up.

They finished brunch. Before the Davidsons retired to their private quarters in preparation for landing, Mark returned with a note about the limo. "All set," he said.

Mark left. The Davidsons left.

Left alone, Alison grabbed Prescott's note. Good, the limousine company's name and telephone number appeared. She promptly dialed the firm to cancel. What if Mark planned to have her taken out? One or more accomplices could easily man the car to detour between airport and hotel.

Alison wasn't taking any chances. She'd make some excuse to the Davidsons, and then call a cab for herself. She might be paranoid, but so what? She didn't care. Better to be safe and alive than sorry and dead.

In Washington, Alison checked in at the All-Nippon-Airways, formerly the Westin Hotel. She showered, donned purple sweatpants and tank top, and set out again. At Twenty-fourth and "M" on the edge of Georgetown, the hotel was ideally situated for Washington's political visitors, from lobbyists to campaigners; a few blocks from Rock Creek Parkway, a great place for joggers. Ali could get in a run along the Potomac River and on to the Lincoln Memorial and back.

Her room on the non-smoking, sixth floor had a wide kingsize bed. She sighed. If Randy were here, if he would only make love to her again, finally, after so many "dry" months, maybe they could get their marriage back on track. She deeply missed the sweetheart she'd once known.

Gazing around, her glance inventoried the room: sofa, easy chairs, a safe for her valuables—pearls, diamonds—a small bar with refrigerator, and an armoire; marble bath, walk-in closet. All the amenities, no time to appreciate.

Following another shower, Alison chose a short brunette wig, much like her own hair—if it ever grew in proper again. The wig was short-cropped and styled in the manner of Geraldine Ferraro, one-time Vice-Presidential candidate.

Before the dinner at the White House that night, she had some stops to make, some senators to visit. First, though, she'd call home. To her double cousin, Lisa, the tiny blonde out in Cheyenne, Alison could now speak freely.

"I should have felt like a fool."

"Why? What did you do now, Ali?"

"I told Julia, and of course she told Dom, that I thought Mark was out to kill them. Mark Prescott. The guy I called you about from Air Force One."

"Wha-aat?" Lisa squealed, sounding like she was in the next room instead of in her palatial Wyoming home. "You didn't tell me that was the problem. You just asked about our Sicilian kin and their pals. I mentioned the Pesci family."

Sitting on the edge of her hotel room bed, Ali kicked off her shoes to curl up on the coverlet. "Yes, well. Pesci, Prescott. Get it? Dom admits that Prescott's real name is Pesci. And not only did I spill my peas to Julia and Dom, but also to one of the President's speechwriters, a former reporter.

Lisa ignored the peas. Ali knew her cousin had given up on correcting her. Peas, beans, what difference did it make.

"Good grief, Ali. Your suspicions are sure to leak out, now. You'll be quoted and blasted all over television land!" Alison could hear Lisa sipping, probably the cousins' favorite cinnamon apple tea. "Ali, Ali, the tabloids will pick it up in a blink, quicker than you can think. Who was the reporter? Not with one of the networks, I hope."

"No, no. Not even a reporter any longer. I'm confused and confusing you. Carl Crosby was a reporter, down in Arkansas. Now he writes speeches for the President. Carl won't tell anybody. Neither will Dom and Julia. Not to worry, Luv. Anyhow, the President and Julia just laughed at me."

"They laughed because you uncovered an assassination plot?"

"No, no. They laughed because I thought I had. They claim to know Mark Prescott well. He changed his name from Mario Pesci. Supposedly he has no connection any longer with his family. Wouldn't matter if he did, Dom said. Julia says Mario, uh, Mark claims the family's gone legit."

"And if you believe that, I've a Stradivarius to sell you, cheap. Right?"

"As I said, I should feel embarrassed."

"You were only trying to protect the President. I hope you didn't apologize. Of course you never do. Anyway, why should you? You didn't do anything wrong."

"Might have hurt an innocent man's reputation, Lisa. That's pretty bad."

"You mean you did say you were sorry?"

"Uh. Actually, what I said was, "Ooh, that was terrible of me to think such a thing about someone whose only concern is for the President's welfare.""

Lisa laughed. "That's my Ali. Twist the language in circles." The little blond out in Wyoming closed off with a quick note about her daughter and Alison's granddaughter, as Beth and Nicole were best friends as well as cousins. Another cousin among the younger set was Ned Fleetfoot, son of Wyoming's Secretary of State. Lisa said Ned was helping the girls get the travel agency ready to launch. Ned Fleetfoot was half-Arapaho, half-Clan, and thus a *double* cousin, but twice removed.

Beth was Lisa's small blond daughter and Nicole was Alison's very tall auburn-haired granddaughter. Alison had married and birthed early, and so had Joan. Thus Joan called herself granny in her early thirties. Nicole too married and birthed young, making of Alison, her Gam, a great-grandmother while barely in her fifties. Conversely, Lisa married and birthed Beth late. Thus Lisa's Beth and Joan's Nicole were the same age.

Beth and Brad Gifford with the BB twins, Brianna and Brittany, lived next door to the Schwartzkopfs, Peter and Lisa, and all of that arm of the family was close as spoons in the knife and fork drawer. Ali sighed. She wished she could say the same for her own nuclear family. Randy and their daughter, Professor Joan Vicente (who'd taken her Grandfather Vicente's name after her divorce), were never going to get along and neither were Nicole and her mother, Joan. Randy could shut up about Joan's divorce of two decades earlier. Joan couldn't quit nagging Nicole about enrolling at the U. Generational battles, born early and continuing to this day as if that were the norm.

Lisa's droning on in Ali's ear about family members abruptly ceased when she realized Alison wasn't listening. "Sorry to get carried away, Ali, but I'm so proud of Beth. Now, back to what you were saying. You didn't apologize, of course, since you never do."

No, Alison said, she wasn't embarrassed. Because she still suspected Pesci, Prescott, of something. Could be jealousy, possessiveness. He resented their affection for her; something like that. Mark didn't like her, though. That much was obvious.

They broke the connection and Alison made ready to depart. At least she'd had the sense to cancel the limousine Mark had ordered. She'd traipse around town by taxi.

Alison set the phone down and this time she chose a gray linen suit with raw silk blouse in lavender. She was headed for the Hart Building to meet with the two senators from Wyoming. The senior, Senator Kevin Macomber, was blocky and balding—but only in front. While the junior, Senator Ronald Perry, was young, dark and handsome, and tall. She knew them both well; had hit the campaign trail with them and their entourage, folded promotional materials, made thousands of phone calls, co-hosted fund raisers. At home in Wyoming, she stood for them, by them, and sometimes against them when she couldn't agree with their policies.

Whenever they were in D.C., the Morisseys made it a practice to drop in on their Senators and Wyoming's only Representative, Patty Pruitt. Her Randy liked to get his photo taken with each one. Framed behind glass, these pictures lined his study walls in Cheyenne like old soldiers left over from the wars.

Senator Perry served on the bipartisan U.S. Commission on National Security. After they'd shared a bit of down-home chitchat about friends they had in common, Ron began shuffling papers. From a security document, he quoted, for Alison's benefit: "Americans are vulnerable to hostile attack on our homeland. We cannot expect our military to protect us entirely."

Sitting in the plush visitor's chair across from Ron, Alison stared, open mouthed. "Which means what?"

"Every citizen must be ever vigilant."

"How much longer must all this last?" Alison worried about people in the metropolises, not about Wyomingites. Surely folk in the hick states were safe.

In Senator Macomber's office, and mounting his own anti-terrorism pulpit, Kevin showed Alison other reports. He cited attacks on and statistics gathered from the U. S. Forest Service, Public Employees for Environmental Responsibility, Americans for Medical Progress, and even the Fur Commision USA. "Essentially, we're talking about other kinds of terrorism in America, besides the strikes and continuing threats coming from outside the country. On the domestic side, I'm talking environmentalist terrorism. Recent incidents in eleven western states have hit us with millions of dollars in damage, from vandalism to arson and bombings. Radical environmentalists use the term, *ecoterrorism*. The FBI says that ecoterrorism is a crime intended to coerce, intimidate, or change public policy."

Alison knew that Dom, like his predecessors since the Oklahoma City, World Trade Center, and Pentagon bombings, continued to use a task force established to study domestic terrorism. Like Ali, though, neither of the Senators from Wyoming had any special worries about their own state. "To quote the President," she said, "the objective of these domestic terrorists is that, like the Unibomber, they want attention to their cause and if they don't get enough publicity, then they try something else. Oh, Kevin. Think of it. It took us nearly two decades to run down the Unibomber. These things go on too long."

"For Americans, patience is a tough call." The Senator pecked her cheek, a gesture of affection and goodbye.

Little time remained for visiting with Representative Pruitt. The two women hugged and exchanged a few words about people they both knew. In particular, several from among Ali's clan members, including Wyoming's Secretary of State, Nasty Three, and the family's good friend, Dr. Sanford, an African-American and the state's Superintendent of Public Instruction.

Alison hailed a cab for her hotel. She barely had time for another shower and a change into evening clothes.

At the formal dinner in the state dining room, arranged with head table and a few round tables beyond, Alison sat between the First Lady and the dignitary's wife from Kzrgyzstan. Ali wore a long black vintage Trigere gown with vee neck and bare arms. Julia also wore black, with a fitted waist and topped with a short, long-sleeved lacy jacket. By contrast, Magna Oblasty wore a lacquered, plasticized gauze gown in white, a couture dress by Josephus Thimister, she whispered. Julia and Ali had adorned themselves with cultured pearls, Magda in diamonds at both neck and wrist. She chattered on and on about American and French fashions.

The Davidsons had first received the Oblasty couple along with accompanying dignitaries, including the Kyrgyzstan Ambassador to America, in the diplomatic reception room, furnished as a Federal period parlor. The rug here, Julia said, contained symbols of the fifty states; the wallpaper, printed in France in 1834, depicted Niagara Falls, Boston Harbor, West Point, the Natural Bridge of Virginia, and New York Bay. The most notable portrait in the White House, said the First Lady, was Gilbert Stuart's 1797 portrait of George Washington. Alison added, for Magda's benefit, that the Davidsons' portraits were also included among the paintings of Presidents and their First Ladies. "All of which line the corridors of the ground floor and the state rooms."

Magda didn't seem to be the least bit impressed.

Although Alison had often accompanied Randy on his global search for oil, she had only visited Kyrgyzstan once. This occasion apparently proved to be a memorable experience for the cabinet member's wife, because Magda had refused to join her husband unless Mrs. Morissey was invited to the dinner.

Julia described the White House as the symbol of the American Presidency. "It is more than the President's home and office. The White House stands for the power and statesmanship of the Chief Executive. Conversely," Julia continued, despite Magda's look of boredom, "The Capitol represents the freedom and ideals of our nation."

Magda appeared more interested in Julia's personal quarters, but the First Lady did not offer to give Mrs. Oblasty a tour of the third floor, nor of the Lincoln bedroom, nor of her and Dom's private rooms. Alison bit her lip to keep from smiling. Seated, now, she caressed the clean white table cloth, letting her finger run idly around the gold ring on the china plate. She stroked the long-stemmed glass of the two Baccarat crystal wine glasses, and stared down at the many eating implements perfectly aligned at each setting.

Education, environmentalism, drugs, and terrorism were among this administration's major themes, and about which commissions were assembled and policies developed. Julia's specialties involved the first two, especially education. The First Couple had recently toured four mid-American states that included Wisconsin and Wyoming, so Dom could listen to the will of the people—a few people, some selected, many at random, from factories to farms, from cafes to court houses. Julia, meanwhile, had her own agenda. She'd met with key state teacher groups, especially high school teachers in the fields of history, literature, and communications. It was from their last stop, in Cheyenne, that Alison had joined the Davidsons.

"The stakes are high," said the CIA's deputy director, still talking, even after the endive salad was served. "The nation can't afford to miss clues of an imminent missile attack in the data that swamp CIA analysts each day." He paused to look around the room, as if to grab everybody's attention. Even his slamming a fist on the table, though, did not distract Magda from primping and fidgeting— pushing her hair about, patting her face, fingering her diamonds. The CIA man concluded: "Foreign crises will continue to spawn atrocities and terrorism." At last he sat down.

Alison supposed that terrorism was the topic of this dinner and the Oblasty's visit. She recalled some of what she'd been told while in Magda's country and, again, in the pre-dinner diplomatic briefing about Kyrgyzstan: capital, Bishkek; government, republic; population, about five million; languages, Kyrgyz and Russian; religions, mostly Muslim with some Russian Orthodox; exports, wool and cotton, some chemicals; currency, the som. Then she remembered an astounding statistic: the literacy rate among the total population, ninety-seven percent; ninety-six for females and ninety-nine for males. Amazing. Especially when compared with the many Afghan illiterates.

When Alison asked Magda why they had been invited to the White House, the woman looked surprised, as if she weren't supposed to know. Julia mouthed to Ali, but didn't speak aloud, "Drugs. Harboring terrorists."

Magda ignored the issues, except to mutter that Kyrgyzstan wasn't involved. She didn't see why everything bad that happened to Americans, at home or abroad, had to be blamed on Muslims. To herself, Ali mused that that could be called *racial profiling*, a sin that she, too, could be guilty of.

Trying hard to empathize with Magda's feelings, Alison suddenly recalled her afternoon's conversation with Wyoming's two Senators. She wondered why Ron Perry had told her, back in his office, that he had reason to believe a terrorist cell could be operating out of Wyoming. Absurd. She tipped her head to ponder. Hmm. Better not stuff her head in the sand. Could be true.

Julia said she would have preferred education as the focus. She leaned forward to ask Magda how they taught world history in her country.

"I'm not sure," Magda said, shrugging her uninterest. A fussy eater, she picked at the endive, shoved bits of the fish about on her plate, settling on the hard roll. Then she chug-a-lugged a full glass of Chardonnay. Flabbergasted, Alison stared under guise of dabbing her lips with a napkin.

No further official talk. The assemblage concentrated on chatting at their own tables and on the delicious dinner of escargot, endive salad, raspberry sorbet, white dover sole with white asparagus and hollandaise sauce; followed by a lovely flan, fruit compote and brie.

Then Magda did a strange thing; strange, for a Muslim woman. She poked around in her tiny handbag to draw out implements and line them up to the right of her plate. Staring at her reflection in the sparkling wine glass, she then applied lipstick and blush. "Gauche," mouthed Julia behind her hand. Ali's lip reading had served the two women well over the years, especially with Julia, who still liked to gossip, yet so often found herself beneath the spotlight of public opinion.

Magda defied the customs of Islam—wearing the burqa, covering her body and hair. The way Ali understood it, clothing was not supposed to be revealilng; people were not supposed to be able to guess a woman's weight within fifty pounds. How different from American styles.

While Magda chattered on about American fashions and Julia nodded and smiled, Alison turned her lipreading talent elsewhere. Mark Prescott (nee, Mario Pesci?) sat at the far end of the head table, past the lectern that separated the women from the men. (Mr. Oblasty's preference, Dom had explained to Julia and Ali when describing the seating arrangement.) Alison detected a sneer on Prescott's face whenever he glanced her way.

Ali felt the bile rise in her throat and goose bumps pop up along her arms. She supposed that among the dinner guests several Secret Service people unobtrusively hovered and circulated, keeping a watchful eye on the Davidsons and their guests. Quietly she sucked in a big breath and let it out ever so slowly. Mustn't hyperventilate.

Oops! She'd relaxed her guard too soon. For just then she dribbled her after-dinner coffee. It trickled down her chin, onto her cleavage, and straight between her perky but ample breasts. Alison shivered, partly with discomfort, partly from self-disgust. She reached with her napkin to soak up some water so she could dab at the dress and perhaps save it from staining.

Distracted from her task by Mark, Alison observed him leaving his table to drift stealthily toward the side of the room. Thus half-discombobulated and half-absentminded, Ali didn't notice Magda's water glass. Mrs. Oblasty had set it, not in front of her own plate, but near Ali's left hand, in Alison's table territory.

Mark bent to speak to a black-haired surly looking fellow, in appearance resembling Prescott himself. The Muslim, Arab, whatever, hunched over his soiled dinner dishes. The man, possibly an Arab, then reached with what appeared great stealth beneath the table. Ali gasped as light from the sparkling chandelier overhead glinted off an implement. She jerked sharply, knocking over Magda's water glass and making a huge puddle.

"My word," the First Lady said calmly, accustomed as she was to her good friend's typical bumbling.

Any normal person, having created such a fiasco in such a public place with such official dignitaries, would have blushed and apologized profusely. Not Alison. She was too busy studying Mark and the other dark-skinned man seated at that far table.

Among the gathering, however, utter silence reigned. Coffee cups paused in mid-air, fingers fiddling with soiled napkins or folding pleats into white linen tablecloths ceased their fiddling and folding. People at every table stared at Alison.

Mark, or Mario, scowled. The Arab at the far table froze. Senators Macomber and Perry from Wyoming smiled. That's our Ali, their exchanged glances suggested.

She wasn't at all embarrassed. She didn't have time.

Without aforethought Alison immediately fell on top of America's honored guest. Just as a sharply pointed blade flew through the air and over the ladies' heads.

Afterwards, in recapping the event, a number of fellow dinner guests would tell the press they were astonished and amazed. Said the CIA director's aide: "The little lady seated at the head table between First Lady Davidson and silly Magda Oblasty jumped to her feet and, with a mighty shove, pushed the gauze-draped Eurasian woman to the floor. It was truly incredible!"

CHAPTER 5

▼

THE AFTERMATH

"I'm on my way to San Miguel de Allende, Lisa. Don't you want to join me?" Alison sat perched on the side of her bed at the ANA Hotel late that night. "If you come, Lisa, all three of the female double cousins will be together. Nasty's in Mexico, too."

"I can't get away right now, Ali. Peter and I are hosting a cocktail party at the officers club," Lisa said over the phone. "Get back to the story. You saved Magda's life. Then what? They catch the killer?"

"In a manner of speaking. Prescott killed him. You won't believe it. Mark grabbed a long, strong, three-tined serving fork off a meat platter and shoved it straight into the assassin's neck. Hit the carotid artery, I guess. Blood gushed like an oil well."

"Ooh, ick," Lisa groaned. "But that's good, isn't it? Kill him before he could assassinate the President?"

"Looks that way. But consider this scenario, Lisa. What if Pesci was in on it and really meant to shut up the assassin before he could finger Mark? The two of them were whispering just a few minutes earlier. And I was lipreading."

"Oh, good." Lisa, too, was hearing impaired and she, too, had taken the lip-reading class. "What did they say?"

"Pesci whispered to the killer, 'Not yet, Ahmud. Wait for a diversion." Alison switched the receiver from her right to her left ear.

"For pity sakes, Ali. You were the one who caused the diversion. You said you spilled Magda's water. Right?"

"I didn't think of that. Oh, dear." Ali kicked off her shoes and curled one stocking-clad foot beneath her. She pulled tight her light robe to stifle her shivering.

"Never mind, Luv. Your diversion also diverted the assassin's knife. You knocked Magda out of range. Isn't that the way you described it, Ali? Ali?"

"I was thinking. What if Julia was the target, not Magda?"

"Then you actually saved the First Lady's life. Terrific! Ali, even as we speak, your courageous deed is on CNN, Fox, and the networks."

"Hey, you and I both know that courage had nothing to do with it. That fumble was pure accident. Typical, but accidental."

"Never mind that, Dear. Get back to your earlier surmise. The one you say the President proposed."

"Dom suggested it might have been an Islamic plot to take out Mrs. Oblasty. For wearing makeup, maybe. Or that goofy, too-revealing dress. If it were up to the fundamentalist Muslims, they'd have her clothed from head to foot—body, hair, face, with only peep holes to see and breathe. Never mind a mouth hole. I don't believe they approve of Islamic women speaking or perhaps even eating in public."

"Good grief."

"Prescott claimed he responded to the Arab's motioning beck, and had only told him where the men's room was and when would be an appropriate time to take a break." Alison pulled back the coverlet to crawl between the sheets, cradling her head in the big fluffy pillow. She still felt jittery.

"Does that jibe with what you lipread?"

"No, of course not. What's a 'diversion' got to do with taking a potty break? And why wouldn't the Arab, Abdul somebody, ask a Secret Service or wait person? Why demand that Mark dance attendance on his bodily functions?"

"He was an Arab, though. You're sure of that?"

"I'm not sure of anything, Lisa. Only of what Dom told me afterwards, and remember he was quoting others, the Secret Service people, perhaps. Actually, get this, Lisa. The assassin, a stranger, was supposedly accompanying the Kyrgyzstan ambassador, who later denied that he even knew the hit man, and nobody else claimed knowledge of his identity either. If Mark knows, he's not talking straight."

"Okay. I'll let you change the subject, now. You're off for Mexico soon?"

"Yes, but that, too, is part of the same story, Lisa. I want to get Aunt Nasturtium's opinion of Mark. Dom insists that I travel on an Air Force plane; not his, of course. For safety's sake, I'm to accompany the Drug Czar and the American ambassador to Mexico. Also on the plane will be Carl Crosby, one of Dom's current speechwriters, who, incidentally, is that Arkansas reporter you met with me in Vermont."

"Sounds to me like Dom is worried about you. The Arabs, or whoever, could retaliate. Have you thought of that? Remember what Shakespeare wrote in the Merchant of Venice—Act III, I believe: *If you prick us, do we not bleed? if you tickle us, do we not laugh? if you poison us, do we not die? and if you wrong us, shall we not revenge?*"

In college, Lisa had majored in literature. Ali ignored the quotation. "Lisa, one question posed from the reporters I didn't appreciate one bit...."

"Don't tell me, I think I can guess: 'Aren't you afraid of retaliation?'"

"Oh, Lisa, if you caught that, what about other people? The media might have planted the seed, if the Arabs hadn't already come up with it." Alison got up to fetch a glass of water, the cellphone still attached like an extra appendage to her ear. "Here's more news, Lisa. Mario Pesci will be traveling with us! Maybe he is one of them and he's looking for his chance to hit me. Not the President. Me."

"Oh, no. Ali, I don't get it. If the President's been privy to your suspicions, why would he saddle you with the very man you suspect; if not of attempting to assassinate himself or Julie, then being in cahoots with the Arab?"

"Beats me. Both Prescott and Crosby are accompanying the members of the international drug-war council, and, since Dom doesn't want me traveling alone, he said I should hop aboard. Then his speechwriter, Carl Crosby, is supposed to accompany me by rental car on up to San Miguel from Mexico City."

"Ali, explain again why you're running off so impetuously to Mexico."

"To check out Mark, of course."

"Okay, but why so passionate about proving or disproving his innocence?"

Alison's voice shouted annoyance. "I'd think it's obvious. I love Dom like a son. I want him safe."

"I can buy that. But one minute you call Prescott a Muslim and the next a Mafioso. Which is it?"

Alison paused a moment. She really couldn't say, except *Mafia* had a more familiar ring, closer to home. *Muslim* reminded her of Osama bin Ladin and the Taliban, the foreign terrorists.

Early the next day Alison pulled on her black pantsuit with lavender silk blouse. Then she returned to the White House for a last chat with the Davidsons and, she hoped, another chance to produce a convincing argument why Mario Pesci should not accompany her to Mexico. Alison had more, not fewer, reasons for mistrusting Dom's Aide.

In Julia's suite at the White House, the First Lady wore a long velvet lounging gown. Before the plane left for Mexico, the two women spent a half-hour pouring over scrapbooks and photograph albums, several of which chronicled the Davidson's early days, from back when Dom had boarded with the Morisseys. More recent albums featured their daughter from birth through adolescence.

"We miss Jerica so much," Julia said. "At least she's out there in Wyoming, where you and Joan can keep an eye on her."

Alison couldn't believe her old friend was really that naïve. Ali's daughter, also Jerica's campus advisor, had told her mother about the Secret Service complaints. Professor Vicente and the D.C. team sometimes compared notes, Joan admitted. Callie was a sweet girl at first and had made some thoughtful observations in class. Then she underwent a personality change, typical of those who succumb to the addiction of drugs.

Now Alison wondered how much to tell Julia. The First Lady squirmed, wadding up her flower-decorated handkerchief in long slender fingers.

"Don't keep me in the dark, dear. Dom and I know what the Secret Service people are saying. Jerica keeps slipping away from them. We agreed, finally, that she could stay with Callie and her parents up in Medicine Bow awhile before coming to Washington." Julia sighed and frowned. "I hope she doesn't want to keep their apartment this fall."

"Might be a good idea. Next year, when she's a sophomore."

"If she lives that long!"

"Julia, darling. Now who's being paranoid?" Alison spanned the short distance between them on the soft, chintz-covered love seat to hug the First Lady. "You can't watch her day and night. Neither can her protectors. Even if the Davidsons were private citizens. Think of Chelsea. She made it through Stanford all in one piece."

"The Clintons' daughter must have understood the necessity for being cautious," Julia snapped.

After more talk, covering the University of Wyoming and some of their mutual memories, the women turned to analyzing the gist of their experience the night before. "Silly woman," Julia said. "Magda didn't even thank you for saving her life, Ali."

When the President joined them, he switched on the television to the Fox news channel. Like hungry mice, the media had picked up the story of the attempt on Magda's life. They'd grabbed the cheese and gobbled, despite the Kyrgyzstan ambassador's request for privacy; namely, a news blackout.

"What did he expect?" Dom said. "This is America, land of free speech."

Everybody connected with the small Eurasian country had quickly vanished from the White House. They were whisked to safety or had evaporated by themselves. With the assassin dead, there seemed no more to the story. The Fox newscaster switched to another story. On to the next crisis.

Dom addressed Alison's upcoming flight. "Mark will be traveling with you, Ali. I hope the two of you will use the opportunity to mend your fences."

Dainty teacup in mid-air, Ali's hand jerked. Her tea slopped over but not, fortunately, on her silk blouse. A waiter discreetly sopped up the spilt tea and then backed off before their table conversation resumed.

Alison had expected to be relieved of Mark Prescott's unwelcome company, because surely the authorities would detain him for questioning. After all, he had killed somebody. Protesting would obviously do no good.

So she changed tactics and topic. "It will be great to have Crosby along. By now he must have many entertaining experiences to share."

Dom and Julia exchanged glances. "After Miguel de Allende, Ali," said the President, "Carl will accompany you by commercial carrier and whenever you're ready to return to Wyoming."

"To Wyoming? What on earth?"

"Jerica likes and respects Carl," Julia said. "Under the pretense of gathering local color and writing a story about the University of Wyoming and Laramie, Crosby can help keep an eye on our precious daughter."

CHAPTER 6

▼

JERICA

After listening to Julia stewing over Jerica, Ali decided to call Joan. She needed to check in with her daughter, anyhow, to see whether there was any news from Randy. While she was at it, she would also inquire after Jerica. If most professors were like Joan, who regularly kept tabs on many of her *chickadees,* they knew a lot more than imagined about their students—from intimate confessions, but also from intra-campus gossip.

To Joan on the phone, Alison said the Davidsons had grudgingly consented to allowing Jerica to spend the early part of the August break with her roommate and family in Medicine Bow.

"Callie's father is a miner and her mother's a bartender," Alison said, quoting Julia, who'd quoted from the Secret Service report. "Hardly a recommendation for proper parental supervision, since both Callie's parents work full time."

"Honestly, Mom, you sound so old-fashioned," Joan objected. "Most women are employed in the labor market these days. Besides, Callie's twenty-one. She hardly expects to be supervised any longer."

"How will the Secret Service keep track of Jerica now?"

Which was what everybody wondered. Except Jerica, who, with her friends, was busy finding devious ways to avoid the Secret Service people assigned to her.

*   *   *   *

"Look, Jerica, here's what we'll do," said Callie in Laramie. "After we get back to town from visiting my folks for one single day, you can get some rest. Butch and I will only be out of town a few days this time. We won't be gone long. Meanwhile, you can keep busy deceiving your shadows. Go to COE Library hauling books. Wear your glasses, look studious. Go out with Bud now and then, to the usual places. Otherwise, lay low until Butch and I get back."

"How's that going to help?" Jerica pouted. She'd begged to go too, but Butch used the excuse that she needed to put off her guards.

"Keep them calm and unsuspecting, kiddo," Butch ordered. "Like Callie says, go to the library, act intellectual." He didn't know what he was talking about, but what th'hell, it sounded good.

"When we're back, Kiddo, we'll all be ready to howl," said Callie, smirking. "The Secret Service will think their little girl won't give them anything to worry about. They'll be calm and off guard. And your social life, my chum, can move into high gear."

First, though, Jerica and Callie used Bud's battered green Ford pickup to drive to the village of Medicine Bow, sixty-five miles north of Laramie. "About four hundred population, tops," Callie said. "Big night on the town is showing up at the bar where my mom works. You'll get a kick outta it, girl."

The "high-rise" Virginian Hotel, three floors only, constructed of sandstone, stood across the mostly deserted highway from the train tracks. Complete with wooden plank sidewalk and century-old wagon sitting out front, the hotel offered both a café and a bar on the ground floor. In the saloon, with its old glass-covered bar top sheltering silver dollars, they perched on stools and peered around at the high walls covered with old western photos depicting early settlers—ranchers and cowboys with their horses and cattle, sheep men and their sheep, miners, oil wells, and the barren lands swept by wind, and by freezing, blinding blizzards.

"My word," exclaimed Jerica, demurely sipping a sarsaparilla. Despite exposure to Callie, Butch, and Bud, the President's daughter was more comfortable using her parents' mild expletives than the foul language erupting like gas from a gas well out of the mouths of her new friends. Sounded cool, but she had not as yet begun to mimic them.

"What on earth?" Jerica pointed to a strange looking animal, stuffed and staring from its glass cage. "What is that creature?"

Callie grinned. "You never saw a jackalope afore? Girl, you ain't lived, yet." So saying, she continued using her version of down-home talk to describe how some early Wyomingite had experimented with cross breeding jack rabbits with antelope, until, "Voila! The jackalope!"

Jerica eyed her friend from beneath slitted eyelids. "You must think me a real dumb city slicker to believe a yarn like that."

Callie's mom wore her long, thick brown hair piled atop her head. She crossed her arms over an ample bosom and retied her apron around a slender middle. "I declare, Callie, you shouldn't tease the President's daughter like that."

"Shh, Mom. Nobody must know." Callie looked around.

"Silly girl. This place is nearly empty. But why not? People round here would be thrilled to know about our visitor."

"Aww, shucks, Ma. Cain't we have no privacy?"

"Now you cut that out, child. You can speak as fine as anybody. Got that scholarship and pledged to Chi Omega, didn't ya? Behave yourself."

"Sure, Mom."

The place was not quite empty. At a tiny table in the dimness of the back room sat Jose Lopez and Juanita Jorgensen, the Secret Service team keeping tabs on the First Miss. Over tall, frosty glasses of Coke, they stifled a chuckle at the joke Callie had pulled on their charge. Short and stocky, Jose, at twenty-seven, was the youngest among the four Secret Service operatives.

"You were fooled, too, weren't you, Jose? Just for a second?" Juanita murmured. She reached across the table to give her dark-complected partner a poke, even while keeping her eyes peeled. Had to be alert in this job, watch out for any untoward action that could endanger Jerica, even if it were no more than some wobbly drunk on the prowl for the pretty and famous coed.

Callie and her mom took Jerica on tour of the old hotel, after which *The Virginian,* by Owen Wister, was named and where, on a wall poster, appeared the quotation: *Smile when you say that.* Upstairs, they found period furniture with red velvet upholstering, tiffany lamps, feather beds, lots of fringe and gold braid, and handmade quilts.

Later, Callie's dad, out of his mining clothes and freshly showered, welcomed Jerica like she was family. Their double-wide mobile home was tidy and clean, nicely furnished and decorated.

"So this is how *normal* people live," Juanita whispered to Jose as they sat in their car beneath a cottonwood tree. Bored with the surveillance detail, Jose made no reply.

*   *   *   *

Back in Laramie, and alone now, the pretty blonde with the heavily lashed, cerulean blue eyes and the naturally wavy, thick, blond hair did as Butch and Callie had commanded. Bud Andrews, the nineteen-year-old redhead, said he didn't understand about Jerica keeping a low profile or wandering around pretending to look studious.

"Let's you and me party," Bud said that night in her apartment.

Jerica declined. She told him she was supposed to stick close to home when not traipsing around making with the *serious student* act. She kicked him out.

Bud lived next door and up one level from Butch's pad. However, Butch Edwards lived in a different building, albeit adjoining, which was owned by another landlord. Which was perhaps why the Secret Service teams hadn't thought to check it out.

Security reports filed in Washington suggested to the Davidsons that their daughter's summer fling with "that questionable element" had been short-lived. "She's settling down," said Caroline over the phone to her boss. She rubbed her nappy head. She wasn't used to it this short. She missed the cornrows.

After completing their reports and observing that Jerica had bedded down for the night, the four agents met at Applebee's to compare notes. They wore casual clothes, designed to make them blend in with the college crowd, numbering over twelve thousand.

"Fall semester starts soon and she'll be back safe again at the Chi Omega house," said short, dark Jose to tall, sandy-haired Robert Schmidt, age thirty-one, and their leader.

"She'll have a new roommate now that Callie's dropped out of school," said muscular Caroline to long-haired Juanita. The women munched green salads while the men chomped their way through huge steaks.

"There was that visit to Medicine Bow to the bar and the Jenkins' mobile home. Plus her lunch with Callie's parents here in town at the Chuckwagon Café near the Interstate," protested Robert dubiously. "Meaning she hasn't cut her ties to Callie yet."

"Nor to Bud," Caroline reminded them.

The popular restaurant on Grand Avenue was a couple of miles from Jerica's temporary apartment. When the team had checked out her rental, they discovered that Jerica was paying the full rent bill, making of Callie a freeloader.

"Right. Bud's been to visit her a couple of times, though," said Juanita.

"And they went out twice," confirmed Robert." He and Jose often shared by rotation the outdoor shadowing duty.

"Yeah, but only to the beer garden at the student union and to dinner at the Cavalryman," said Jose.

"The kid has to have some social life," Juanita reminded the others. "Seems harmless enough."

"Yeah, if Bud hasn't got into her bed," said Caroline with cynicism. She still liked the idea of bugging Jerica's premises. The others resisted.

Four people couldn't be everywhere at all times of the day and night. What they didn't know (besides the information on Butch they'd missed) was that Bud regularly crawled through the window of Butch's garden-level apartment at three in the morning.

Jerica didn't know it either.

Bud was very quiet hauling in and stashing in the locked hall closet their cache of guns, ammunition, and materials for building explosives. In boxes labeled "Popcorn."

CHAPTER 7

▼

MEXICO

"The way she dresses and lives, you'd never know my Aunt Nasturtium is independently wealthy," Alison told Carl Crosby aboard the plane.

"How's that?" asked the President's freckled speechwriter, his face seemingly as transparent as onion skin. Blotchy, too, from sun or embarrassment, thereby reminiscent of a thermometer, with the blood of his face rushing up and back down.

Sipping tea, while occasionally glancing out the window at the puffy clouds billowing below their plane—and periodically peering over her shoulder for Mario Pesci's lurking presence—Alison described her old aunt. "Aunty Nasturtium wears weird things, Carl, like pleated jersey dresses with sneakers and socks, umbrella and poncho shawls and floppy hats, reading glasses on a gold chain round her neck. She invariably carries a crocheted bag of cotton yarn, though she never crochets. Doesn't know how. Uses it as a guise, under which she hides her wallet."

Carl Crosby smiled. They had already quizzed each other with personal questions, along with sharing their hypotheses about the assassination attempt of the night before. They also talked at length about the First Family.

Carl said he liked Jerica. "She's so pretty," he said wistfully.

Meaning he had a thing for Jerica? Who wouldn't, she was so sweet and innocent. Alison, like the Davidsons, hoped the girl would be safe out in the wilds of backwater Wyoming, where "nothing (in this century) ever happens."

Ali closed her eyes and leaned back to rest, albeit uneasily. Where was Mark Prescott? He could be a sleeper, like the Taliban terrorists, awaiting his call to attack. After the foiled assassination in the White House, if Mark was involved he surely wouldn't attempt another hit so soon. Oh, but he could attack her personally, perhaps verbally, psychologically, to put her off his scent. In college, she had majored in psych-soc, and, because she kept up on trends and topics, and analyzed and shared her opinions with Randy, her husband had more ammunition with which to criticize her. He accused her of sounding pedantic while uttering all that psycho-babble and socio-mumble.

She hadn't meant to think of her husband. She felt like muttering, *Get behind me, Randolph Morissey,* as if he were the Devil to shunt away.

When she asked Crosby if he'd seen Mark while she was napping, he looked surprised. "Didn't anybody tell you? Mark was detained for questioning; for killing the Arab. Prescott's not aboard this plane with us."

Pity sakes. All this time, all these nerves. Julia, if not Dom, should have told her.

"Said he'd catch up to us later, though. He's flying to Mexico City and will rent a car to make the trip to San Miguel de Allende on his own."

Good grief. Up in the air, down in a hole, up with the nerves again. She gasped, caught her breath, wondered if this was what an anxiety attack felt like. "Why, Carl? It doesn't make sense. Surely, if Mark's needed on this trip at all, it would be at the conference table in the Mexican capitol. Why would he be directed to follow us to San Miguel?"

"To keep an eye on you?" Carl suggested candidly, posing the unspoken notion that her quest to save the President's life all by herself was absurd.

As for himself, Carl had instructions to accompany Alison until she was safely ensconced with her aunt and cousin. Why? Alison wondered again. Was Dom worried about an Arab retaliation against her? She thought it might have been Pope who said, *For fools rush in where angels fear to tread.* Or was it Shakespeare? Cousin Lisa would know. At any rate, she didn't think Lisa thought she was foolish, rushing about and wringing her hands like this.

Carl drove their rental car the two-hundred-fifty or so kilometers north out of Mexico City. Although she used her compact mirror to periodically peer behind them, it appeared they weren't being followed.

Soon Crosby met Ali's aging aunt and gossipy double cousin. After hugs and squeals, the quartet sat down to tea on Aunty Nasturtium's patio terrazzo. Carl would check in at the Casa Murphy, a bed and breakfast. Nasty Two promised to escort them about town the next day to her favorite restaurants, the El Campanario for Mexican food and the La Pinata for their vegetarian lunch specials, and to churches, including the Templo del Oratorio de San Felipe Neri.

Alison fidgeted. Thinking she might hyperventilate from her fears about Prescott, she breathed deeply, though quietly and unobtrusively.

"You'll love it, Ali," gushed her aunt. "There's such a clash of architectural styles—neoclassic, baroque. The inside of the church is absolutely beautiful."

"Parks, too," Nasty Two said. "You'll appreciate the Jardin Botanico, I'm sure. It's a premiere botanical garden with over nineteen hundred species."

"I need to get in some power walking. Any ideas?" Ali asked.

"Sure, same place; the Jardin has over five miles of walking paths."

Nasturtium said she regularly rented the same suite in this same hotel, year after year. Within a mile of the city center, the run-down hotel way past its prime sprawled haphazardly, like an abandoned ship leaning to port. Over six-thousand feet in altitude, the town felt familiar to Ali; much like Laramie. Nasturtium said that this year she was determined to learn the language. Enrolled for the third time in Spanish One, Aunt Nasty was barely getting the pronunciation right.

"*No es un policia. Es un profesor,*" she muttered.

"What are you saying, Aunty?"

"Something about a cop and a teacher, I guess. Or how about th: : *Que son ustedes, alumnos?* Which takes the answer: *Si, mosotros somos alumnos.* I think." She laughed at herself. Then she added that she was blessed with an abundance of serotonin, the "happy" chemical.

Seventy-two-year-old Nasty Two thought her ninety-two-year old mama ought to stay home. Nasty Two wanted to talk about her grandson, Ned Fleetfoot. She missed him, she said; also her daughter. "I don't trust that new husband of hers, either. There's something fishy about him." Again Nasty Two begged her mama to return home.

"So go, a'ready. Who's stoppin' you?" the old lady squawked, as if she didn't know her daughter was suffering from getting squished in the sandwich generation, torn betwixt and between what she perceived as her familial obligations. Hard to separate needs from wants; which generation needed Nasty Two more, or which direction she would prefer being pulled into. Alison suspected it was hard for her double cousin to admit that the Secretary of State didn't need her mommy any more. Or her grandson Ned either.

Nasturtium, experienced in ignoring anything she didn't want to hear, turned away. Taking Alison aside, the old lady demanded to hear the real scoop. "What's your purpose in coming here so suddenly? And don't try to fool me."

"I'm following a lead, Aunty. The President or his family could be the target of a terrorist plot."

Nasturtium gasped, one gnarled hand flying to her bosom.

Approaching, Nasty Two harrumphed, shaking her head in disgust. "In that wig, Ali, you look like Little Orphan Annie."

All the Nasties—One, Two, and Three—were redheaded; also balding, but only at the crown. At last Alison could empathize. With her own hair burnt off to the roots and hesitating about growing back, she had chosen a red curly wig for this trip to Mexico.

Redheaded Nasty Two, otherwise the image of her tiny white-haired mother, quickly changed the subject to lean forward eagerly. Obviously she was anxious to glean some chewable and tasty quotes she could sprinkle on her back-home gossip. Well, she could suffer alone. Alison would have to be out of her mind to share her secret objective with double cousin Nasty Two.

The hotel's central patio, now overgrown with weeds, must have been a beautiful garden. Bougainvillea still spilled their scarlet blossoms down the walls and over wrought iron railings on the second floor balconies. Parrots, colorful as rainbows, squawked from the trees. Uncaged, they couldn't fly away because their wings had been clipped.

"Sounds cruel," opined Carl.

Aunt Nasty's suite crouched crookedly at garden level. It, too, with door hanging half off its hinges, appeared ready for the demolition crew. Breakfast and lunch were provided with the rental and the Nasties heated soup on a hot plate for supper when they didn't go out. All of them drank bottled water, said Nasty Two.

"Gotta watch out you don't catch Montezuma's revenge," Nasty Two told Crosby knowledgeably. "Else you'll spend half your time running to the toilet."

Carl's thermometer switched into high, the red creeping swiftly from beneath open shirt collar to the top of his head.

The Nasties escorted Carl and Alison to the central plaza. Hustling her ducklings down the dusty road and along the cobblestoned streets, Nasty One pushed forward. They passed a lone farmer sidling along beside his burro, two milk cans tied to and bumping the sides of the sway-backed, scarecrow animal.

"They don't pasteurize or even refrigerate their milk," Nasturtium whispered. "But after a few days of diarrhea, your system builds up immunities to the bacteria. You'll be just fine, then."

"I can't believe the courage of your old aunt," Carl muttered to Ali. "Taking off from the safety of home to face all these challenges? All by herself?"

Alison said most of her kin had the clan's *wanderlust*, a real bent for travel. Nasty Two described the golf courses, bars, exotic foods, and the colony of Americans who regularly made San Miguel de Allende their home.

"All sorts of great things to see and do," said Nasturtium from her seat on the park bench. They'd reached the central piazza, concluding their power walk with the old lady beating everybody, but willing to rest awhile on the rusty bench. Meanwhile, Alison had a stiff neck from twisting it round this way and that, on the lookout for Mario, or some other thugs resembling Pesci in coloring and physique. He must know she wasn't staying long, which must mean that if he were coming, he was bound to arrive any minute.

"Carl, you were talking about the President's daughter," said Nasty One. "Sounds like you know Jerica well. She's a great youngun, though maybe she's got to experience a slice of life for herself before she starts to grow up. Her mommy and daddy are altogether too over-protective. In my opinion."

"They have to be, Ma'am. With all due respect, as the President's daughter Jerica is way too vulnerable to attack. Kidnapping for ransom, or for political leverage—those are the first two things that come to mind."

Alison arched an eyebrow. So Carl too had worries like her own.

Nasturtium squirmed on the hard bench, fidgeting as though the young man's words made her nervous. In one hand she gripped her crocheted bag, yarn spilling over, with her wallet hidden underneath. She wore a mid-shin length cotton print dress with full skirt, black ankle socks with white sneakers, and several necklaces, one of which was handmade from seashells, another of miniature pine cones. Topping these were two twenty-one-carat gold chains. Somebody could mug the woman for her goodies!

Must she fret over Aunty's safety, too? Ali stewed, but kept her lips sealed.

Just then a pigeon's after-lunch splash smacked near the old woman's shoulder. The bird poop hit Carl instead. Up went his thermometer.

"Tch, tch. Happens all the time." Pat, pat went one hand, gnarled with arthritis, while with the other she checked her daisy decorated hat for splatters. She grinned at him. *"Accept that some days you're the pigeon, and some days you're the statue."*

"Hey, that's pretty good," Carl said, whipping out his notebook and uncapping a pen. "Maybe I can use it in one of the President's speeches. I'll credit you, of course."

"Can't lay claim to it, Sonny. It was Roger C. Andersen," said Nasturtium, with no further elaboration. Abruptly, she arose. "Let's get out of here. I want to take you kids round to my favorite bar. I need a drink."

She meant a tiny sherry. Plopping down at a picnic table inside the gated courtyard outside the dim saloon, Nasturtium waved a hand at her daughter. Nasty Two was delighted to introduce Carl to the American regulars, adding his *nom de plume* as the U.S. President's "right-hand man, the guy in the know," thus triggering his thermometer.

People gathered around the table. While Nasturtium sipped from her tiny glass, she winked at Ali. Alison grinned back. She wasn't at all offended that her aunt and cousin spotlighted Carl as the star and herself as bit player. Aunty lived here. She needed to harvest the hay of Carl's visit as currency in her social arena. Ali mused that this could just as easily be the VFW hall back home, where veterans of foreign wars gathered to spin their yarns from battles past, like new wool into thread. In Wyoming, double cousin Lisa's retired Air Force Colonel liked to linger and listen and unravel his own war stories.

"Tell us the scoop, Mister," said one old but rather fit codger, his thin white hair pulled across a pink scalp. "Will the President send us into another dad-blamed war maneuver where NATO and the European generals call the shots?" Down here in Mexico among the expatriates, Alison noted, the consensus appeared to match that of many people back home. "Go to war, Mr. President! But with American generals in charge!"

Before Carl could reply, the oldtimers quickly challenged each other. Some demanded to know why Arabs hated Americans. Others responded that they called us infidels, a decadent society; or, that they envied us our affluence; or, that they resented America's support of Israel; or, they despised Western influences on their women.

With their pleasant tour and the challenging saloon chitchat behind them, Alison had grown complacent. What she should have been doing was try to prepare herself for the disaster of coming face to face again with Mario Pesci!

Right the first time!

Back at Nasturtium's hotel, Mark Prescott sat on a tilted iron bench among the weeds on the patio. He sipped lemonade, one leg crossed over the other, swinging a foot and rocking one patent leather shoe back and forth. He glanced briefly at Alison without smiling. Then he smirked at Carl before rising and turning to Nasturtium.

"*Mama, mia!*" Pesci exclaimed, rushing to greet and encircle the old woman with arms stretched wide.

Alison felt like she'd been socked with a wet tortilla. "What's going on?" she squeaked, in a voice rusty as old bedsprings.

"*Numero uno. Tengo paciencia,* Mario." Have patience, Number One. Aunt Nasturtium hugged him back.

Alison and Carl stared, first at the tableau, and then at each other. Quickly, they both turned to Nasty Two, who, shrugging, glared back at them.

"Sit down, sit down, my boy," Nasturtium said, extricating herself from Pesci's grasp. "Nasty, order lemonade for everybody. And some cookies."

At last the story unraveled, though in pieces that made little sense when juxtapositioned next to one another, like stitched into a crazy quilt.

Nasturtium was Mario's godmother. She knew his family well, she said.

"Mario Pesci was named for our Mario, Ali. Mario Vicente, grandfather of Cousin Alberto Vicente, the latter a resident of Sicily, nowadays. Our Mario—the grandfather, that is—was *consigliere* to the Don; Pesci, I mean...."

"Let me, Godmother," Mark Prescott said, now looking perfectly harmless with his face split in a huge grin. Turning to his audience, he took up the story. "Several Vicentes served several Pesci Dons as *consigliere*; namely, advisor, counselor, friend. The *caporegimes*, heads of the family, depended big on the Vicentes. Hence, my friends and fellow kinsmen, the Pescis will forever be in the debt of the Vicentes. You in trouble? Come to the Pescis."

"What kind of trouble?" Ali murmured. "Rub somebody out, is that it?"

Mark grinned. "You mean like *zotz, zap, whack,* or *off* someone?"

"Whatever." She dismissed the notion with a shrug, but her mind zoomed into overdrive. Along with her heart and every pore in her body, which immediately commenced sending droplets of perspiration swimming free to puddle in her arm pits. If she couldn't bring Randy around, persuade him to stop abusing her, she could just call the Sicilians. They'd come and *zotz* him for her. Ali shivered at the horrid fantasy.

"We don't do that kind of thing any more," Mario countered, thus returning Alison to reality. "Our people are lawyers, business people, computer programmers, what have you. I don't personally even know any *vindictores*—hit men. No, I meant you can call on us for legitimate help, like legal advice or representation."

Alison didn't believe it, not for a second. Mario didn't <u>know</u> any *vindictore*? What did he call himself? He'd just killed a man, right there in the White House, right in front of God and everybody. Or didn't stabbing an assassin count? Or was such a terrible thing so common he didn't notice?

Nasturtium was Mark's godmother. The invitation had been made and accepted when the boy was named Mario after a long succession of Sicilian Vicentes. And his father had been instrumental in "putting away" members of the *Costa Nostra*, when he'd appeared in Federal Court to testify against them.

"When I say the family's legit these days, I mean legit!" Mark insisted.

Nasty Two appeared as amazed as Alison. The Family Gossip said she thought she knew all the family's secrets.

"Hardly, my dear," said her mother, lifting one eyebrow at Alison behind Nasty Two's back. Everybody in the clan knew Nasty Two was an incurable gossip. Tell her something and you might as well broadcast it on Fox news. The arched eyebrow suggested her mama wasn't about to tell Nasty Two everything she knew.

Alison invited Mark to take a walk with her. "Alone," she said, glancing at Nasty Two. Only her Aunty noticed.

Supportive, old Nasturtium agreed. "You two must get acquainted."

Alone together on the mostly deserted gravel road, Alison couldn't resist taunting him. "What about the assassin, the Muslim at the White House?"

"Like you, I sensed something wrong," Mario admitted. "Also, I got a glimpse of his blade beneath the tablecloth. I didn't know when, didn't know what he was up to, but whatever it was I wanted to divert him. Pierre Corneille said, and I quote: *All evils are equal when they are extreme.* It's good to be prepared, Mrs. Morissey."

"Call me Alison."

"You've got the nose for trouble, too, Alison. I like that. A true Sicilian can sniff out trouble. When you suspected me, you had the wrong guy, that's the difference."

She could have told Mark this wouldn't be the first time her instinct for trouble had got her into hot water. With her husband in particular, but also with the thugs she'd helped bring to justice. Alison could have talked about her old friend back home, Detective Walt Fletcher, and how, between the two of them, they'd captured a ring of bank robbers. But this was not the time nor the place. As some of her former escapades flashed across the screen of her memory, Alison smiled. Randy had good reason for trying to keep his wife at home and out of trouble.

"Why didn't you tell me about the kinship between our two families. About your godmother, all that, when you discovered on the plane that I had pegged you as sinister?"

"Didn't think you'd believe me. You didn't believe the Davidsons when they told you I'm an innocent. Besides, I hadn't seen Nasturtium for a long time, and thought this would be a good opportunity. See her, and explain to you, with your aunt's help."

This time Alison apologized, genuinely and sincerely. Never again would she allow herself to accuse somebody merely on the basis of the color of their skin or the shape of their features. She dropped her head in shame and remorse. Pausing to pat her shoulder, Mark paid no attention to the roadway, to which his back was turned. He said, "Of course I forgive you, Alison. You care about the President. Every citizen must be alert to danger and to suspicious characters."

Around the corner careened a high-powered, speeding car. His back to the street, Mark continued to stare into Alison's troubled face. Spotting the danger, she quickly shoved Mark out of the way to hurl herself onto the side of the road, where she skinned both knees and elbows, ripping her pants.

"A hit and run!" yelled Mark, sprawled on his belly.

While Alison sat rubbing her knees and grimacing, he leaped to his feet.

"Man, alive! You saved my life!"

She shrugged, apologized again, and painfully arose.

"I owe you one, Alison."

She couldn't speak. He helped her to her feet and slowly the two of them commenced the long stroll back down the street to Aunt Nasturtium's hotel. She took his proffered arm. Both of them fell silent, as they leaned on one another.

Granted, Alison had taken a 180-degree turn. She felt so relieved, however, in having discovered a home-grown former Mafioso, not an international terrorist, that she willingly accepted Mario as friend. If he was good enough for Aunty, he was fine with Alison. She felt more relaxed with him now.

Besides, the Mafia seemed familiar, less sinister than a terrorist cell of Muslim sleepers awaiting the call to attack the President and his family.

"As I said, Alison, I feel as though the Nasties, you, Lisa, the whole Vicente clan, are my family, too," said Mario. "The Sicilians are loyal and protective of their own. Just remember that. In case you're ever in need, I'm witchew. Got that? Know what I mean? You need help, you need the Pescis, you call. Remember that, Alison. I'm witchew."

CHAPTER 8

▼

LARAMIE

Back home in Cheyenne now, Alison didn't know whether to panic or collapse with relief. No sign of Randy, the cantankerous old fool. No mail or messages on either voice mail or email. No evidence he'd come and gone. Clara, their live-in housekeeper, said she hadn't seen hide nor hair of him.

"Why, Ali? Were you expecting him back early?"

"No, of course not. I just thought he might check in with you."

If it were true that no news was good news, she'd relax and forget it. Why look a gift horse in the mouth? For whatever reason, Alison had been handed a gift of another few days, without him ordering her around, criticizing every last thing she did, and raining guilt trips on her head.

Alison chatted awhile with Clara over tea. The woman with the iron-gray bun at the nape of her neck was practically family. Naturally Clara wanted to hear all about Alison's harrowing experience.

Later, Ali bathed and left for Laramie to meet her daughter and the President's speechwriter, as if she had not a care on earth. With no messages or news of Randy, she was free awhile longer from her sniping husband. Time enough to worry about her marriage when he returned.

"No, I haven't seen Jerica lately," Joan admitted to her mom and Carl. Wearing tee shirt and blue jeans with black leather boots and blue linen blazer that set off her blue eyes and wavy auburn hair, the professor suggested they go to the Coal Creek Coffeehouse in historic downtown Laramie.

Dressed to play golf, Ali wore a lavender cotton blouse with purple skirt. She preferred these hues, while the Nasties usually chose blue, and Lisa, pink.

"I'd like to invite Jerica out for dinner," Carl said. "Think she'll come?"

Joan shrugged in dismissal before recommending a variety of international coffees, their aroma permeating the big room. The trio took seats among the chatting twos and threes and singles reading poetry, textbooks, newspapers and journals. The high ceilings with fans twirling slowly in the old building with the bookshelf-lined walls below stained glass windows was homey, Crosby said.

Once settled, he re-introduced his questions. Apparently Carl needed reassurance. Personally, Ali couldn't see anything obnoxious about the man. But with Jerica currently tuned into the scrubby misfits Joan had described, the girl might dismiss the President's shy speechwriter as a paltry milquetoast. Or she would suspect that her parents had sent Carl out to campus on purpose; to spy on her.

Determined to share some local history, Joan said that Laramie was an old railroad town. "The Union Pacific Railroad came through the territory from east to west back in 1868, in a rush to beat the California Pacific, whose workers busily hacked over and through the mountains from west to east. The U.P. laid 540 miles of track between Cheyenne and Utah, using 2,400 ties per mile, weighing 300 pounds apiece. The *Tie Hackers* cut and hacked ties from the trees in Medicine Bow National Forest, for which they were paid up to sixty cents per tie in boom times, compared to just seven cents later."

Carl interrupted Joan to suggest that if it were modern day times, the tree huggers would be out en masse with placards and demonstrations to protest the cutting of trees.

"And the ecoterrorists to blow up the tracks," added Alison dryly.

Crosby agreed to a game of golf, so they went to the club next to make up a foursome, including the golf pro. In that high altitude, over seven thousand feet, August is warm and sunny but seldom hot. Carl found the weather delightful. The day was beautiful and the course, surrounded by evergreens and dotted with sand traps and water hazards, came with rolling green hills.

Alison and Carl won the golf match.

After a driving tour of the University of Wyoming campus, they settled in the Student Union. Joan went to fetch goodies, returning with a tray laden with tea, cheese, fruit, and Ritz crackers. To Carl's visible relief Alison proposed they talk about Jerica.

"Recapping what we know," Joan replied, "Jerica and her roommate Callie checked out of the Chi Omega Sorority house in May, got an apartment, and Jerica enrolled in summer school. Now the President's daughter is supposed to be up in Medicine Bow staying with Callie's folks. What could those girls be doing? It's just a wee village."

Carl shrugged. Apparently he knew no more than the two women.

Joan shook her head, selecting a grape from the fruit bowl to nibble while staring solemnly across the room. Impatient, Alison leaned forward, grabbed both their arms, and gave them a shake.

"Hey, listen up, you two. I'm frightened for Jerica."

"Why?" Joan asked. "She's been safe all along; all her whole life, in fact."

"She wasn't running with the bunch she is now."

"About fear, Mom," Joan said. "Pierre Corneille said, *Do your duty, and leave the rest to heaven.*"

"That's what I'm trying to do, dear. 'Do my duty—to the First Family."

Carl appeared discomfited. He turned to Joan, as if willing to play the one-upmanship game. "In the words of Honore de Balzac, *The heart of a mother is a deep abyss at the bottom of which you will always discover forgiveness.*"

Joan stared at him, mouth agape. Alison laughed. Carl started to blush, but gulped water and air instead. "I meant Alison. She's acting like Jerica's surrogate mother."

Before Ali could reply to that, he leaned forward eagerly. Hands clasped below his chin, he addressed Joan. "Tell us what you know about Jerica's friends. Like, uh, her roommate."

From his hesitation Alison guessed Carl didn't want to know about boyfriends. She smiled behind her hanky, blowing her nose as a diversion.

"Callie. Callie Jensen. And a boyfriend they both seem to share. Callie was flunking my class. When I gave her the *F* she deserved—she hardly ever came to class, rarely turned in an assignment—Callie dropped out of the University. I'm Jerica's advisor because her dad requested me, via the University president. Jerica hasn't declared a major and is therefore assigned to the Arts & Science College, my university home. Academic advisors aren't personal counselors. If and when Jerica wants to talk, I'm there to listen. Mom and I visited her in her sorority house last spring, Carl, but otherwise I've no real excuse to pry."

Joan said she wanted to drop by her office in Hoyt Hall before leaving campus. Turning to Carl, she clarified. "The home of many English professors, Hoyt Hall was named for the U's first president, who was also the territory's third governor, prior to statehood in 1890. Mrs. Hoyt was among the most educated of all the state's first ladies. With a Ph.D., Elizabeth Orpha Sampson Hoyt taught philosophy and logic."

Alison dropped her head. Ever the professor, Joan often waxed pedantic.

*   *   *   *

At that precise moment, Butch and Bud were slumping down low in Butch's tan van, parked across the street from Hoyt Hall, Merica Hall, and, farther down, the Administration Building, otherwise known as *Old Main*. "See, Bud?" Butch said, pointing his finger off in the vague direction of Hoyt. "That's our target. Do you remember the reason? 'Cause the son of a timber tycoon works there. We're gonna hit the S.O.B. where he lives. Knock out one a his own."

"Hey, man, great idea. Pass over that thermos. I need more brew."

CHAPTER 9

▼

THE EDWARDS
BROTHERS

In Milwaukee, Butch's older brothers made ready to recall Lil Bro, the only Edwards boy who knew anything about building bombs. Their target, which Ellery had chosen himself (but had put off on *The Man's* decision), was the U.S. Federal Courthouse on East Wisconsin Street, in historic downtown. Actually, the boss was pretty vague when he commanded the Edwards boys to *wreak havoc*. Ellery figured he had enough moxy to decide for Cell Number Two.

The Edwards brothers sipped coffee and munched pastries from their perch at a hotel café. Their huge haunches squashed across the plastic-cushioned benches with the stuffing poking out. Ellery scarfed his third roll, while Eden stuffed his mouth with his fourth. Another few minutes and they must leave for the airport to pick up Butch. The fragrance of fresh brewed coffee along with pork roasting and apple pies baking commingled with the stink of stale grease from the grill.

Ma Edwards had home-schooled her sons, but only Ellery recalled much of the city's history. By the late 1800s, because of the influx of so many German immigrants, Milwaukee was referred to as the most German among American cities. Earlier, the feud between Juneau and Kilbourn—one of whom had staked out the area to the west of the Milwaukee River and the other to the east—produced two sets of streets that did not meet when they greeted each other across the river. Subsequent builders constructed bridges that, instead of running straight across, ran catty-wampus. That's how Ma told the story. Then she said that the three small villages of Juneautown, Kilbourntown and Walker's Point had merged in 1846 to form the City of Milwaukee.

Eden shook his head when Ellery reminded him. "Who cares? I wanna know about this courthouse building we're supposed to blow up."

"Later. We gotta get a move on." Ellery paid the check, leaving a nickel tip to clatter across the Formica-topped table.

Out at General Mitchell International Airport, Ellery drew up at the curb designed for quick loading and unloading. He pulled in, cutting off and nearly running down a man in a wheelchair, who shook his fist at them. Ellery flipped him the bird, yelling "Outta the way, cripple!" He found a spot where they could keep an eye on the exit. Shouldn't be long. He'd keep the engine running. He wasn't about to pay for parking or move his ass to go greet the returning hero who'd blown up a mere gas station. Jeez, Eden couldn't stop praising Lil Bro. He could have made Butch's personal cheerleading squad.

In the back, Todd smoked a toke. "Wake me when Butch pulls in," he said. "I'm gonna catch a few winks."

Scooting down to rest on his tailbone, Eden demanded more information on their assignment. In particular, how tough would the old building be to bring down?

Ellery sighed. Eden nor Butch remembered nuthin' from Ma's teaching. "Constructed between 1892 and 1899 of Mount Waldo granite, from Frankfort, Maine, the U.S. Courthouse is fireproof throughout and well guarded."

"Never mind that. Butch will find a way." Edward Edwards, Junior, was obviously Eden's hero. "I bet he'll get inside on the sly to check it out. Then he'll know how and where to place his explosives."

Ellery was no believer. Certainly not in *Junior*, the brother what got their Pa's name. "Listen, dummy. The building has granite walls, which intersect with hipped and gabled roofs. You know the place sports a huge, impressive tower. It's not gonna be easy to blow. Butch'll prob'ly miscalculate."

Eden looked appalled, then mad; finally, he cooled down. "You're pullin' my leg, right? Trying to impress me with the size and structure of the building. You're thinkin' Butch ain't up to pullin' off this job."

"Not at all. I jus' want you to realize how tough it'll be." Which was one among several reasons why Ellery had chosen the famous old Federal Courthouse as their target. With *The Man* recalling Butch to do the job, preempting Ellery in the process, Big Bro wasn't going to make it easy. If Butch failed, no skin off his ass. Butch could make his own excuses to their boss.

The federal building, Ellery droned on in Eden's ear, was an excellent example of Richardsonian Romanesque style architecture. The interior was arranged around a vast central arcade, "You know, Eden, like the Hyatt Regency lobby" (that was a target he'd considered and then discarded). The arcade, Ellery lectured further, was surrounded by broad corridors and surmounted by an iron and glass skylight. "This arcade appears substantially as it was at the turn of the Twentieth Century. And so are the adjacent public areas, having many-hued terrazzo and tile floors, multi-colored marble paneling, wainscot, and door frames; paneled wood doors, mosaic, wood-paneling, and plaster ceilings. The building today is filled with the chambers and courtrooms of the U.S. District Court, the U.S. Circuit Court, and the U.S. Bankruptcy Court, along with suites that house the U.S. Attorney, U.S. Marshall, and U.S. Probation offices."

Eden sat up and shoved his baseball cap around backwards. "Jeez, Ellery, shut th'hell up. You sound like you memorized some dadblamed brochure." Which was exactly what Ellery had done. Eden wasn't the only one he wanted to impress. Forget Lily and Todd, they were too stoned to notice. *Bonnie and Clyde* weren't worth tiddly, either No, it was Butch that Ellery hoped to snow.

Ellery ignored the airport exits with the hosts of travelers bursting through the doors hauling their wheelies, their snot-nosed kids, and all the rest of their crap. He wasn't going in to meet Lil Bro, either. Let Butch find their beat up RV on his own. Ellery also discounted Eden's protests about his *lecture.*

"Eden, listen up. One of the most impressive rooms in the federal building is a two-story judicial chamber with oak-paneled walls and ceiling and intricately carved oak trim." This beautiful and historic chamber was Ellery's specific target. "Above and to the left of the judge's bench hangs the State of Wisconsin seal; above right is the City of Milwaukee seal, and above center is the federal emblem. The stained glass lamps are period originals, only now they have modern fixtures in them. Eden, you must recall this court house!"

"Oh, shut up, Ellery." Eden closed his eyes.

$$* \qquad * \qquad * \qquad *$$

When he learned he was expected to do the bomb job, Butch issued orders over the phone for Ellery to follow. "Now hear this. You or Eden, one, gotta get inside. Check out the ventilation system. Identify where the original gas lights used to be." Ellery had told him that following the installation of the modern-day light bulbs, which had to be changed through a crawl space above the ceiling.

When Ellery protested, demanding how that information would help, Butch proposed to impersonate the janitor or whoever was in charge of the piddly chore. "Nobody will suspect an employee."

Like the Oklahoma City bombing of another federal building, Butch said he would use fertilizer and kerosene, plus detonator and timer. Unlike Oklahoma and the World Trade Center, though, they did not plan a daytime strike. Killing a whole batch of people would bring in too many authorities. The media, too. The latter was okay, *The Man* said. That's what he wanted, for the boys to publicize their cause.

Ecoterrorism! Tree hugging. *Save the Trees!*

Then Butch would return to Wyoming, before moving on to Oregon and Washington. "You'll be hitting the timber industry big time, then," said *The Man.*

But not before the Edwards brothers did the job on the U. S. Federal Courthouse in Milwaukee. Butch and Eden agreed with the target. "Couldn't suit our own purposes better," Butch had yelled over the phone when he heard.

*   *   *   *

Northern Wisconsin was home to the Edwards boys and their kin. Pa had met his Maker from an early and untimely demise. "May he rest in peace."

Ellery had specifically targeted this particular court house and the famous oak-paneled courtroom because that was Judge Donald Sullivan's bailiwick. The mid-height, mid-girth, graying Sullivan was the judge in American Timber, Inc. vs Edwards, back when Pa Edwards worked as a lumberjack in northern Wisconsin. Pa Edwards had fallen, breaking both legs and crushing three discs in his back. The court, meaning Sullivan, had ruled for the defense. According to the plaintiffs, the corporation continued murdering men, and they still killed Wisconsin and Minnesota trees, while the Edwards family and their compadres got the shaft. Which was when the three brothers hooked up with the tree-hugging ecoterrorists to teach corporate America lessons they'd not soon forget.

This same federal building also housed the bankruptcy court, where Pa Edwards had lost his life's savings following his accident. Shortly thereafter, Pa had hanged himself off a rafter in the shed back of the house. Double reasons, then, personal and public, as Ellery saw it, for blowing up Milwaukee's fine old building. Butch gave Big Bro no argument. Eden shrugged, lost in his own fog.

Neither Ellery nor Eden could do the dirty deed of positioning the bomb, because they'd grown too fat since their Pa had lost his lawsuit, and all the

Edwards men, including uncles, had lost their lumberjack jobs. Eden weighed in at two-ninety and Ellery at three-forty-three.

"Hey, man," Eden suddenly yelled, sitting upright and looking over his shoulder. "Where th'hell is Butch? Here come the cops to run us off."

*   *   *   *

Lily had promised Ellery she'd keep an eye on *Bonnie and Clyde*, though she hated the assignment. "Jerky old people," she'd fumed. Now she was eavesdropping. She studied the menu, turning up her nose at the odor of sizzling meat on the grill. Badly wanting a toke, she settled on white toast.

On the west side of the Milwaukee River at the once elegant Wisconsin Hotel on Old World Third Street, Bonnie and Charles sat fuming and fussing at the counter of Maxie's Café. The long-married couple, middle-aged, middle-class, middle-girth in middle America, weren't young enough to do the work demanded of Butch, Ellery, and Eden. What the husband-wife pair were good at was legitimacy—stuffing envelopes, making phone calls, creating homemade protest signs and staging demonstrations. What the two soft little doughboy-shaped dumplins were mad about now was this federal building blow-up. Pull it off and they'd all have to disperse like ants under a dose of boiling water.

"I don't get it," Bonnie wailed to her husband. "If we want to bring national attention to our cause, why do it like a bunch a thugs?"

"Because we've dadgum well hooked ourselves up with thugs, Bonnie. We'd be better off finding some other group."

"Too late now, Charles." Bonnie looked around the ordinary little café with the red plastic seats (but with very tasty food) at the group of tourists from Germany who'd reserved ahead of time and thus took up every table, leaving the eco pair to shove their haunches on the little stools. Bonnie worried that somebody would overhear them, especially Lily, or even the top dog, whoever and wherever he was. "They said they'd take us out if we left." Bonnie giggled. "*Take us out.* What a funny way to say 'kill us'."

Charles sighed. He wondered if his little darlin' was entering the first stage of Alzheimer's. Whatever happened, he aimed to take care of her.

They were too old and semi-crippled, they said, to take their naps on the floor of the RV awaiting Butch's arrival, despite Ellery's aim to keep them all together, like overripe tomatoes that might squish and leak their juices if left alone. Bonnie and Charles would like to leak all right; leak the news of the terrorist plot to the cops or the press. Stop this horror before it was too late. Besides, they told each other, they were retired postal workers on civil pension and social security, so they could afford a hotel room.

Bonnie peered this way and that while dipping her toast in runny yellow egg yoke. Observing, Lily wanted to barf at the sight of those gloppy eggs.

"It'll all be over, soon, Charles," Bonnie said. "Then we'll go home."

"Haven't you been listening, Hon? We can never go home again. Got to relocate."

Bonnie shrugged. "Oh well, we've already sold everything of value." Then she paused to wipe away a salty tear. "Wish we had our son back, Charles. Somebody to remember us. We could get ourselves kilt, you know."

"I know." Charles sighed again, this time a big one. They'd already posed to each other their worst nightmares—cops after them, car chases, shootout in the streets. Lying bleeding and half-dead, but not quite. All that pain. "But if we had our son back, we wouldn't a got our butts stuck in this quicksand we can't seem to get out of."

"And for what?" Bonnie demanded.

"For the cause, sugar." They'd worked hard at stopping the timbering since their son was killed. "Can't be tree huggers without putting our mouth where our money is."

"I think you got that backwards, Charles."

"No, I meant it the way I said it. First we contributed small amounts of money. Remember? Before we committed ourselves, and started shooting off our mouths about stopping the big timbering companies."

"Yeah, I know. We were overheard; next thing we knew, we're charmed into making a full-time commitment."

Their son, Kent, was killed while stopped at a stoplight. The logging truck in the next lane lost its logs and dumped them all over him. An overloaded truck, its chains had snapped. Down rolled the logs, tumbling off the truck to bury Kent Castle before he could accelerate across the intersection. Smashed him flat as a waffle.

"Don't you mean pancake?" Bonnie had asked Charles at the time. He, not she, had gone to the morgue to identify their son. She couldn't bear it.

"No, I meant waffle. What was left of Kent had dents and marks all over him from the logs what bashed him. Kent's remains looked like a waffle."

When she realized, through her shock, what they were talking about, Bonnie burst into tears. Her son, lost to them forever. Squashed like a waffle.

*   *   *   *

The Edwards brothers and their Cell Number Two ecoterrorist gang needed Butch in Milwaukee. Which was why Butch had commanded Callie and Bud to blow up Hoyt Hall on the UW campus by themselves. And, also, he ordered, "Get Jerica involved!"

The President's daughter. Blamed for the bombing. Man, what a coup!

Butch had left Laramie driving Callie's blue Dodge Intrepid for Cheyenne. He planned to catch a plane from Wyoming's capital city, change planes at DIA out of Denver, and be in Milwaukee before nightfall. Meanwhile, he had ordered his older brothers to be at the airport waiting for him. No sense wasting time.

Except that Butch Edwards got picked up before he could get out of Cheyenne. He was stopped at an intersection, for "probable cause," by police rookie, Bobby Gilbert. The baby-faced, apple-cheeked youngster was determined to impress his boss, the guy with the eighty-percent arrest-to-incarceration record, Detective Sergeant Walt Fletcher. The blue Dodge Intrepid was riding low in the back, Gilbert told Fletcher.

The baby-faced rookie didn't know it, but Callie's car springs were sprung from carting around all that ammunition and explosives in crates labeled "Popcorn."

Bobby told Sergeant Fletcher he'd figured maybe the Dodge, with the dirty haired chap with the nose earring hunched over the steering wheel, might be smuggling drugs into their fair city.

Gilbert said he aimed to put a stop to that!

CHAPTER 10

▼

CHEYENNE

At home in Cheyenne, Alison was set on cleaning. "Top to bottom, Clara dear. We mustn't settle for anything less."

The raw-boned, gaunt widow was working as a motel maid when Alison had rescued Clara three decades earlier. Ali's home was hers, too. Clara said she loved Ali's kinfolk ("Well, most of 'em"), along with the occasional stray Alison brought home. Clara had particularly cottoned to Dom, back when Dominic Alexander Davidson came to board for the summer.

Commissioned in the late 1880s by Rose DuMaurier, the double cousins' great-great-grandmother, the house was built on what once was known as "Millionaires' Row." With three floors plus basement, the house Ali inherited through her paternal kin (because the other two doubles-line "girls and boys" already owned fine houses) was where she'd hoped to raise many children. Joan alone arrived before Randy's grown-up case of mumps put finis to that plan. He was diagnosed sterile.

Which was perhaps why Alison filled the grand old place with what her husband called human strays. "Look what the cat dragged home this time," he'd not so fondly proclaim, like back when Dom Davidson came to board with them. The future president had lived on the third floor. So did Clara.

Now the two women labored from room to room and floor to floor. Clara's efficiency methods had taken root in her employer; the only seeds to ever sprout, apparently, for otherwise Alison consistently bumbled, tripped or spilled.

"Only because her mind is invariably somewhere else, on something more important than housework," the German woman loyally defended her employer to anyone who dared laugh at Alison within her earshot.

Vacuuming, dusting, scrubbing, changing linens, they could gossip and giggle without missing an inch. "Who's moving in this time, Alison?"

"Only Carl Crosby, overnight. But we're having the clan for cocktails."

"Great. I haven't seen any of the family while you've been out of town."

Clara whipped through the last bed with sharply cornered top sheet, gathering into a carry basket and the pockets of her apron the cleaning supplies that Ali couldn't handle. They also had plenty of cooking to do before the party.

With the house clean and tidy, the pair welcomed Clara's niece, the baby sitter for the small children. Beforehand, the girl would help prepare the menu of baked cheese puffs, caviar and toast tips, bacon-wrapped chicken livers, shrimp with sauce, cauliflower and broccoli flowerets, celery sticks stuffed with pineapple flavored cream cheese or peanut butter, slices of honeydew melon and cantaloupe, purple grapes, stacks of assorted cheese squares, meatballs in sauce, hot wings, and everybody's favorite, Alison's cheese ball, concocted of three cheeses, and garnished by rolling it in chopped pecans and serving slices on a variety of crisp crackers. Various chocolate concoctions, from seven-layer cookie bars to walnut brownies and "some-mores" for the younger set, rounded off the adults' food fare. Also, for the teenagers and children, hot dogs and burgers grilled on the back patio, with soft drinks, dips and chips. Although it was billed as a cocktail party, few would need dinner later or leave early.

Clara ordered the liquor and checked the larder to ensure there was plenty of tea and coffee; also milk for the youngsters, and for Nasty Three's new husband, who claimed to be a teetotaler. "Proud of it!" Harold the Hayseed often crowed, like a lone rooster in a chicken house full of horny hens.

Wilma Sanford, Wyoming's Superintendent of Public Instruction, wasn't kin but she was "family." She was descended from the famous black settler, Willamena Jackson, friend and lifelong companion of the clan's ancestor, Rose DuMaurier. Wilma, with the velvety milk-chocolate skin, and Nasty Three, with the pale and transparent-like, easily mottled skin, were as close as their forebears had been. As were Alison and Lisa, or Nicole and Beth. Whenever the clan gathered, there was widowed Wilma, with her teenaged son, Mark.

Meanwhile, the tall, elegant State Superintendent and the short, crown-balding, hearing-impaired (double cousin once removed) Secretary of State often left their offices late to share a drink in the Cloud Nine Lounge at the Cheyenne airport, which squats in the middle of town, a sling-shot throw from the complex of state government buildings. Thus the bar was a hangout for the capitol crowd. And for other wheeler dealers, including wealthy ranchers, powerful business people, lawyers, and the political brokers, from lobbyists to the backstage people who operated from the wings rather than from within the spotlight of public awareness.

Although Nasty Three was a recent bride, she hadn't changed all her habits. The Secretary of State continued to join Wilma at the Cloud Nine, but without the groom. To clan gatherings, held at the Morisseys if not at the Schwartzkopfs, Nasty Three now brought her silly little husband, Harold Morton. Nobody—in the family nor in the whole state, for that matter—could see what Nasty Three saw in Morton the Mutt. Morton the Manikin, Harry the Huffy, Harold the Haberdashers' dream customer. All these were labels Alison and Lisa, amidst giggles, periodically produced out of earshot of Nasty Three.

A former bank teller, Morton the Mordant was now one of the veeps at Cheyenne's First Bank, a promotion, the clan suspected, arranged as a concession to the Secretary of State. The bank president and most of the Vicente-Aulds were country club members, having shared a long history of personal experiences and favors exchanged. (If that's what Nasty'd done, got her new husband his job, Harold either didn't know or failed to acknowledge.)

True to form, Harry showed up at Alison's wearing a three-piece charcoal pinstriped suit with starched white shirt and white on white (more stripes) tie, shining patent-leather shoes, and doffing a top hat. The others, save for those who came straight from work, had dressed informally.

"It's a wonder Harry's not in tux with ruffled pink shirt," whispered Lisa to Alison, as they giggled behind their hands like two little girls. Lisa smoothed the jacket of her pink linen pantsuit.

Alison wore a lavender cotton pantsuit and Nasty Three a blue floral summer dress with pleated skirt. Wilma, too, had come from work, her large executive suite and complex of department offices in the Hathaway Building, where she'd been in conference with the deputy superintendent, an Asian woman Wilma chose because of their similar educational theories and workaholic natures. "As Thomas Carlyle in *Past and Present* said," Wilma said to Nasty Three, who cheerfully chided her friend for working too hard, "*Blessed is he who has found his work, let him ask no other blessedness.*"

Nasty had replied, "Yes, dear," since that was her way.

Alison and Lisa giggled again. They knew that Willamena Jackson, over her whole eighty-year history with Rose DuMaurier, had never managed to persuade their great-great-grandmother to commit to memory any of the Bard's famous writings, nor any other from among the classics, any more than modern-day Wilma had convinced Nasty Three to memorize apt quotations.

Armed with sports bags, the family arrived in bunches, like concord grapes. Peter and Lisa Schwartzkopf came with their daughter Beth and her husband, Brad, and the BB twins—who were promptly escorted by Clara to the big, sunny, toy-filled, third-floor playroom where Clara's niece was in charge. Nicole's four-year-old, Stevie, ran to squeal and run circles about the pretty little blondes. Typically, he would tease and carry on until his grandmother, the professor, popped in for hugs and admonitions about good behavior.

Hundred-year-old Hepzibah clutched her yarn and knitting needles, and her daughter-in-law, Isabelle, whose husband, Rudolph (he of the bulbous red nose and not to be confused with Ali's Randolph) was off somewhere looking for a church that would have him and his hell-fire brand of preaching.

Harold the Hun clung to the Secretary of State, as Nasty Three held fast to her daisy-decorated straw hat. Dr. Wilma Sanford arrived with Mark, and her son came armed with his guitar. Nasties One and Two lingered in Mexico.

Lisa whispered to Alison: "You've so much to tell me about your trip. I can't wait to hear how the Nasties are doing. Cousin Nasty Two must be having a fit. I can believe that Aunt Nasturtium didn't get around to telling you and me about the family's connection with the Pesci family. But not tell her own daughter?" Lisa paused to nod and smile at Harold the Haughty, but her courtesy fell flat. As though Harry had never learned his manners, he did not complete the pleasant transaction.

"Good grief," Lisa continued in Ali's ear, dismissing Harry as if his huffy shrug in her direction were no worse than a pesky gnat in the face. "Mario Pesci is one of the President's aides? And Nasty One never told Nasty Two that she's Pesci's godmother? Unbelievable."

Unable to await regaling Lisa with the details, Alison had called her soul mate before leaving Mexico. Now she had no time to reply nor Lisa to continue, because running up the steps of the Morisseys' screened-in, wrap-around front porch came Jeff Vicente, Nasty Two's brother from Casper, with his son, John, presently of Laramie.

Clapping her hands, Lisa squealed, "I didn't know you guys were coming."

"More double cousins," said Alison, exchanging hugs with both tall men.

Jeff and John were both tall like Jeff's dad, Thomas Jefferson Vicente, Nasty One's deceased husband. All of these people—the Nasties, the men they had married, and their children—sprouted red hair.

Jeff's son, John, was a physicist, or would be, when he completed his doctorate at the University of Wyoming. An ectomorph in shape, tall and slender, with a full head of wavy, reddish-brown hair, John Vicente could have passed for John F. Kennedy. With good reason; this arm of the family had inherited their Irish looks from Grandfather Luther Auld. Nasturtium One, John's grandmother, was Essie and Luther's eldest flower-named daughter, which made Nasty Two John's aunt.

Led by Alison, Carl Crosby was introduced as the President's speechwriter. "One of them, just one of them," he corrected Alison. She noticed him fighting like crazy to keep his thermometer under control.

"Sounds like an important job," John replied easily. His ready smile spoke of self-confidence and acceptance.

"Nice guy," Carl told Alison later. "Hope we can get to be friends. John agreed to show me around campus and Laramie, help me locate some good sources to quote as background for my story on Jerica and her current habitat."

Alison thought Carl made Jerica sound like a protected specie. Ali sincerely hoped and prayed that Jerica was well protected.

Mark Sanford, Wilma's son, Beth Gifford, Lisa's daughter, and Nicole Taylor, Ali's granddaughter, went outside to play Frisbee on the wide sweeping lawn at the side of the house. Most of the clan members were fit from their various games of golf, tennis, downhill and cross-country skiing, power walking, and touch football. Softball was the game of choice this time, with the arrival of the men— Peter, Brad, Jeff, John, and Carl. But not Morton the Meticulous, who set off to roam the house uninvited.

The men were soon challenged by a team of women—Alison, Lisa, Beth, Nicole, Nasty Three, and Wilma. But not Hepzibah and Isabelle, who continued sitting on the front porch, in silence, knitting and crocheting.

The men won two innings, the women the third. After a few laps in the pool, everybody hopped into party clothes, ready to be wined and dined. They could have been baby birds awaiting mama bird to pop in the worms. With Randy still in absentia, Peter Schwartzkopf, Air Force Colonel, retired, and his son-in-law, Brad Gifford, played hosts, manning the bar and mixing drinks in the dining room. Alison and Lisa shooed people into and through the large rooms with the high, Victorian ceilings and on to the sun-bright, sun-yellow kitchen where the big antique round oak table held the array of hors d'oervres.

All but Hepzibah and Isabelle filled their own plates. Tall, skinny Hepzibah stayed put; out on the wicker sofa on the front porch, where baskets of azaleas and chinese lanterns hung, swaying gently in the light summer breeze. Hepzibah knitted a long, multi-colored scarf that now appeared to be approaching its full length of twenty-six feet. Soon, as everybody knew—except Carl Crosby and Harold, the would-be Highbrow—Hepzibah's equally skinny, mostly silent, arthritic-gnarled daughter-in-law would be commanded to quit her own crocheting to unravel and rewind all that yarn so the old lady could start anew with the same wool. Isabelle, in turn, regularly produced colorful poncho shawls that she passed on to her female cousins-in-law.

Carl Crosby, fascinated by these two old women, volunteered to serve them. Colonel Peter objected. "They like their plates filled 'just so,' Carl. Leave it to me." Peter left the bar to Brad.

State School Superintendent Wilma and Secretary of State Nasty Three accepted their martini and scotch-rocks, declined everything but broccoli flowerets and pineapple-cheese stuffed celery, and took their drinks and veggies to the living room. Wilma's son, Mark, left to get his guitar out of the car. His mom suggested he wait to see whether the other boys would arrive. Dr. Sanford meant the four sons—Matthew, Mark, Luke and John—of the just-plain-first cousins, Martha Washington and Betsy Ross.

"Right the first time," Lisa whispered to Alison. Ali knew Lisa could barely tolerate the first cousins. These two women and their four teenage boys finally showed, late as usual. Martha, wearing a cloche atop her stringy hair and dressed in black crepe, carried a macaroni and cheese casserole. Betsy, in a pleated brown jersey dress, proffered a bowl of green Jell-O with fruit cocktail.

Alison sighed, rolling her eyes at Lisa behind the backs of the *just-plain-first* cousins (as opposed to double cousins). "I thought I told you this was a cocktail party, not pot luck," Alison said with strained courtesy.

"You didn't tell us nuthin'," snapped Martha. "As usual."

"We wouldn't have knowed about the party if Nasty Two hadn't told us when she called from Mexico," grumbled Betsy in her typical whiny voice.

"Of course you were invited," Lisa said. "Ali asked me to do it. She was out of town. I called and talked to Luke. Perhaps he forgot to mention it."

"Oh, sure, like it's our fault," said Martha, the short wide one.

"As usual," pouted Betsy, the short narrow one.

"Just because we're not *double* cousins, we get rejected alla time," growled the older Martha in black crepe to her younger sister Betsy in brown jersey. The two petite double cousins just stood there, immobile, biting their tongues and twisting their hankies.

Alison took charge of the casserole and Lisa the cold Jell-O. "I'm sure the children will love this stuff," said Lisa. "I'll take it out back for their picnic."

"Ain't fit for nobody but kids, eh?" pouted Martha.

"Not good enough for the grown-ups," muttered Betsy.

"Never mind," said Alison. "We'll set your dishes right here on the kitchen counter. For everybody."

"Yeah, I get it," wailed Martha. "Our contributions ain't good enough for your precious antique table."

"I'll just switch the caviar," whined Betsy. "Move this disgusting stuff to the counter and then there'll be room on the table for our dishes."

"Okay," said Lisa, sighing.

"Good idea," said Alison, turning away.

Ali wondered why they bothered. Forget to invite the just-plain cousins and they'd have it all over town that the *doubles* were again discriminating. Include them, and they invariably endeavored to spoil every party, constantly howling to everybody that the double cousins didn't want them. True enough, they didn't!

The best reason for including Martha Washington and Betsy Ross was to give Mark Sanford company. Neither Lisa nor Alison would dream of omitting Wilma and her son from the guest list. Their friendship went back three generations. Even as this ridiculous tableau played itself out in the big kitchen, the five boys had gone off to do their own thing.

Led by Wilma's son, Mark, the teens would charcoal hotdogs for Stevie and the BB twins, and hamburgers for themselves on the back patio. Tall, handsome, nappy haired Mark Sanford, computer nerd and football jock, also played an expert guitar. He would later entertain the crowd in a sing-along; from old-time gospel to the oldie-goldies that the Morisseys, Schwartzkopfs, Nasties, Wilma, Hepzibah and Isabelle preferred.

Peter Schwartzkopf, Brad Gifford, and Jeff Vicente joined the knitting and crocheting ladies on the front porch. Greetings, followed by nods but not conversation from the women, left the men to talk politics and sports. Their debate grew heated when they switched from the Denver Broncos to the potential showing the UW Cowboys would make on the football field that fall.

Beth Gifford and Nicole Taylor vanished upstairs to check on the children. They carried Disney-decorated plastic mugs and a pitcher of milk to pacify Stevie, Brianna, and Brittany until the hotdogs were ready. The young mothers exchanged hugs and squeals with their four-year-olds, and family memories with Clara, who had temporarily deserted the kitchen for the nursery. The older woman had helped raised both Nicole and Beth.

Harold the bank veep Morton prowled every room. He didn't care for football or any other sport, so the men on the porch didn't interest him. He didn't like blacks, especially the government woman who was so close to his bride, so he avoided the living room. Upstairs, he eavesdropped on the President's speech-writer and another chap, from Casper, kin of the Nasties, which meant his wife. Harry heard Nicole and Beth talking about their travel agency partnership. This was his new family, though he felt as alone as Little Orphan Annie. Actually, he'd rather talk <u>about</u> them than <u>with</u> them.

So that's what Morton the Masterful did; he set out to brag about his in-laws. Harold slipped into Randy's study, closed the door, and poked in the numbers he knew by heart. Dollie Domenico, downtown bartender, and Harry's real sweety, picked up on the first ring. She was off work tonight and home in her trailer dec-orated with pictures of felt bulls and roosters, plastic doilies, and red and orange paper flowers.

"Guess where I am, Honeylips," said Harold, giggling like a school girl. "The important and powerful in this town are holding a wing-ding at the Morisseys' house. I'm calling from the study." He paused to listen to Dollie's sputters, but not for long. "Of course I was invited. I married the Secretary of State, right?"

While Harry the Holier-than-thou chortled and bragged and hardly half lis-tened to Dollie's complaints that he hadn't been by lately, he switched on the computer on Randolph's desk. Maybe he could access the uppity man's records. Morton the Manipulative knew, from checking the Morisseys' bank accounts at "his" bank that Randy was up to something; a lot of recent activity—a few depos-its along with huge withdrawals.

Before he could crow further in Dollie's ear or prowl deeper into Randolph's financial secrets, Peter walked in. The retired colonel topped out at well over six feet, with broad shoulders, wide chest, and thick wavy gray hair. Scowling and harumphing, Schwartzkopf demanded to know what Morton thought he was doing. Harry the Hacker backed off, but he neither blushed nor explained.

Alison and Lisa poked their heads into the living room to see if their company was desired. Nasty Three and Wilma motioned the "girls" to join them.

"Okay, cuz, tell us about my mom, grandma, and Mexico," said double cousin (once removed) Nasty Three.

"And tell us how you foiled the assassin in the White House," said Wilma

Just as Alison backtracked to describe Mark Prescott, whom she'd met while aboard Air Force One, just-plain cousins Martha and Betsy walked in.

"Oh, of course," said short wide Martha. "Bragging about people you know in high places."

"Naturally it didn't occur to you to invite us aboard to tour the President's plane before you left Cheyenne," accused short wiry Betsy.

Lisa glanced at Alison, who stared at the floor. Wilma harumphed and Nasty Three scowled. Ali quickly excused herself.

Upstairs on the second floor, where Carl Crosby would spend the night in one of many guest rooms, Alison discovered John Vicente sitting in a wing chair near the window visiting with the President's speechwriter. After greeting her warmly, the two men resumed their discussion of the First Miss.

The JFK look-alike grinned. "Jerica is certainly lovely," John said. "Back when the President was a U.S. Senator from North Dakota, they had more time for old friends—our extended family. They came to Wyoming frequently. As you can guess by now, Carl, they were always welcome with Alison. I met the Davidsons when I was no taller than a jackaloupe." John smirked, as if willing to share a big secret. "You heard about our famous Wyoming critter? The one that's a cross breed between jackrabbit and antelope?"

Impatient, Crosby nodded. "So, you've known Jerica for some time."

"Right. T'tell the truth, Carl, I think I fell in love with her when she was a tiny six-year-old and I was a scruffy ten."

CHAPTER 11

▼

CELL NUMBER TWO

From the Cheyenne jail, Butch used his single phone call not to call a lawyer, but to ring up his brothers on their cellphone in Milwaukee. The Edwards brothers and Todd continued sitting, half-asleep, in their scratched up, banged up, recreational vehicle out at the airport, awaiting Butch's plane. After describing the delay, Butch ordered his brothers to call Callie in Laramie. "Tell her and Bud where I'm at. They gotta come spring me."

Afterwards, Ellery, Eden, and Todd fumed and cussed. Todd said, "Here we got all Eddy's stuff—fertilizer, nitroglycerine, kerosene, detonator, cheap alarm clock to wire up to the whole shebang as a timer. And he's stuck in jail?"

Ellery said they had a backup plan. "I got the recipe off the Internet. What we need with little brother?"

"Yeah, but...." Eden said.

"But, nuthin'," snarled Ellery. "Lily can crawl through the ceiling vents in that old building. She's skinny enough."

Todd protested. "I'm with Eden. Yeah, but."

"What about the Castles?" Eden said. "I don't trust Bonnie and Clyde."

"Bonnie and <u>Charles</u>, Eden. What about them?"

"They want out."

"That pair's out all right. We'll off em later. You can shoot 'em."

"Naw, let's don't do that. I never shot nobody."

"What, then?" Todd said. "Eden, you know they'll rat on the rest of us."

"Make 'em the fall guys."

*   *   *   *

The subject of their debate, Bonnie and Charles, along with Lily keeping tabs on the Castles, had checked out of the Hotel Wisconsin and were waiting for the Edwards brothers to come get them. They figured Butch would be in tow by now. In the foyer, Lily lit up. She laughed when the doughboys wrinkled their little chubby noses. She blew a long, full-bodied cloud of smoke in their soft, round, unworldly faces, as if to say, "So there, too."

Lily Thompson and Todd Campbell, her main squeeze, looked like a pair of basketball players, or player and cheerleader, or king and queen of the prom, all of which they had been, once upon a long time ago. Blond, slender, their eyes mostly glazed over now, from whatever they could lay their hands on, from tobacco to cocaine. They differed mostly in gender; plus, Todd had hazel eyes flecked with green, while Lily's were azure blue.

One more thing about the young blondes that also set them apart from their earlier prom-going-athlete-cheerleader distinctions: they were often dirty, unkempt, seldom bathing or shampooing. Too much bother. So their once attractive, naturally wavy hair hung long and ragged, oily and stringy.

*   *   *   *

Todd left the airport in his own car. He'd run out of patience, he said.

After loading everybody and everything from the hotel, Ellery pointed the RV toward Lake Michigan. He outlined his plan to Lily and the Castles in back. "Constructing the bomb shouldn't be that hard. We got the formula. Read it to us, Eden."

"Okay," said Eden. "*One type of explosion is the expansion of highly compressed gas and throwing of fragments following brittle rupture of a pressurized container.*"

"Huh?" Ellery said. "Read slower."

"Buncha garbage. Okay. *Rapid deflragation of a gas-producing pyrotechnic mixture such as black power; detonation of a charge of chemical explosive like TNT.*"

"Don't make no sense, Eden."

"Never you mind. We know what to do. I think."

Bonnie was seated on the frayed cushion at the table behind the driver's seat. She burst into tears.

"We didn't bargain for all this violence," Charles said, sitting across the table from his wife and reaching over to clutch her hand.

Lily, curled on the lumpy couch on the opposite side and behind Eden in the passenger seat, ignored the middle-aged amateurs. "Bomb? Singular? I thought we were going to plant a whole bunch," she said, her eyes foggy.

"Not without Eddy, uh, Butch. He's the explosive expert, from blowing up stumps when we was all loggers. Besides," said Ellery huffily, "I've changed the plan. Just one bomb. Set it to go off tonight."

"That's stupid," Lily said. "I thought you guys were set on taking out Judge Sullivan. Set it for night and he'll be home with the wife and kiddies. Or all tucked in going beddy-bye."

Furious at having his every statement challenged, Ellery accelerated. He ran a red light, heading straight down Wisconsin toward the lake through heavy traffic and right on past their target, the U.S. Federal Courthouse.

Charles held tight to Bonnie's hand. She sniffled, coughed, and sneezed, using her blouse tail to wipe away her tears.

"Did you check with Todd?" Lily demanded. "Where'd he go?"

Ellery suspected Todd had left them to drive his own car so he could call *The Man*. It was obvious Todd didn't trust him or appreciate that he was supposed to be in charge of Terrorist Cell Number Two. Ellery yelled at everybody to shut up, quit fussing about where they'd meet Todd. "We'll catch up with him, probably, at the War Memorial building overlooking the lake."

Ellery was downright disgusted, what with Todd dashing off on his own and the old couple chickening out on him. Up until Lily had overheard them complaining, Charles and Bonnie were an integral part of the team. Eager to create and print colored flyers off their computer, design and letter protest signs, solicit funds by making phone calls to their long list of fellow tree huggers—all that milk toast stuff.

If Charles was to be believed, the innocent Castles really thought that it was a downtown demonstration they were making ready for. The dumb dodos didn't even realize they'd joined a small select terrorist cell. Ellery had given up the secret when he let the Castles view the ingredients for making explosives. Now the whining couple was no more than excess baggage, and no less than hostages. No help at all.

He couldn't be bothered with the Castles no more. Ellery whispered to Eden to tie them up and tape their mouths. "Handcuff them to the bed in the back, like a couple a sausage rolls."

Lily interrupted Ellery to demand that he step on the gas. No mystery why she was so all-fired bent on finding Todd. He controlled their drug supply.

Ellery headed straight for a quiet area near the lake. "Get yourself in the back, Eden. Then finish assembling our bomb. We're gonna do it by ourselves!"

CHAPTER 12

▼

THE FIRST FAMILY

"Hey, cut me some slack, Mom," said Jerica over the phone to the First Lady. "I'm fine. No problem. Take off your worry hat."

"We want you home, Sweety. We miss you." Julia motioned to Dom through the open doorway that connected their suites in the White House.

"One more week, Daddy, please," Jerica begged, after sharing greetings and assurances with the President.

"I don't know, Little One. There's so little time before the fall semester starts." Then Dom suggested a compromise. "Go stay with Alison Morissey in Cheyenne. I'll call your advisor to pick you up. Joan will go over with you, take you to her mother's."

The First Couple might have wondered why Jerica agreed so readily. Except this was the daughter they knew; quiet, ladylike, acquiescent to parental requests. What Jerica was really thinking was, Great! She and Callie were heading over the mountain for Cheyenne anyhow. Though she didn't understand the mixup, as Callie called it, the pair of roomies were on their way to make bail for Butch.

"Mistaken identity; something like that," Callie had said lamely, in explaining Butch's "false" arrest.

Jerica had plenty of money, her own bank account and credit cards. She offered to put up the funds to get Butch out and back with them. He was fun, and their foursome didn't seem complete without him.

It was bad enough Jerica had been all alone for several days while Butch and Callie were away, who knew where, who knew doing what. Sometimes the pretty protected blonde didn't understand anything; why they were so open one minute and so utterly private the next. Bud, without Butch and Callie, could be a nuisance. Cool on the dance floor, too surly and demanding off it. With just the two of them, he wasn't nearly as attractive to her as she'd first thought. She knew he wanted to have sex with her and she wasn't nearly ready for that kind of commitment. Bud's overt advances frightened the young virgin. No, better to get Butch back. He could keep Bud in line.

Phone to her ear and sitting cross-legged on the floor of their apartment wearing faded cut-off jeans and white tee-shirt, with the slogan, *I'm proud to be a tree hugger,* Jerica grinned, circling thumb and index finger in the Okay sign at Callie. Going to Alison Morissey's house in Cheyenne for an evening sure beat getting recalled to the White House.

"Look Dad, Mom, I'm a big girl," Jerica said into the phone. "Callie and I will drive ourselves.

Julia said she'd rather that Jerica ride with Juanita and Caroline, the Secret Service pair. "Or Robert and Jose," Dom proposed.

Jerica refused to capitulate. "No doubt one or the other team will trail along. But look, let me at least pretend for awhile that I'm a normal adult person. On my own."

"But you aren't, sweety," Julia gently remonstrated. "No more than your father and I are. Don't you think that we, too, look forward to the day when we can be private citizens again?"

"We'll never be that, Julia," Dom said to his wife from his own suite, though both were supposed to be communicating with their daughter. "Jerica, your parents are always going to have Secret Service people around. I thought you were used to it by now."

"Oh, Daddy, I hate it! Just hate it. Why did you ever have to run for the Presidency? You never once thought about me, I bet. Just your own selfish ambitions."

"Jerica! What a perfectly dreadful thing to say," Julia protested. "You know how much your father cares about you. Both of us do. Besides, you surely know we believe that your Dad is good for the country."

"Jerica, dear," Dom said. "I thought my choosing to run was a family decision. Don't you remember all those late-night and over-dinner talks? You were the one, Jerica, if you'll please recall, who urged me to go after the job."

"Yeah, sure," Jerica moaned from Laramie. "What did I know? I was just an ignorant kid. How could I have known your winning the election would make of me a perpetual prisoner?"

Quoting an Icelandic proverb, Dom said, "*He who lives without discipline dies without honor.*" Then the President added, from Shakespeare's *King Richard II, act I.* "My darling daughter, *Take honor from me, and my life is done.*"

"Yeah, well, I feel like my life's done and I haven't even got started yet."

Dom said he'd get back to her, after talking to Alison and Joan.

He did, and this time Jerica agreed to travel in Professor Vicente's car, with Jose and Juanita along to ride shotgun.

The pretty coed agreed without further argument, because, in the interim (with Bud's arrival and the trio's conference), Callie had said the President's plan for Jerica would draw fewer suspicions.

"Bud and I will drive Butch's van. We'll pick you up at the Morissey house," Callie promised. "Just be a few hours. Some old lady won't give you a hard time and, meanwhile, after a nice chatty visit with you, Mrs. Morissey can entertain the Secret Service pair. Keep them occupied and out of our hair."

Jerica wondered who was being naïve now. Jose and Juanita distracted from their appointed duties by old-lady gossip, tea and scones? In a pig's eye.

ALISON'S PARTY

Joan and Jerica, with Juanita and Jose in the back seat, traveled to Cheyenne. The young people chattered until Joan interrupted to share highlights along the way. First she described Telephone Canyon and the Ames Monument.

"What once was a canyon with a narrow dirt trail about ten miles east of Laramie is now a major traffic corridor carrying Interstate 80." Joan said it was named Telephone Canyon because it was the first canyon in the west through which a telephone line was strung. "I find facts like these quite fascinating. Don't you?"

Juanita leaned forward, poking her face over the seat. "You bet."

"The Ames Monument," Joan continued, "is a sixty-foot limestone pyramid built in 1881 to honor Oliver and Oakes Ames, who were influential in the construction of the transcontinental railroad. The Union Pacific Railroad built the monument, despite a scandal about the brokers and the mismanagement of railroad money." She pointed to the south, off I-80. "It resembles a huge Egyptian pyramid sitting off in the sand by itself."

Jerica paid no attention to her university advisor. She closed her eyes to keep from repeatedly glancing out the window or in the rear view mirror. If Callie and

Bud were ahead of them or behind, surely there were too many cars intervening for them to be spotted by the Secret Service. Caroline and Robert might also have joined the train of vehicles, but Jerica chose not to worry or even think about it. She had decided to pretend she was a normal person, make believe her protectors were invisible, or friends she'd made in college. She was polite, as trained to be, laughing at Juanita's jokes and listening to Jose's tales of hair-raising survival and protection of the mighty.

They arrived at the Morisseys' house while the party was still in full swing. Alison came out on the front porch to greet and capture the First Miss. Clutching an elbow, she led Jerica around, making introductions to those who had not already met her. She made sure to especially include the just-plain-first cousins, along with Nasty Three's new husband, Harry the Handful.

Peter had told Alison he'd caught Morton snooping in Randy's study, trying to break into his computer files. So now she and Lisa had another nickname for the offensive oaf.

Martha Washington and Betsy Ross oohed and cooed, vacillating over proper protocol. Martha curtsied, as if in the presence of royalty. Betsy lay aside the hot wing she was gnawing to grab Jerica's hand in her own two greasy palms to bend over it as if to kiss Jerica's high school graduation ring.

Carl Crosby blushed, his thermometer rising, as if Martha and Betsy were his own kin. He was embarrassed in the presence of their faux pax.

The double cousins—all of them, men and women alike—gulped back snickers, and Martha glared at them. Betsy stalked off, motioning at Martha to follow. As if nothing untoward had happened, Alison proceeded to introduce the Secret Service pair.

With the just-plain cousins' absurd behavior as a model to avoid, Morton the Melodramatic nevertheless gushed and wheezed over the First Daughter. "Such a pleasure, Ma'am, uh, Miss. Such a delight," Morton mumbled mushily, completely and totally flabbergasted.

Wilma's son, Mark, trailed by Matthew, Mark (the other one), Luke, and John, with Nicole's Stevie and Brad and Beth's BB twins, trooped through the house and onto the front porch, where everybody, except for Martha and Betsy, had gathered.

"Sing-along time," announced the Secretary of State.

Jose and Juanita, having been introduced to everybody and made to feel at home, sat cross-legged on the porch floor with the other young adults: Beth and Brad, each cuddling a twin; Nicole with Stevie; and John Vicente, double cousin (once removed). Carl Crosby, from Arkansas via the White House, and the Secret Service pair were already acquainted.

Jerica sat with her back against the screen of the porch. Jose scowled before moving over to suggest that she remove herself from this vulnerable position. The First Miss grudgingly complied. Carl and John scooted apart to make way for her, and now the three of them sat in a row like the three monkeys: *See no evil, hear no evil, speak no evil.*

The Schwartzkopfs and Alison, Aunt-in-law Hepzibah and her arthritic daughter-in-law, Isabelle, Nasty Three and Wilma, sat on wicker chairs, sofa, and the hanging porch swing. Martha and Betsy returned, dragging straight chairs from the kitchen. Morton the Miserable was missing again, Ali noted. She hoped he wasn't back on Randy's computer.

While some people argued over which songs they wanted Mark to play for them, the double cousins struggled to hear. Every one of them had inherited Luther Auld's hearing impairment.

"Huh?" said Nasty Three.

"What?" squawked Lisa.

"Speak up!" bellowed Jeff Vicente.

With her plan to slip about the house reading lips, Alison said nothing. She noticed the two young men, Carl and John, nearly swooning under Jerica's attentions. Crosby managed to control his blush. Handsome John Vicente, normally confident, periodically stuttered in her presence.

Conspicuous by her absence, Joan had gone missing. Every clan member (with the possible exception of Morton the Mischief) suspected what had happened to Joan. Those who were not witness to their greeting soon heard the gossip zipping about the congregation. Joan had disappeared with her ex-husband, Big Jack Jacquot.

Everybody had been privy much too long and much too often to Randy's claim that Jack still carried the torch for his foolish daughter. Also, however, every single clan member was a born romantic.

During all those years since Joan had divorced Jacquot, their relationship appeared amicable. They shared parenthood, after all, of Nicole, and grandparenthood of Stevie. Usually something to talk about. Moreover, it was Jack who had paid Joan's tuition, and her and Nickee's living expenses, for all that long time it took for the young former Jacquot bride to get all those degrees. It wasn't a court order, either, for Joan had refused to accept both alimony and child support. Besides, she had long ago paid him back, plus interest, from book royalties and consulting fees. Her academic salary was more than enough to live on, for Joan's needs were basic and few.

With the emotional threads zithering between the two of them like fine silver strands, never to be broken, some of the clan inclined to playing cupid kept their fingers crossed. Nasty Two, Chief Clan Gossip, had once sworn to Alison and Lisa that she could feel the electricity crackle between the two of them whenever Joan and Big Jack showed up in the same place.

Perhaps the Nasties, Lisa and Randy were right, Alison mused. Neither Joan nor Jack had ever re-married. She wasn't aware of any other man, another real romance, beckoning her daughter in the intervening years. She didn't know about Big Jack. If he'd dallied here and there, a time or two, the liaison, singular or plural, had gone unnoticed and unremarked.

Joan and Jack with brandy-laced coffees and tiny plates of *canapés* were ensconced in the third-floor playroom. When Alison peeped in at them, they smiled and said they'd come up the big front staircase that opened off the marble-floored foyer to see Stevie. Meanwhile, Jack said, grinning at Alison like he knew exactly what she was up to with her spying on them, their grandson had disappeared with Clara and the BBs.

As Alison backed out of the room she overheard Jack's deep voice posing questions to her daughter. "How've you been, Love?" So he still used the endearment. Ali sighed, wishing that some romance would soon return to both their lives; to Joan, living alone in the university town; to herself, with her bitchy old man, whose youth and loving tenderness had disappeared on the wind.

Jacquot's *Big Jack* handle was a natural, for he was huge. Bigger than Peter Schwartzkopf (at six-four), Jack stood nearly seven feet tall when wearing his custom-made leather cowboy boots with the heels, and high Stetson atop his red curls. Broad, gruff, scowly unless specifically smiling. Rancher and auctioneer, Big Jack, with his father, Jason, owned a sprawling spread of over twenty-thousand acres; also a livestock auction market, known in the vernacular as a *sale barn*. It was from Big Jack that their daughter, Nicole, got her height and the thick auburn hair; from Ali's mom's side too, as from Essie, with the red hair and from Luther Auld, with the long slender bones.

Big Jack had degrees in Ag-econ and BusAd. He had studied the classics on his own. Hence Alison was hardly surprised to witness the next segment, Jack dropping his gruff voice to a softer, more charming register.

"*Wine comes in at the mouth And love comes in at the eye;*
That's all we shall know for truth Before we grow old and die."

"Yeats," Joan said. "From *A Drinking Song.*" Then the professor countered with a La Rochefoucauld quotation. "*Philosophy triumphs easily over past evils and future evils; but present evils triumph over it.*"

"Touche," he said. "So you see, Dear Heart, I am always interested in what you're interested in. And you are, as always, interesting."

Alison tiptoed away, her heart thumping a fierce pitty-pat. Love in the air all around her—Carl versus John over Jerica; Joan and Big Jack. Ali sighed with longing for the return of her own, once-sweet romance.

Next, she slipped into the shadows in the back of her husband's den. She'd been right about Nasty Three's husband. Harry the Handful was snooping again. This time it looked as though he meant to break into Randy's desk. Hah, fat chance. Paper clips and dried up pens in the top drawer, the bottom one was locked. She would have liked to prowl in there, herself.

Alison wasn't worried about Morton. Let him play little boy getting into mischief. She turned away, just as he picked up the telephone to dial. From the one-sided conversation, she concluded that she'd stumbled onto another love scene. Good grief. Harry, married to her cousin, giggled and cooed into the phone like a junior high kid with his first girlfriend.

Who was the woman who had stolen Harry's heart away from the Secretary of State? Should she tell Nasty Three?

Love, romance, humph. Her cynical side returning, Alison backed out. Love, and falling in love, only got a person in trouble.

CHAPTER 13

▼

CELL NUMBER ONE

Out in Laramie without Callie, Butch, or Jerica, Bud decided to make a bomb; get ready to blow up Hoyt Hall. Butch was no longer here. Bud was.

As soon as the girls got back to town they'd go into action. Man, would Butch be surprised about what the rest of them could accomplish without him.

Naw. The whole idea was to get Jerica involved. And she wasn't his yet. If Bud knew anything, he knew women. Make her his and then she'd be committed for sure.

The girls had gone to Cheyenne with bail to spring Butch. When they returned, so would their leader. The guy Bud now hated. The man who'd taken Callie from Bud. And threatened to get Jerica, too. The First Miss obviously yearned for the taciturn older and more experienced man. Why was that?

Hell, Butch hadn't even been to college. Bud had, though not for long. Great with numbers, he was majoring in accounting, but hadn't even got to his sophomore year, yet, where he'd get to enroll in the first of his major courses. No, he was put off by language. Never had been no good with English, so when he got several Fs in a row on his written papers, looked like he wasn't going to make it as a college man. Callie dropped out, too, though, so no big deal.

What were the girls doing over the mountain? Shouldn't be taking this long. Drive seventy-five on the Interstate to Cheyenne, park, hop out of Butch's van, do the paper work or whatever. Bring Butch back to Laramie.

In Edward's garden-level apartment, Bud paced. Scratched his oily hair badly in need of a shampoo, and stewed. With his key to the closet, he hauled out the makings for a half-dozen bombs. Only needed one, though. Plant it in the janitor's closet, right next to Professor Vicente's office. He didn't know no more than that. Bud had never been there in person. He was going on Callie's description of the layout. Joan's office, Callie had said, was mid-way down the second floor. Next to the cleaning closet in Hoyt Hall.

No big deal. Follow Butch's instructions. A pipe bomb with lots of nails to shoot like shrapnel straight into the human body, all those human bodies, students and professors alike. Hit the despicable Vicente woman. When the professor had flunked both him and Callie, she'd written her own death warrant. Joan deserved to die. Be like a bunch a crucifixions, a dozen or so times over. Wow! Imagining the scene, Bud could see all the blood and guts splattered around like spilled beans in a catsup sauce.

Busy with his job—scowling over Butch's recipe, sweating, repeatedly wiping damp palms on dirty jeans and swiping a shirt sleeve across brow and eyes—the hour hand crawled round the clock; once, twice. He expected Butch to walk in any minute. Catch him working on the sly. Bud didn't want that.

Ahh, finished at last. Bud peered through the wide picture window. He dare not walk through the front door. With his luck, he'd run smack into the trio on the entrance steps. His pickup in the alley behind the complex of several adjoining apartment buildings (each owned by a different set of landlords), Bud unlocked the big chromium box mounted in the truck bed and loaded his precious cache. Hot damn, he'd done it. Without getting caught.

Then he remembered. He'd made a mess in Butch's kitchen. Jeez. Back through the window again. Why couldn't Edwards come through with a key? He hung out at Butch's pad often and long enough; felt like the place was his too.

Indoors, he couldn't recall the arrangement of Butch's stuff. He'd hauled in and stored most of it himself. Using Ajax and Lysol's bacterial spray, he scrubbed countertops and floor like he was a Dial-A-Maid employee. Disgusting, all this woman's work.

Finally. Clear of the building the second time, Bud drove his green Ford pickup sporting a *Tree hugger and proud of it* bumper sticker around to the front, where he parked on the cement driveway.

Bud sat in the driver's seat listening to tapes, some he'd recorded himself from his mom's precious stash: *Set Him Free*, co-written by Skeeter, Helen Moyers and Marie Wilson, originally a Top Five hit back in 1959; *It Wasn't God Who Made*

Honky Tonk Angels, a Number One hit when sung by Kitty Wells, who'd broken the male streak on August 23, 1952. Bud beat a steady beat on the steering wheel.

Then he tuned the radio to a country western station, where he found John Denver singing about a *Rocky Mountain High*. Made him cry. Bud missed Denver. Why'd he have to die? John Denver, JFK, Jr., Payne Stewart, the professional golfer. All of them had met their Maker while piloting their own airplanes.

When Bud made it big—which he was sure would happen any time now, if he stuck with Butch and they ever got going with their big-money heists, hitting banks and such. One thing Bud wouldn't spend his own money on. No private little plane or big Learjet for him.

Nosiree Bob! Bud grinned. That was one of Jerica's favorite expressions. (Taken from her dad, who got it from Alison Morissey, long before Dom became President). Bud knew what he'd do with his share of stolen loot—shower Jerica with diamonds and furs, travel to an island in the South Pacific, lounge around on sandy beaches with cocktails beside them. And make sweet love.

No, scratch the gift of furs. Jerica didn't believe in killing little furry animals. Which came, she'd admitted once, from her mommy, the First Lady, who chaired the National Conservation Council.

Humph. Bud and Butch and Callie had something in common with the White House. If Butch said he was against the big timbering companies, then they all were.

Why else would Bud be driving around with this dumb bumper sticker and flaunting the tee shirts with the same slogan that Edwards demanded they wear?

Bud stopped daydreaming long enough to look out the truck window, fore and aft. Where th'hell was everybody? The songs finished, Bud continued to sit. Jittery with nerves, he resumed beating on the steering wheel, this time in frustration. If they couldn't get Butch out a jail, why didn't the girls come on home without him? Tonight was the night. Bud was eager to get laid. And not with the half-stoned Callie. Once he'd had Jerica, Callie would be past tense.

Then he remembered. Oh, yeah. The girls weren't going straight to the jail, and they hadn't left together. Jerica had to ditch her shadows first; Jose and Juanita this time. Meanwhile, they were stopping off at a party, given by Mrs. Morissey.

Right, Mrs. M—that nosy little lady who kept poking into Jerica's personal life. Visiting her at the Chi Omega House, calling, sending notes and cards. Why was that? Bud wondered. More thinking, enough to give him a headache. Then he remembered that Alison Morissey was Professor Vicente's mother, and Joan Vicente was Jerica's advisor, and the whole pack and passel had been friends with the President's family for God only knew how long. And He wasn't talking. God, that is. He; or She, as Callie referred to the Creator. Damn sacrilegious, that gal. Funny, though.

Yeah, Alison Morissey was Joan's mom. Hot damn, the nosy old dame would sure be surprised when her professor daughter got all blowed up.

CHAPTER 14

▼

IN CHEYENNE—THE JAIL AND THE DOWNTOWN SALOON

Sergeant Walt Fletcher needed an excuse to hold Butch over night. The guy looked like he'd been left over from the Methodist rummage sale the day following their two-dollar-a-bag discounted day.

It wasn't his pony tail and rag-tag clothing nor the nose earring that made the Cheyenne detective suspicious. It was attitude—surly, obstreperous. No priors on Edward Edwards, Jr., though.

The big, burly, crew-cutted detective, wearing rumpled brown suit and crumpled brown fedora straight out of the fifties, sometimes got a gut feeling. This was one of those times.

Edward, Eddy, "Butch"; Wisconsin driver's license. No other documents, papers, or even a credit card on the guy. A single suitcase in the back seat.

"Going or coming?" Walt had demanded.

"None of your bees wax," Butch sneered; then proceeded to use language a lot stronger than that. Walt didn't find the flight packet because Butch hadn't picked up his roundtrip tickets for Milwaukee yet. He planned to pay for the reservation with cash at the airline counter.

No knives or other weapons, though Wyoming was one of thirty-one states that permitted the carrying of a concealed handgun. For personal defense. Plenty of pickups also sported a rifle, shotgun, or both in the rack above the back window. For hunting or defense. Plenty of isolated country out there between the few scattered villages and ranches.

Maybe things were similar in northern Wisconsin, from whence heralded the lad in his thirties. But, from Walt's fiftyish perspective, Butch was a kid.

While Edwards sat fuming in a holding cell, Detective Fletcher sat at his scarred wooden desk. He propped his feet in their scruffy cowboy boots in an opened bottom drawer while he leaned back, arms clasped behind his head, chewing on a toothpick.

Smooth-cheeked, baby-faced Bobby Gilbert arrived to pace in front of the desk. Every other time the rookie paused, to rock back and forth from heels to toes as he turned to face his hero.

"What we gonna do with him?" Gilbert asked breathlessly.

Fletcher switched the spindly pick to the other side of his mouth. "What do you recommend, Bobby?"

"Me? Uh, let's book him. Let me tell the boys in the yard to strip that damn car. Bet they'll find drugs!"

"Bet they won't. Guy looks clean."

"You're still holding him, though. Gotta charge him with something."

"The Chief's out a town. So's the municipal judge. That was my excuse. I told Edwards he'd have to wait over the weekend to see the judge. I'm keeping him for contempt. May be a weak excuse, may not stick, but meanwhile I bought us some time."

"Whew. That'll give us a chance to go over the car."

"So get out of here. Go on and do it." Walt figured he was going to look damn stupid, come Monday. Guy and his car, both, were clean. He'd bet a plugged nickel on it.

The phone rang. Walt removed the toothpick to toss it overhand into the trash bin before choosing a fresh one from the pack on the blotter. He picked up the phone. On the other end was Mrs. Morissey, an old friend and the one who had helped him catch a pair of bank robbers back in the spring; back before she'd left Wyoming for Vermont, where her hair caught aflame in a forest fire.

Fletcher grinned, unwrapping the new pick from its plastic cover. He could see Ali in his mind's eye, wearing some new glamorous wig. "What's up, Ali? You all right?"

"Fine, Walt."

"No bank robbers to report?" He laughed; with, not at her. Without her jumping into the back of the get-away pickup, the whole regional bank community would have been up spit creek.

Alison gave him a girlish giggle that quickly flipped to somber voice of concerned citizen. Not of the state and region, but of the whole United States this time. "I've got the President's daughter at my house, Walt. Thought you ought to know."

"Jerica Davidson? Well, I'll be a horn-swoggled toad. She in trouble?"

"Not at all. Two Secret Service people are here with her. Really nice young people. Thought you might want to drop by for the party."

"I'm on duty."

"So? Make it semi-official. If nothing urgent is pending at the moment. You all tied up?"

"Not really."

Which was how Detective Sergeant Walt Fletcher happened to be at the Morisseys at the same time Jerica's roommate, Callie, was sitting on a saddle-topped stool in the dark, seedy, downtown saloon with the long long glass-covered bar. She sipped her third or fourth beer with shots of whiskey, straight.

"Perhaps you've had enough, Miss," suggested the bartender, hesitantly. Dollie Domenico, tall, slender, with stringy, greasy hair, wore soiled tee shirt with faded blue jeans. Dollie was Harry Morton's sweetheart. Or had been.

The bartender refused to believe that Harry was no longer her Honeylips. Just because Morton had married Nasty Three, Wyoming's Secretary of State, didn't mean he'd stopped dropping by the bar on his breaks from First Bank down the street, or had quit stopping at her trailer house, either. The former teller had been promoted to vice president—no doubt, Dollie figured, correctly, at the request of his new bride. You betcha, Dollie was still attached as if by bungee cord, to Morton the Magnificant—one of her handles for the little guy who strutted around like a little baby male peacock.

Dollie Domenico used her own last name, which Harry her Honeylips insisted she go by now, instead of her rightful handle of Mrs. Morton. She knew exactly where Harold the Horrible (horribly insensitive) was at that very moment. Over at the Morissey house hobnobbing with what he called "the really classy people in this city and state."

Wobbling, nearly falling off her saddle-topped stool, Callie Jenkins told off the bartender in four-letter words. She'd decide when and whether she'd had enough, she said. Meanwhile, the loud-mouthed drinker vacillated between blaspheme and maudlin muttering. She needed a fix and had no idea where to get one. Butch was her supplier and he kept a mum lip about his source.

Monday! That's what some cop had told her. They were keeping Butch over the whole damn weekend. So he could face the judge when he returned. She would die before that. Might even be tempted to raid the grocery store to sniff cleaning products: glue, nail polish remover, hair spray, room deodorizers, lighter fluid. Maybe hit the office supply for markers, computer spray, or correction fluid. Nah, let the kids get high, or die, on that garbage. Callie knew what could happen short of death, including limb spasms, bone marrow or liver or kidney damage, even permanent brain destruction. Stupid kids.

When Dollie Domenico's replacement showed up, she left through the back door to pick up her sixteen-year-old battered Buick. She planned to head for the Morissey house. Dollie wanted to grab a look at those rich-bitch folk Morton the Maniacal now called kin. Get a peek at his new wife and her cronies. What did Nasty Three have that Dollie didn't?

Money, power, social position, sure. Bet she's no match for me in bed, though, Dollie cried out loud as she pumped the pedal trying to persuade her beauty of a Buick to get going. Tears streamed down her cheeks. She pounded the steering wheel in frustration; angry with Harry, upset with her old car.

What Dollie really wanted to do—instead of sneaking around the house and hiding in the bushes to secretly spy on the party—was to barge right in and yell at the top of her voice, "Harry's my Honeylips, not yours, Miz Smarty Pants Secretary of State. Morton the Monster's a bigamist! We never did get no divorce."

Before she'd left the saloon, Domenico passed on to her replacement the news that their lone bar customer was a drunk and probably a junkie. He said he could handle that. Benji refused Callie service and hustled her out the door.

Nerves jumping, eyes rolling, steps staggering, Callie Jenkins tried to remember where she'd parked Butch's tan van. Jeez, in front of a fire hydrant. Not one but three pink tickets fluttered like aspen leaves in the breeze from beneath her windshield wiper. She jerked them loose, glancing around furtively for the meter maid. Stomping the accelerator, Callie took off, ramming the back left fender of the new silver gray Lincoln sitting like the Queen of England in the space ahead of her.

"If I can't get Butch out of jail, at least I can spring Jerica," Callie mumbled, roaring away down the street.

CHAPTER 15

▼

CELL NUMBER TWO

In Milwaukee, everything was proceeding as planned. The plan was Ellery's, not whatever scheme little brother Butch might devise.

"Here's what we're gonna do," Ellery said from beside the U.S. Federal Court House, where he'd found a good place to park the RV. "Tie up and tape up the Castles, Eden. Throw 'em on the bed back there." While Eden complied, Ellery said, big brother would outline Lily's instructions for her.

Turned out, it wasn't that easy, for Charles resisted and Bonnie wept, clinging to the table behind which she sat. Eden socked Charles in the nose and then cursed at the blood spurting over the two of them. Charles shoved, Eden pulled.

Bonnie sobbed louder and Ellery whirled around on the driver's seat, yelling "Stifle yourself!" in the manner of Archie Bunker to his wife, Edith, the "dingbat" wife on *All in the Family*. Bonnie screamed.

Ellery drew his 9mm Beretta with the polished blue finish and gold accents. He meant to give the old broad a light rap to the temple. Instead, his hard sock to the head caved in her skull. Silenced for all time, Bonnie slumped sideways like a sack of mushy melons.

The wind went out of Charles. He moaned in despair, reaching with both arms outstretched in a fruitless attempt to revive his wife by his will alone. Like a sail gone limp on a windless day, Charles' energy collapsed, all spirit gone with his dear one's soul.

Eden shrugged before completing his brother's assignment by tossing the lumpy doughboy on the floor next to the bed. Quickly he turned to hear the rest of Ellery's plot.

"We're in luck, you guys. Look up there on the second floor."

Though late in the afternoon that Friday, lights still burned in the famous old courtroom. Also in the Judge's chambers next door. "Sullivan's up there, still!" crowed Ellery. "We got to move fast."

Not quite five o'clock, when the building would be closed and locked for the weekend, Lily was supposed to walk nonchallantly through the front door to take either the stairs or the elevator to the second floor. When stopped, as she would be, by one of the men guarding the entrance, she was to say she'd been in the courthouse earlier, when she must have left her wallet.

Ellery handed Lily a brochure describing the historical significance of the building. "Or you could ask for a tour."

"Jeez, Ellery, then they'll know who I am. They'll see my face and can identify me later. Besides, what if they search me?"

"Shut up, girl!" Ellery told her to wash up and change clothes from their supply in the closet. "No time to shampoo your grungy hair. Wear that blond wig Todd got for you. And hurry."

"What about Bonnie?" Lily asked, stepping gingerly over the inert form.

"Forget her. We'll dump her body later."

Near his crumpled wife, Charles groaned.

Ellery snarled, "Shut th'hell up back there."

Meanwhile, Eden's fingers shook as he wrapped the bomb Ellery had put together out at the lakeside park. The middle brother shoved the deadly package into an innocent-looking woman's carryall covered in needlepoint.

Lily grabbed the handbag, tears gathering in her eyes. She didn't want this job. When Ellery yelled at her to hurry, she flipped him the bird, her hand turned over. "Hey, man, can you read upside down!"

Carryall in hand, Lily started through the side door when Ellery stopped her. Reaching into the glove compartment, he grabbed a small .22 Smith & Wesson. "Just in case," he said, telling Lily to conceal the shooter in the back of her waistband or her bra.

*   *   *   *

Upstairs in Judge Donald Sullivan's courtroom, he and the bailiff, Gus Schuman, chuckled like a pair of schoolboys let out for recess. Contrary to Lily's supposition, there was no wife or little kiddies at home awaiting husband for cocktails, or a daddy to read them bedtime stories. A recent widower, unblessed with children, Donald was all alone. Moreover, he had all but forgotten what it felt like to laugh. Mid-height and graying, the Judge's shoulders slumped with grief from the recent loss of his wife; also with the burdens of covering too many civil lawsuits and trials over his long career.

By contrast, Gus stood as a mighty tower, vibrant with life and invariably tickled by small things; delighted to take people on tour and describe their marvelous building. An ex-cop, Gus served as bailiff in Sullivan's court and otherwise conducted tours or stood guard at the front door.

Donald and Gus had spent the last three days suffering through a particularly boring court case. Nowadays, Sullivan liked to dawdle after court. Gus didn't mind, he had nowhere to go, either, and asking the Judge to join him for a drink didn't seem appropriate. So they talked about the participants in the last case while scanning Gus's funny drawings. He kept art paper with pens and pencils in the bailiff's table. Sketching helped him pass the time.

Judge Sullivan scrutinized each sketch carefully. "You've sure captured the plaintiffs and defendant well," he said. "I can recognize them in a minute."

"Their features were distinctive," Gus demurred. "Somewhat oddball; weird, if you recall. Easy to caricaturize."

*   *   *   *

At the front door, Lily met little resistance. Wearing a light fragrance, "White Diamonds," with Elizabeth Taylor's imprint, she had dressed respectably in blue blazer over white blouse with gray flannel slacks. Wearing a long-haired, wavy, blond wig and shuddering at her appointed assignment, she carried the handbag Eden had prepared for her. Perhaps the lone guard at the entrance wanted out of there, for he gave Lily only a cursory glance and no argument.

"The Judge and Bailiff haven't come down yet, Ma'am," said the guard. "If you left your wallet in Sullivan's courtroom, Gus will let you in." He waved her through.

Heart pounding, palms sweating, little trickles running down between her breasts where she'd hidden the .22, Lily entered the elevator and punched the button for the second floor. She wished they hadn't left Todd behind.

CHAPTER 16

▼

ALISON'S CLAN
PARTY

When Joan and Big Jack—smiling, walking together—rejoined the front porch crowd, people smiled while singing even more lustily. Lisa poked Alison. Wilma winked at Nasty Three. Hepzibah raised an eyebrow without missing a stitch. Harry the Huffy huffed and puffed with curiosity, but Isabelle, seated on the wicker sofa between her knitting mother-in-law and Nasty Three's groom, seldom said anything and she didn't this time either. Ali watched and lipread.

Juanita asked Jose in a whisper to identify the big man. Jerica, who overheard the pair, mumbled, "Dr. Vicente's ex-husband, Jack Jacquot."

Martha Washington and Betsy Ross, seated on their straight chairs, sat up straighter. Not known for their tact, Martha jumped up to stand, arms akimbo. to raise her voice. "Well, about time you two got back together. Right, Betsy?"

Mark stopped strumming. Everybody quit singing.

"I'll say," Betsy said, rising to stand beside her sister. Like two generals, the pair confronted the whole battalion.

Joan didn't look at the loud-mouthed pair nor at Jack. Head dropped, she wedged herself between Carl and John on the floor. Peter offered Jacquot his chair, with the excuse that he was going after more coffee.

When Clara motioned to the children, the three youngsters vacated their parents' laps for more play time before baths, bed, and stories. "We're having a sleep-over," squeaked Brianna excitedly.

"Me, too," echoed her twin, Brittany.

"Yeah," yelled Stevie, giving his Granddad Jack and Grandma Joan hugs.

Mark abruptly arose, followed by Matthew, Mark, Luke, and John. The basement with its pool table, video and computer games beckoned, like fresh hay to a herd of cattle.

Silence reigned.

"What'd I say?" Martha Washington wailed.

"We didn't do nuthin'," pouted Betsy Ross.

"Oh, do shut up, girls," mumbled Hepzibah, for once breaking her self-imposed silence. "Sit back down and behave yourselves."

"What'd she say?" Lisa said.

"Speak up, Aunty Hepzibah," Alison said.

"Why don't the double cousins get hearing aids?" John suggested.

"Lisa already has one," Joan replied. John was Joan's second double cousin. "She doesn't always wear it, though. Don't ask me why."

Peter returned to the porch with the coffee pot. "Anybody want a refill?"

"I sure do," Morton muttered. He had pushed his bride over on the swing to plump himself down between the Secretary of State and the State Superintendent of Schools. "What's happening in the schools these days, Wilma? The kids getting spaced out on drugs? Or are they building bombs and terrorizing their teachers?" Harry chortled at himself, like he'd made a funny.

Juanita and Jose gasped.

John whispered to Jerica that he'd like to talk to her. Alone. The First Miss looked surprised, but she arose without protest to trail after her childhood friend.

Jose, too, started up, but Juanita pulled him back down. "Leave them alone, Jose," she whispered. "John's okay. We checked him out, remember." Verifying, checking, these were among the Secret Service people's first chores upon arriving at Alison's and discovering the size of the clan. She had given them a printed list of the party people, on which she had included identifiers and particulars.

Alison was familiar with protocol and security procedures, also with the computer and their laser color printer. Her mind wandered from the porch commotions. Surely Jerica was safe here with the clan. Detective Fletcher would arrive soon, too. Walt, plus Juanita and Jose, and Colonel Schwartzkopf, of course. Plenty of protection.

Alison wasn't at all sure about Randy's safety. Why didn't her husband call? Let her know he was okay and tell her when to expect him? Tomorrow she would make fresh bread; also cookies, and maybe a key lime pie. She must remember to buy heavy cream for whipping. Clara could put on a pot roast. They'd be ready to feed Randy if he popped in without warning.

Peter, Brad, and Big Jack huddled over football plays, pondering the potential success of the UW Cowboys' new quarterback. On the swing, Harold the self-proclaimed Historian, commenced telling Wilma stories about the old days in Wyoming Territory, ignoring on his other side his wife's scowl and nudge, or Ali's smirk behind her hand. Tell these stories to the descendant of frontiers-woman Willamena Jackson, who'd amassed a fortune right along side Rose DuMaurier? Absurd. Alison turned away to keep from laughing aloud.

Carl whispered to her that he was making frantic mental notes. He wished he'd concealed his micro-recorder on his person, so as to capture all this clan clamor and camaraderie. He could use some of it as background for the series of articles he intended to write about Jerica's life away from the White House. His stories, he said, would be more colorful and believable if he added personal anec-dotes.

Lisa distracted Alison with a poke to the ribs, while nodding her head at Wilma. The poor dear sat there, continuing to suffer under the squeaky voice and wild gestures of Harry the Histrionic. He sounded worse than a fingernail scratching a chalkboard.

Ali promptly jumped up to grab a tray of chocolate delights to shove beneath the nose of Morton the Misbehaving. She caught Lisa grinning at her.

Fletcher's voice suddenly boomed at them, as if he were calling for surrender through a bullhorn. Startled, Alison jumped. The tray tipped, and gooey, half-melted chocolate squares plunked onto Harry the Horrible, the mess bounc-ing off his chest, leaving sticky brown smears, and onto the knees of his sharply creased pinstriped pants. Harry jumped up, knocking Alison backwards, and her lovely, glamorous platinum wig slid to one side of her head.

"Good grief," said Lisa.

"My word," said Beth.

"Oh, Gam," said Nicole. "Let me help you."

"And you tell us to behave?" shouted Martha Washington at Hepzibah.

"Yeah, what about her?" said Betsy Ross, pointing at Alison.

Ali laughed merrily, thus relieving the tension and giving everybody an excuse to snicker, giggle, and guffaw.

Nasty Three and Wilma quickly addressed the mess, while Harold the Haunted rushed off, presumably to the powder room. Ali greeted the detective.

"I'd introduce you to the President's daughter, Walt, but she seems to have momentarily disappeared. I believe you know everybody else, except the Secret Service team." She pulled Jose and Juanita forward and did the honors.

"You'd better go see about Jerica, Juanita," Jose said afterwards.

"I'll go," said Ali.

She discovered John and Jerica sitting at the round oak table over twin bottles of mineral water. They didn't appear to notice her slip behind the kitchen counter. Laughing, talking, sharing common memories of their youth, Jerica suddenly sobered.

"I wish I were a man, John. A free man, and anonymous," said Jerica. "You can do whatever you wish, go wherever you choose. Me? I live under a microscope, like a bug in the biology lab."

Tall, handsome John Vicente, a JFK look-alike, said he'd like to see more of her. He blushed, but unplagued by Crosby's thermometer, it hardly showed.

Alison knew plenty about cousin John, for they were close. His academic life had kept him busy in the physics and chemistry laboratories and, until recently, he hadn't paid much attention to women. Friends, coworkers, fellow students, yes. But this could likely be his first blush with romance since he was fifteen.

"Sure," Jerica said lightly, replying to his hesitant proposal. "We'd better make it quick, though. I've got to join my parents soon in Washington. But I'll be back in Laramie again this fall, living at the Chi Omega sorority house. Call me, now or later."

John nodded, grinned, and blushed. Otherwise, he grew speechless, as though he couldn't think what to talk about next. Jerica relieved his agony by suggesting they log onto the computer in Mr. Morissey's study.

"Play computer games?" he proposed.

"Or get on the Internet," she countered, suggesting a couple of chat rooms.

Nearly hidden behind the high divider separating food preparation area from eating table, Alison maintained silence. If would be awful if the young people suspected her of spying. Nevertheless, she trailed silently after them.

Harold used the excuse of scrubbing his clothes for leaving the clan. Instead, he bypassed the powder room to head for the study. His purpose: unravel the mystery of Randolph Morissey's finances. He would sure like to get something on the snotty Mrs. Morissey, too. He had labeled her snotty, not because she snubbed him, but because he figured people from her class regularly poked fun at people from the lower classes, like him and Dollie, his real and true sweety. Had

Harold been privy to even one among the many nicknames Alison and Lisa and a lot of other people called him, he would have been appalled, and convinced that he was right about these snobs.

Phooey. He couldn't use the computer. The President's daughter and her boyfriend had beat him to it.

*   *   *   *

Unknown to Morton the Miserable, his Dollie was at that moment prowling the perimeter of the Morissey mansion. The bartender at the downtown saloon with the long long bar could hardly peer onto the high porch. Listening from around the corner, she'd heard her Honeylips' voice droning on about Wyoming history, but since then he'd been silent. Must have gone indoors.

The first floor windows were too high for Dollie to see through. She'd have to find something to stand on. No boxes, no chairs. She couldn't get onto the back patio or around by the swimming pool, as the high fence and locked gates prevented access. After a bit, she discovered a garbage can on wheels. That would have to do. Filled with party trash, the can was heavy but movable. Dollie kicked off the open-backed spike heels she'd slipped on in the car (as if anticipating an invitation to the party), and, barefoot with chipped-paint ragged toenails showing, she clambered up to the study window.

In time to see her Honeylips backing out through the open doorway.

Uninterested in the young couple sitting and laughing together in front of the computer screen, Dollie didn't realize she'd caught a glimpse of the First Miss. Too late, anyhow. She slipped and fell, with the can overturning and crashing with a shot, like unexpected thunder booming over the neighborhood. Or a car backfiring. Or a gang of international terrorists setting off a bomb.

*   *   *   *

On the porch, Juanita grew restless; not quite apprehensive, but nervous. She turned to Jose. "What do you think, partner? Was Jerica's departure merely a ruse to escape us? Why hasn't she returned?"

He smiled indulgently. "Sounds like you're getting a case of paranoia."

Juanita ignored his ridicule. "You canvass the house, Jose. I'm gonna check around outside." Both young people got up and left the porch.

Just then came the crack, like a gunshot. With her long, straight blond hair swinging, Juanita retrieved her Glock Model 27 from the waistband holster concealed beneath her baggy summer sweater. She was onto Domenico before the bartender could say squat.

When Alison and Fletcher noticed the Secret Service pair departing, Walt poked her. "I'll follow Jose, Ali. You tail Juanita." The detective and Alison had been informal partners a few times already. He knew he could count on her to follow orders and meanwhile keep her cool. When he arose, scowling, Ali silently followed him.

"What's happening?" she asked when they were out of earshot of the party people.

"Got a gut feeling...."

Alison, Walt, and Juanita rounded the corner simultaneously, like the front three members of a parade band. They discovered Dollie buried beneath a heap of rubbish, veggies, and kids' paper plates smeared with catsup and mustard. Pausing in mid-step, Juanita gasped.

"What on earth?" Alison exclaimed.

"On your feet!" Walt commanded, one hand on his holstered Colt .45.

"Up against the wall, legs spread, hands over your head," barked Juanita, recovering quickly and pointing the Glock at the bartender's head.

"For heaven sakes," said Ali, nothing in her hands, save a helping gesture. "Let me help the poor girl get out from under all this debris."

"What's going on here?" yelped Harry the Harasser as he burst onto the scene like the Lone Ranger. Recognizing Dollie, he joined Walt and Juanita in harassing her.

CHAPTER 17

▼

CELL NUMBER TWO

In Milwaukee Lily couldn't make up her mind what to do. Todd would insist, as he had all along, that she find the passage way above the courtroom, the one used by the employee charged with changing light bulbs. Plant the bomb, set the timer to go off in the middle of the night, and get th'hell out.

Make a statement with their ecoterrorist attack, but kill nobody. Ellery had said *The Man* said they should call the media and take the blame; not personally, but on behalf of dedicated environmentalists the world over.

Lily knew that Ellery had his own agenda: take out the Judge. Make him pay for what he'd done to old man Edwards with his ruling for the big corporation instead of the little guy. Bomb Sullivan's courtroom and shoot him smack between the eyes, while yelling, "That's for Pa Edwards!"

Lily smiled, despite her case of nerves. Yeah, like she cared about old man Edwards. Oh, well, taking out the Judge should be fun, even though she had no personal vendetta against Sullivan.

As for herself, she wasn't crazy about Ellery's plans. Butch should have been here to do the dirty deed. Why did it have to fall on her? Then she remembered. The Edwards boys were too fat and the old people out of it. And Todd had deserted her. Where th'hell was he? Woolgathering, hesitating, she stood in front of the closed door to Judge Sullivan's inner sanctum.

At that moment she heard footsteps approaching from behind a narrow door at the side of the courtroom. Slinking backwards, Lily scrunched herself tight against the wall, as if willing herself into invisibility.

In a rush to quit for the weekend, a janitor wearing coveralls and carrying a sack of used bulbs that peeked from their perch pushed through the narrow door, leaving it ajar. With no glance about, he hurried away. Opportunity yawning and indecision waning, Lily made up her mind. Time to instigate Todd's plan. Get this over with.

Halfway along the dusty overheated overhead tunnel with spiders threatening, Lily paused in her cautious crawl to swipe at cobwebs. Nervous, upset, frustrated, her hands began to shake. She stopped to drag out the explosives. Except she dropped the alarm clock devised as a timer, When it went clink, clang, she held her breath.

In the courtroom below, Gus gathered his drawings to replace them in the single drawer of the bailiff's table. "I'll put the finishing touches on these sketches during the next boring trial," he said.

Still in his black judge's robe, Sullivan nodded. He started to reply, but just then Gus held up a hand for silence.

"What's that noise?" Gus cautioned.

"Probably the janitor changing light bulbs," Donald said. "Haven't you noticed it's been getting dim in here? I put in a request a week ago. Takes them long enough to replace the duds."

"No, wait, Judge." Gus glanced at his watch. "We've stayed late this afternoon again. Nobody should be in the building by now except us."

Silence reigned. Gus scowled.

Judge Sullivan shrugged. "Rats, maybe."

"I don't like it." Gus reached for his cellphone. "I'm calling for backup."

Above them, Lily squatted in the crawl space trying to retrieve the pieces she'd dropped. A rat skittered across her hand, sending her into a shudder.

Suddenly she changed her mind. No way was she following this plan. Backing out and hastily gathering timer and tools as she went, Lily made a racket. Hardly caring, she was getting th'hell out. She'd already set the charge to go off, although there was no time to set the clock. She'd got it backwards; supposed to be the timer first. The bomb would explode any second!

As she emerged through her door, Gus burst from his. "Watch out!" Lily yelled, tossing the bomb ahead of her and over Gus's shoulder. Straight into the arms of Judge Sullivan who had barged up close behind the bailiff.

Simultaneously, Gus and Lily drew their guns. A standoff.

"It's a bomb, Judge! Get rid of it," Gus hollered.

Sullivan immediately obeyed. He ran to the window, open to let in some fresh air since the air conditioning had gone off. He shoved up the sash and threw out the bundle. In the moment that Gus took his eyes off the strange woman to look at Sullivan, Lily got off a shot.

Straight into the back of the Judge's head. Sullivan reeled and collapsed. But not before the bomb went sailing through the summer evening.

Gus gasped as sirens split the air with their approaching whoop-whoop wails. His call demanding backup had come through fast. Turning from the Judge and the open window, where a giant-size explosion whooshed up dust and debris from below, Gus took aim at the terrorist.

Too late. Lily didn't wait to see if her bullet had sent the Judge into the ozone or to worry that the bailiff's bullet might catch her in retreat. She flew through the chamber door, Gus dashing after her.

She took temporary refuge behind a narrow door, pulling it closed and into locked position behind her. A SWAT team stormed the building, while outside on the street, cops circled the bombsite, holding back the gawkers.

Along the west side, the old federal building didn't appear to have suffered more than a few scratches. Perhaps indignantly bulwarking itself against such sacrilege.

Lily waited what seemed a long while. In reality, only a few minutes had elapsed before she slipped out and through another door, this time into a cleaning closet. Here she shed her clothes and stylish wig, donning coveralls and arming herself with mop and bucket. Her grungy hair helped her pass easily for a tired, unkempt cleaning woman. Stealthily, she made her way down the long corridor, open on its front side to the huge central arcade, up to the fourth floor, and across and around to the opposite side. When finally approached by a cop, she cussed the management who'd assigned her to extra cleaning duty with no blankety-blank overtime pay. The policeman sent her on her way, with orders phoned on ahead to "Let the poor old lady out of the building."

"You got your wish, Ellery," Lily snarled, when the two of them reconvened at the back of the curious crowd. "I killed the Judge for you."

"Yeah, but look at how you screwed up the rest of the job."

Eden was dead. Bonnie was dead.

Ellery was saved from the bomb that blew up the RV and everybody in it because he'd left to take a leak, he told Lily. What Ellery was really doing was checking on Lily. He didn't trust her to even go inside the building, much less follow through the way she was supposed to.

"Wh-what happened to Ch-Charles?" Lily asked, stuttering with nerves.

"Got all blowed up, too. Must have done. Lookee there."

Where the RV had been they saw only mangled metal, smoke and dust.

"You killed him! Eden's dead, Lily. First my Pa and now my brother."

"N-not me, El-Ellery. It was the Judge what threw it out the window."

Then Ellery shared more bad news. "Todd showed up just in time for the bombing. So you killed your boyfriend, too, girl." Ellery knew, because he had spotted Todd sneaking up from the back of the vehicle. Ellery had also borne witness to Todd's freeing Charles. But the poor little man must have died, too.

While the cops awaited the cloud of smoke and dust to settle and while their backs were turned to corral the crowd, Charles had pulled the tape from his mouth. Bent over and confused, he stumbled away to lose himself among the bystanders. Bonnie dead, he was having nothing more to do with this bunch. Charles Castle, retired doughboy minus his equally round and soft wife, caught a series of city busses. He located the Greyhound station and bought a one-way ticket to Tucson. Time he retired in the sunshine on his pension and social security. He had no priors. Nobody could ever connect him with the radical ecoterrorists.

Ellery proposed to Lily that they hitchhike to Wyoming. "Gotta spring Butch, the only family I got left," said the oldest Edwards brother.

Lily shrugged. No reason not to tag along. She too was all alone.

CHAPTER 18

▼

CELL NUMBER ONE

She missed having her own car and wondered where it was. Impounded by the cops, probably. Callie's blue Dodge Intrepid sported two bumper stickers, back and front. The front one proclaimed her allegiance to tree hugging, but the back one was personal choice: *Subvert the dominant paradyme.* Similar to the sixties, her mom said, who also said it was just another way of saying "Down with the Establishment."

Butch was stuck in jail over the weekend, so there was nothing more Callie could do for him in Cheyenne. She'd spring Jerica, preferably on the sly, and they would return to Laramie without the girl's keepers. Have fun with Bud.

When Callie had called Bud to report, he said he had some great ideas. She couldn't wait. This sitting around twitching her toes was dumb. She needed a fix, bad. She bet Bud had a source. Butch shouldn't have left her like this!

Now, how to collect Jerica. Spy on the Morissey house and wait for an opportunity? Jerica would be alone when she went to the john.

Callie lettered a sign to stick up in front of the powder room window, in case it was too high to see into. Jerica would spot it and come out. Voila! they'd be on their way. Or, maybe not. Jerica might disagree. Then where would Callie be? She decided to come up with a backup plan. Hey, man, would Butch ever be surprised at her ingenuity.

First, though, she would appeal to Jerica as a fellow tree hugger. The President's daughter was so gung-ho on their gang staging a protest. What a nuisance,

Jerica's pestering. Callie and Bud had nearly let the cat out of the bag a time or two. Okay, now she would tell Jerica they were finally going to put action behind their braggadocio, back up the slogans on their tee shirts and bumper stickers. She would insist that the others needed Jerica to help them plan a big demonstration.

Uh, what if the babe-in-the-woods wanted to know where and when?

Answers: on campus, this fall; at the capitol, in the meantime.

Yeah, but.

Suppose Jerica wasn't all that committed to saving trees?

Ah, tell her they would include some little furry animals.

Like, which ones?

Um, how about the Preble's Meadow Jumping Mouse? Callie didn't know when or where she'd heard about it, but what did it matter if she made it up off the top of her head? Jerica wouldn't know the difference.

Enough, already. Callie had plenty of verbal ammunition, enough to entice Daniel into the lion's den. Should be easy to get Jerica out of the house.

Only, what if, after all that garbage, she still didn't want to come?

Callie couldn't wait to cross that bridge before she blew it up. So she crawled into the back of Butch's van for some specific ingredients. Just in case Jerica gave her trouble, Callie planned to present the First Miss with a special concoction for the girl to drink.

CHAPTER 19

▼

CELL NUMBER TWO

At a truckstop between Lincoln and Omaha off Interstate-80 and six miles south of Ashland, Ellery and Lily placed a phone call. Back to Milwaukee, to *The Man.*

The newspapers had the bomb story, but the disheveled pair hadn't had access to television. "Gotta check with the Boss, Lily," fussed Ellery. "See if he knows more than the papers are reporting."

Intermittently sobbing and sniffing over Todd's death, the blonde with the strong body odor nodded.

The Man was mad. Disgusted with the amateur bomb bumblers, angry that Ellery had used his private line. "Don't ever call me again. I'm through with the lot of you," he said, from his plush suite in his high-rise office building. "Everybody else is dead. I wish the pair of you were, too. It's over. Disappear. And leave me alone!"

Ellery said okay, that was just fine with him. He didn't want anything to do with ecoterrorism again as long as he lived. Get to Wyoming, Butch, and start over, somewheres else. Not Wisconsin nor Wyoming, that was for sure. As for *The Man,* let him go elsewhere to find the suckers to do his dirty work.

That's what Ellery told Lily, and she readily agreed. Without Todd, what good was life anyhow?

Over burgers and greasy fries before they hit the road to wag their thumbs again, Ellery began to wonder. "Ponder this, Lily. Who th'hell is *The Man,* that he's so all fired up over saving trees?" Ellery talked and chewed with his mouth open. Lily couldn't bear to watch, so she stared at her plate. "You listenin'?" Ellery demanded. "Look at me. Who is this guy?"

"Who cares? We're shed of him. And he of us."

"I'm not so sure, Babe. We've got his phone number. He might be afraid we can identify him. What if he sends somebody after us?"

She shrugged and left her fries. Excused herself for the ladies.

*   *   *   *

Ellery was right. Even at that moment, *The Man in Milwaukee* placed a call that produced a contract on the hitchhiking couple. He couldn't take the risk. They could be picked up at any time for any dang-fool reason. Under police interrogation, their answers could lead to the man who didn't give a hoot in hell about saving trees.

He wanted to hit his competition and hit them hard, so his own megabucks timbering company would be closer to his long-time goal of monopoly. If Bill Gates could do it in computers, he could do it in trees.

▼

CHAPTER 20

CELL NUMBER ONE
AND ALISON'S PARTY

His bomb would work, Bud knew it would. What'd he need Butch for?

Callie had called his cellphone number to explain the delay. She planned to pick up Jerica, she said, and would return within a couple of hours. "Got any fun ideas for the weekend?" she asked Bud.

"Yeah," he said, with no further elaboration. Reluctantly, he agreed to go find her a fix. He wasn't sure how to do that either. Oh well, hit one of the bars, start hintin', somebody would know.

While roaming the bars, the greatest plan of all time burst like a bomb from Bud's fevered brain. Excited, he postponed looking after Callie's need for drugs. Bud was too engrossed in getting ready to blow up the world. He'd show both girls that he was as good an explosives expert as their hero.

In Cheyenne, Callie parked Butch's tan van a half-block away. Dark now, she could slink around the Morissey house searching for Jerica. Try to catch her alone. Meanwhile, steer clear of the girl's snoopy jailers.

*   *   *   *

Alison's party began winding down. The silent knitter-crocheter pair leaned back in fatigue. Peter Schwartzkopf left to take the old ladies home.

On the third floor, the children slept soundly. In the basement, the boys had had enough of pool and video games and singing along with Mark Sanford's guitar strumming. They raced upstairs to the main floor.

John and Jerica, however, hadn't even begun to get reacquaintanted. Their covert glances and blushes suggested they'd like to get away, be alone.

"You two ever going to get off that computer?" squawked Harold.

The spell broken, the young couple quickly excused themselves and left the room. John said he'd look for Alison to thank her for inviting him.

Juanita told Jose about the snooper crashing the garbage can.

Alison told Lisa about their encounter with the bartender from the downtown saloon with the long long bar.

"What on earth?" Lisa said.

"Should we tell Nasty?" Alison countered, after describing the silly scene with Dollie buried under all that rubbish.

"What's to tell?"

"That the Domenico woman has the hots for Nasty's husband."

"Good grief, Ali. The way you talk."

The double cousins returned to the kitchen. Clara was upstairs near the sleeping children, having dismissed her baby-sitting niece for the night.

Martha Washington and Betsy Ross, with their four sons trailing along, left with their bowls of macaroni-cheese and Jell-O fruit cocktail still intact. "What's our stuff, poison?" Martha complained.

"They probably saw us coming," Betsy said. "I don't know why they don't like our food. Or us."

Nicole and Beth gathered up dirty dishes scattered in several rooms. Two of the men returned chairs to their rightful places.

Carl Crosby scribbled furiously in the dining room. When Alison wandered by, he told her he had a great idea for the hook to his article. (Which he would soon change to something quite different.)

Juanita and Jose exchanged relieved glances at spotting Jerica and John emerge from Mr. Morissey's study.

Wilma and Nasty Three emerged from the living room with serious expressions. Talking shop, Ali mused, or sharing capitol gossip. Probably some lofty topic. She decided to keep mum for the moment about Harold and Dollie. The Secretary of State would discover the truth soon enough about her husband's girlfriend. Let it not be from the lips of a double cousin (once removed). Nasty went to collect her new husband, but couldn't find him.

Mark Sanford came out on the porch to tell his mother he had another party that night. Wilma and Mark left together.

"So, what do you think, Ali?" Lisa said. "Should we tell Nasty about her husband and the bartender?"

"Dollie Domenico must be nuts. What's she see in Morton the Mutt?"

"For that matter, what does Nasty?"

Alison pulled Lisa down to sit with her at the antique oak table gleaming from many generations of polishing with Old English oil. "Tell me. Have you ever seen the newlyweds actually talk to one another?"

Lisa looked pensive. "You're right. I haven't even seen them smiling at each other. Beats me what Nasty's doing with him."

Detective Fletcher popped up, in time to catch the last knot on the tail of their conversational kite. He laughed. "No accounting for human nature," he said. "Domenico could be the jilted woman."

"Spying on an old flame, though. That's a bit much," said Lisa.

And that's all there was to that.

Dollie had chickened out at the last moment. She couldn't bring herself to tell the chief of detectives and a Secret Service person that one of First Bank's vice presidents was a bigamist. Her Honeylips, her very own husband, would kill her!

Alison left Lisa and the kitchen to check on the remaining guests.

Alone on the front porch, Joan and her ex-husband, Big Jack, resumed where they'd left off, before Martha Washington and Betsy Ross had accused the former marrieds of acting like a hot new item again, which rapidly cooled their ardor. As usual, Ali noted, spying, her daughter and Jack enjoyed a lovely chat that would probably go nowhere in particular. It never did. That it sometime might, Jack Jacquot might (or might not) continue to hope.

Lipreading, observing, Ali sighed. She wished her daughter would get back together with Jack, finally. When would the stubborn pair ever admit they still loved each other, that destiny meant for them to be together?

When Lisa interrupted Alison to ask about the First Miss, Ali replied that Jerica would occupy one of the guest rooms, next to Crosby's on the second floor. Juanita and Jose said they were eager to turn over the watch to Robert and Caroline for the weekend. They would return with Joan to Laramie, they said, and then be free until Monday, when they'd take over again from the other pair.

Jeff Vicente asked his son when he was returning to campus. John looked at Jerica and she at him. "Soon," John said vaguely.

Aha, Alison thought, more romance in the air. Maybe this one would work out.

After making a date with his physicist son for lunch in Laramie for later the following week, Jeff too went to his room on the second floor. He said he would return to Casper on the morrow.

To Alison, Juanita and Jose, Jerica excused herself for the powder room.

And that was the last that any of the party people saw of the President's daughter. Except on the many late-breaking television news shows broadcast around the world.

▼

CHAPTER 21

CELL NUMBER ONE

Bud knew somebody who knew somebody who owned a log cabin in the mountains beyond Centennial, up in the Snowy Range Mountain area, where the altitude ranges from nine thousand to over twelve-thousand feet, where lodge pole pine and a variety of flora and fauna unique to the mountains flourish, and where bears and mountain lions vie with elk, deer, moose and many other wild creatures for survival. And where visitors throw snowballs in August.

Easy to lose yourself in this vast wilderness and many people had, from small children to experienced mountain climbers and backpackers. Many to die, from freezing or hypothermia or from getting ripped apart by wild animals.

Bud and his buddies could use the isolated cabin awhile, said their host, as nobody else would be up there until hunting season that fall. The owners were off on an extended tour of Europe, including a Mediterranean cruise.

Meanwhile, Butch cooled his heels in the Cheyenne jail. Lying flat on his back on a thin, stinking mattress, he dreamed of robbing banks, like his hero, Butch Cassidy.

Cassidy got his nickname because he worked as a butcher. He and the Sundance Kid were famous for robbing trains and banks. Edwards proposed to carry on the tradition—robbing banks, if not trains, although the latter appealed. Instead, here he was, stuck in the Cheyenne holding tank, stinking of urine, vomit, and strong disinfectant; incarcerated with a bunch of drunks and junkies and perverts, or that's how he labeled them. Well, they had also thrown Butch

Cassidy behind bars awhile, over at Wyoming Territorial Prison, in Laramie, now restored and targeting tourists and their money.

If Butch Cassidy could stick it out in jail, so could Butch Edwards. Then he'd get back in business.

It didn't occur to the unkempt, mid-thirtyish thug with the red pony tail and nose earring that the cops would be going over Callie's car (the blue Dodge Intrepid he was driving), like they were searching for lice on a migrant worker invited to the mansions of Wyoming's most powerful.

*   *   *   *

Back before he'd left for Alison's party, and while seated at his scarred wooden desk, his boot-clad feet propped up, his toothpicked-mouth salivating, Detective Fletcher fumed and fumbled, undecided.

"So you found what looks and stinks like a tablespoonful of fertilizer," Walt said, plopping boots to floor and rising abruptly to tower over Bobby Gilbert, the rookie with the jitters. "So what? This here's ranching country. Anybody could have a good excuse for carting fertilizer around. Nothing else?"

"Few loose wires."

"Come Monday and the return of the municipal judge from his fishing trip, we have to let the creep go."

"I guess."

*   *   *   *

During the sixty or so hours before the weekend closed and the Judge returned, Butch did a lot of thinking. Mainly about how his gang would blow up Hoyt Hall when he returned to Laramie. Then he could report to his brothers back in Milwaukee that little brother had come through after all.

*   *   *   *

Out west and up in the mountains above Centennial, Bud too was doing a lot of thinking; and grinning, as he circled the log cabin on indefinite loan, and while unloading the supplies and provisions that might have to last their gang a long time. Butch was gonna be surprised at Bud's ingenuity. So would Callie.

The one person up for the really big surprise, though she didn't know it, was Jerica! She might not like it, but then again she could fool them. Add those little furry critters to the mix and she'd be hooked for sure on their cause.

And Bud would get her in bed. Then she'd make a commitment, for sure. Bud shrugged, hauled stuff, sweated. And grinned.

CHAPTER 22

▼

ALISON'S CLAN PARTY

At first they didn't notice anything amiss. Pretty girls often linger in front of the mirror, freshening their makeup, brushing their hair.

When muscular Caroline and ectomorph Robert arrived to take over for Jose and Juanita, the latter said they were out of there. Caroline said just a minute, you haven't yet turned over our baby to us. So all four beat on the powder room door. Silence.

A strong breeze had arrived with nightfall. The door rattled, with age or something else that couldn't be determined, Alison said, joining the rappers with her own dainty rat-a-tat. Silence.

"Got a key?" Robert asked.

"Sure," said Alison. Except she couldn't remember where it had got off to. Lisa tried prodding her cousin's memory.

Trailing his wife, who trailed Alison, Peter had more ideas: Randy had put the key in his desk? How about the kitchen key rack? In Clara's apron pocket? In the background, Joan and Jack lingered, looking on, looking at each other.

On the front porch, Walt Fletcher and Brad Gifford were swapping stories. Privy to cousin Alison's White House adventure, Brad shared a few personal particulars about how she had foiled the Muslim's assassination attempt.

Robert said he couldn't wait any longer. He and Jose went outdoors to peer in the window, while Caroline and Juanita continued knocking on the door and calling loudly for Jerica. All astew, John paced the floor. Sweat droplets popped out on his forehead. He mopped his face with the sleeve of his shirt. Why wouldn't Jerica come out?

Carl vacillated between filming with his videocam and jotting notes in his notebook. This could be an historic moment.

It was When they burst into the powder room, it was empty. Apparently Jerica had crawled out the window to vanish unseen by anyone save her co-conspirators.

First order of business for the four Secret Service people hired to protect the President's daughter: a conference of high priority, deciding what to do and in what sequence. Call their boss first? That meant admitting they'd failed. Miserably. Instead, maybe they should launch their own search. Caroline perspired. Robert cussed. Jose scowled. Juanita cried real tears.

"Call the President," Caroline insisted.

"Alert the detective," Robert said.

"Put out an APB," Jose added.

"We could split up," Juanita contributed. "You guys comb the city, while Caroline and I return to Laramie."

Fletcher, when they told him the First Miss was gone, put out an All Points Bulletin. Colonel Schwartzkopf said he'd race to the base for a helicopter.

"I'll go with you," said Brad, the other pilot in the family.

Piercing the terrible fears gripping the Secret Service people, Alison recommended they postpone calling Dom. "Jerica has likely run off with her friends for the evening and will return soon."

"But what if she's been kidnapped?" Juanita moaned.

"By terrorists," Caroline proposed.

"Or by genuine kidnappers who'll demand a big ransom," Jose said.

"Or by people with a political agenda," Robert suggested ominously.

"Or perhaps by aliens," Alison said dryly.

Juanita and Jose, who'd come with Joan, said they would return with her. Robert and Caroline, officially on duty now, said they'd stick with Walt and Mrs. Morissey.

Beth and Nicole said they aimed to hit the Cheyenne bars.

Nasty Three said she was calling the Governor and the Mayor.

Alison repeated that everybody should wait a bit before running off half-cocked, and meanwhile she and Lisa would stay put to man the phones. Big

Jack poured a stiff brandy, offering the decanter to the ladies. Lisa accepted. Joan and Alison declined.

Martha and Betsy and their four boys and Wilma and her son were long gone. So were Hepzibah and Isabelle.

Harry the Hyena demanded to know *What's happenin', man,* and why were they always leaving him out of things. The Secretary of State pushed him out the door ahead of her, telling Alison to call with any news. "Don't worry about waking us."

John was too stunned to say or do anything. Minutes earlier Jerica seemed eager to get better acquainted. And now she was gone. "Unbelievable!" he said to Alison.

Carl's feelings came clear from the reaction of his thermometer, alternating between blushing and paling. He was torn between his personal feelings of concern for the First Family and the chance to be front row and center with what could be a wow of a story, whatever it turned out to be.

The telephone rang. Alison leaped like shot from a cannon.

Lisa said, "I'll get it."

"No, I will." With trembling hands, Alison picked up the phone. "Yes?"

"Hey, Gal, bake me some cookies," said Randy. "I'm on my way home."

CHAPTER 23

▼

MAGDA OBLASTY

Before Alison could search for Clara to alert her to the imminent arrival of the *Master, the Head of the House,* the phone rang again.

This time Lisa took the call before handing over the instrument to Alison. Lisa said it was Magda Oblasty. In Kyrgyzstan it was noon; midnight, Wyoming time. Exactly twelve hours difference.

"What on earth?" said Alison.

"You've got to help me, Mrs. Morissey," wailed the dignitary's wife from half-way around the planet.

How in the world could she do that? Ali had too many cups wobbling around on her saucer right now. "Yes, dear," she said, circling one ear with index finger, signaling to her double cousin with the universal sign that she was listening to a dingbat.

"House arrest! I think that's what you Americans call it," Magda said. "I can't leave the house. My husband says I embarrassed the whole country. The government says I humiliated them in public."

"Why is that, dear?" Alison suspected she knew the answer.

Lisa lifted the brandy decanter, raising an eyebrow at her soul mate, who shook her head while pointing to the water pitcher. The Colonel's wife complied, using tongs to add a few ice cubes from the covered silver bucket.

Magda droned on, with Alison periodically mumbling her standard placebos of Yes, dear—no, dear.

With the call completed and nothing resolved (in Kyrgyzstan), or promised (from Wyoming), Alison and Lisa ventured several suppositions:

Magda's outlandish, semi-see-through plasticized gauze gown and her garish makeup had set back the Kyrgyzstan women's rights by several decades, if not a century.

The Muslim fundamentalists would seize power in the country to impose their ultra-strict religious dictums on the Kyrgyz women. Magda's husband would be ousted from his position, the couple ostracized from society, perhaps exiled from their homeland.

Alison and Lisa could see it all now: American women who cared—like the clan cousins—would again be embroiled in a massive campaign of phone-fax-email-telegram and fund raisers to gain world-wide attention and sympathy for the beleaguered women far from American shores in a country smaller than Dom's home state of North Dakota.

But not quite yet.

First on the stack of their wobbly cups was locating Jerica Davidson.

C H A P T E R   24

▼

THE PRESIDENT AND
FIRST LADY

Saturday, Sunday—nothing. No word of, from, or about the First Miss.

The Davidsons panicked. They called in the Federal Bureau of Investigation, the Central Intelligence Agency, the National Security Czar, the Secretary of Homeland Security, Betty Lukowski. Then they took off in Air Force One for Wyoming.

The action had moved from Cheyenne to Laramie, home of the University and Jerica's summer residence. Jerica's Secret Service people thought they would lose their minds; their jobs and reputations, too. They dreaded facing the President and First Lady.

The local police and county sheriff's deputies combed the area. In Laramie, the city and university police and the county deputies conferred, followed by setting up roadblocks and calling in reinforcements of state patrol and National Guard. Nothing. No signs, no clues, no demands for ransom.

Federal law, said Peter Schwartzkopf, prohibits the military from becoming actively involved in domestic law enforcement matters, unless explicitly directed to do so by the President. However, this was different. This was an immediate emergency; both personal and public. This was the President's daughter. Without aforethought, Dom agreed with Peter that the military could assist. Colonel Schwartzkopf called personnel at F. E. Warren Air Force Base out of Cheyenne.

Then Peter and Brad, in separate helicopters and in company with a dozen others from the base crisscrossed the county. Then they expanded their search beyond Albany and Laramie Counties; west and north into Carbon and Natrona counties; south into Colorado, east into Nebraska.

By Monday, the Laramie motels were packed solid. First, with the tourists passing into and through Wyoming. Next, with the President and entourage, the FBI and CIA, and, of course, the media from the nation and around the globe.

Accompanying Dom and Julia were Presidential Aide Mark Prescott (nee, Mario Pesci), Davidson's private secretary, Rose Washington Lincoln, and speechwriter Carl Crosby, among others including Secret Service personnel. This group took over the entire Park Inn off Interstate-80 in Laramie.

The media at first swarmed Laramie's Comfort Inn on the east end of busy Grand Avenue. Hundreds of reporters and photographers—including CNN's Marci Carmichael with photographer Phillip Schatz—booked rooms at Super 8 Motel, Foster's Country Corner, Days Inn, Econo Lodge, Camelot, Sunset Inn, the Travel Inn, the Gas Lite, and out at Stone House Stables. As these accommodations rapidly filled, the rest of the press and the many gawkers tried bed and breakfasts, or they headed out of town to western guest ranches, including the Two Bars Seven and V-Bar, Brush Creek, and Old Glendevey, Bit-O-Wyo, and Rawah. Finally, they doubled up in the last few rental cars to drive the thirty miles west of town to tiny Centennial; population, 101.

"Sounds like a psychology course," Marci said to Phillip. "You know, Phil, Psych 101." The two tall slender CNN brunettes couldn't be tagged as doubles, for they were woman and man; the former, neat and tidy; the latter, slouchy and rumpled. Marci wore her dark hair in a pageboy with bangs.

Across the Interstate and next to Motel 6, the FBI had already filled up the Holiday Inn, commandering a big suite for their communications and command center. Here was where the UW trustees stayed too.

The University president, Roe Bryan Kennedy, stayed home in what was euphemistically called *The white house* (lower case), because his three-story, near-white house loomed over the town's northeast landscape. On a hill above the Kennedys' Victorian style mansion stood a huge Mormon church.

Everybody else—all the leftovers and lesser bodies including tourists raced back east forty-five miles to grab rooms in Cheyenne.

When CNN's Marci remembered that Jerica's campus advisor was Alison's daughter, the Ace field reporter called Joan Vicente at her office in Hoyt Hall. Getting no answer, she next tried her home. Bingo!

"You don't know me, Professor Vicente," Marci began, after introducing herself.

"Of course I know who you are, Ms. Carmichael. I'm a fan, in fact."

That established, Marci moved from the personal to the occupational. "I'm trying to locate Alison Morisey. She's your mom, right?"

"She just walked in," Joan said into the phone.

Slamming the door behind her, Alison said she was plumb tuckered out. Having completely forgotten her husband's imminent arrival, she too had taken up residence in Laramie. She had barely slept since Thursday night. Her head ached from all that babble in Dom and Julia's suite. She needed a nap, preferably straight around the clock.

She cared about Marci, though. Which was why Alison agreed to meet. "Give me a couple of hours, and then I'll come to your room."

Ms. Carmichael objected. "Too many other media reps here. Can you think of somewhere more private?"

"There's a little café out on Snowy Range Road, called the Beanery. Good Mexican food. Lot of people, but they won't know either of us."

Shower, shampoo, and nap. While Alison slept the sleep of zombies, Joan fielded phone calls, catching each on the first ring; from clan members, at first, in search of news. Shortly thereafter, she heard from the university's President, then the Wyoming Governor, followed by U.S. Senators Kevin Macomber and Ron Perry, and Congresswoman Patty Pruitt. Everybody sought the professor's mother, and assumed she would be at her daughter's. Also obvious was their assumption that Mrs. Morissey, the President's *Surrogate Mom*, would have personal knowledge of this mysterious and possibly deadly situation.

With each caller Joan was courteous, but concise. She knew no more than anyone else, and her napping mother could not be disturbed.

Except that Randolph Morissey insisted he speak to his wife. "Tell me what you think you're doing!" he squawked at Alison over the phone from Cheyenne.

Bleary-eyed, Alison swiped a hand across her face and sighed. "About what?"

"Everything! First off, tell me why you think you had to go to Mexico."

"Oh, that." Odd, she thought, that he wouldn't want to talk about Jerica's disappearance. Everybody else did. "You suggested it, Randy."

He blubbered that he'd done no such thing. Skipping over his protestations, she said she was after saving the President. "Aunt Nasturtium has the scoop on everybody. Mario Pesci, or Mark Prescott—the name he's using—looked pretty darn sinister to me. I suspected him of setting about to kill the President...."

Randy interrupted to sputter and yell at her:"Good God, woman! The President has a whole flank of people watching over him. It's not <u>your</u> job! And neither is this missing-daughter business. Come on home."

Alison couldn't understand her husband's inability to appreciate that Dom was like a son to her. It should be obvious that she must do everything in her power to look after him.

"Your place is here at home. You should be baking cookies and casseroles. Taking my dictation."

"Don't be silly, Randy. You're retired. Where's the dictation come in?"

More sputtering in her ear. She was so tired. "I'll be home soon, Dear." He could have suggested he'd like to have her in bed. What had happened to the romance in their marriage? How she longed for those wonderfully passionate days of yesteryear. He could be so exasperating, even back then—criticizing her, fussing about every little thing not of his own making. All that marvelous bedroom action must have overshadowed the obvious. Randolph Morissey was a most despicable person!

Alison hung up in the middle of his ranting and raving and returned to bed. She needed sleep.

*   *   *   *

In a log cabin beyond the village of Centennial (elevation, 8,086 feet), nestled beneath tall lodge pole pine trees and far from civilization, someone else slept.

But not Bud and Callie.

CHAPTER 25

▼

CELL NUMBER ONE

"Eden is dead?" Butch said. He couldn't believe it. First Pa, now Eden.

It was Monday afternoon before they released Butch. By then Ellery and Lily had arrived

None of them had tuned in or read the news. No interest to them what happened around the world.

At the truckstop south of Cheyenne the trio ordered lunch and loaded up on snacks before heading for Laramie. "You guys can meet my gang," Butch said, puffing out his chest with pride at garnering a group with allegiance to himself.

Lily rolled her eyes and left the table; to make a potty stop, she said.

Ellery reached over to slap his younger brother on the back. "You don't look no worse for wear, Eddy." Then he twisted around to watch Lily wagging her behind through the café in her tight, elasticized, micro-length skirt, and shook his head back and forth, like he was watching a tennis match.

"I know Lily stinks, Eddy. But she don't like baths. Weird, eh. Says 'natural body odors' ain't nuthin' to be ashamed of."

"'I go by *Butch!* Would you th'hell call me Butch!" Mad enough to chew nails, Butch belched and rolled his eyes. "So, you been beddin' that broad?"

"Not me, Eddy. Uh, Butch. Lily is Todd's woman. *Was,* I mean. He's dead now too. But doin' it with Lily with Todd fresh dead don't seem right."

"That's better. *Butch!* I like t'be called Butch. Ellery, you know Butch Cassidy was from Wyoming? The one what robbed trains, banks, and such."

"Okay, sure. So you named yourself Butch after Cassidy. So how's about you? You getting any?"

More relaxed now, Butch grinned and puffed out his chest anew. "Yeah, man. More'n I can handle. My main squeeze, Callie. Plus—get this, Ellery; you listenin'? I'm 'bout to lay me some real pipe, man."

"How's that?" Ellery took a big bite of chicken-fried steak, swabbed around the big glob in the gravy and stuck it in his mouth. He chewed with his mouth open.

"The President's daughter!"

"President of what? Who?" Chomp, chomp.

"President of these U-Nited States. Of America. That's who."

"Go on with you." Another big bite poised on the end of Ellery's fork, it sat there waiting, gravy droplets dripping off the fork onto the table.

"Really, Ellery. I'm not kiddin'. See, over in Laramie, where I recruited this bunch, my gang: Bud and his girl, Callie—she's my girl, now—well, she lived with her rich-bitch friends at the sorority house. Well, uh. Never mind all that. But Callie's 'roomy,' as they call each other, is ripe. Ripe for a real man and ripe for the ecoterrorist movement. And, this *roomy* of Callie's is, yeah, man, I mean it, honest-Injun, Jerica Davidson, daughter of the President."

"And she's one of your gang, now? Go on with you."

"She doesn't know she is, but she is. That's for sure." Butch munched his burger and dipped a wad of fries in thousand-island dressing.

"Makes no sense, she is or she ain't."

"She's with us, at least while the good times roll. She don't know nuthin' 'bout no bombs, though. Nor what we're going to do with them."

"Listen Butch, about all that bombing business. After Milwaukee, me and Lily want nuthin' t'do with all that tree-hugging stuff no more. Too dangerous, too scary…."

"Ah, Ellery, what are you saying t'me? I thought we wanted revenge?"

"Got that, boy. Lily shot the Judge. Sullivan's dead. End of story."

Butch suddenly remembered. "Wait a minute. Back up. You say Eden's dead. Right? How'd he get it? Lily shoot him, too?"

"Naw. Judge threw our bomb out the window of his courtroom. Landed on our RV. Boom. That's all she wrote."

"Wait a minute. No more Eden. No more RV, either? Then how'd you get from Wisconsin to Wyoming?"

Ellery jerked his thumb in the hitchhiker's gesture just as Lily returned, preceded by her body odors. Butch wondered how they'd ever caught a ride, or kept it. Stink up their car, drivers would dump her right back out on the highway. Talk about rank.

Butch meant to roll down all four windows of Callie's blue Dodge. If they ever got going. Here in the truckstop with its showers for truckers, he wanted to tell Lily to go bathe and shampoo before they hit the road. His girl wasn't much cleaner, though.

Soon he'd be using Callie to haul his ashes, or maybe he'd try Jerica, instead. He bet the <u>clean</u> blonde couldn't wait to jump into his bed; all that cutsy-flirty stuff from her in the bars lately. What was with these other girls, Lily and Callie, moseyin' around, actin' like flower children, or what?

Over coffee, Butch outlined his plan to bomb Hoyt Hall on the University of Wyoming campus. "See, Ellery, this job also speaks to the tree huggin' issue. *The Man* says to me that one of the professors housed there is the son of a timbering tycoon. That's the assignment. Turns out, Callie has a personal reason for this particular bombing. Her communications professor flunked her. So, ya see, Ellery, that dame with an office in Hoyt Hall will be gittin' her come-uppance, too."

Standing, Butch said he had to go make some calls. Abruptly he left the table to head for the foyer and the bank of public pay phones.

Out in the lobby, one hand on the phone and the other fishing for change, Butch got to thinking. In Milwaukee, the *Big Bang* hadn't come off as planned. But a prominent judge was murdered. They'd got rid of Sullivan. That was good. Maybe a lot of other people out on the street got killed, too. Great. He felt like cheering.

Meanwhile, *The Man* had said he wanted media coverage, lots of attention. He'd charged the Edwards brothers with alerting the press and the cops to take credit on behalf of tree huggers everywhere.

Right after the Milwaukee bombing, so the plan went, Butch was supposed to set off his charges in Wyoming. Claim the environmentalists had done it again. That way it would appear that the ecoterrorists were well organized, with lots of cells all over the country, about to go Pop! Boom!

Unless the big timbering corporations stopped cutting down the trees. Yeah, like an ultimatum. Jerica oughta go for that, she was the one what was quoted in the press saying she didn't see why anybody wanted to cut down pretty trees. So, Butch mused, it was apparently a bunch of *political statements* they were making. Instead of demanding the release of foreign nationals held captive, we're supposed to demand the release of trees. Hah, pretty good—exchange trees for their agreeing to stop the bombing.

With all this summarizing rushing like Niagara Falls through his cranium, Butch's head ached. What was he doing out here holding the phone in his hand?

Oh, yeah. Call Callie in Laramie, tell her to get Jerica, keep ahold of her until he got back to town. Then he'd figure out what to do next. It was his call.

No answer. Callie's machine wasn't even on, so he couldn't leave a message. Oh, well. Bud had probably left a note in Butch's apartment to let him know where to catch up with Callie, Bud, and, hopefully, Jerica.

Next, Butch called his boss. (Ellery hadn't had time to tell Butch that he and Lily had broken with *The Man,* or that he and Lily were afraid the big shot might try to take them out as a result of their defection.)

*   *   *   *

Surprised, the man in Milwaukee just listened. When he hung up, he stood up. Too late to halt the contract he'd arranged, to hit the remaining Edwards brothers and Lily. *The Man* had gone through two intermediaries, plus who knew how many others they had contacted before choosing the hit man.

No matter. They could take out the trio and be done with it.

Meanwhile, Butch had spilled the beans when he gave *The Man* the whole upcoming scenario.

The lumber tycoon paced back and forth over his expensive oriental carpet. No hitting little white golf balls across the long expanse of the room. Not today. Too much to think about.

The President's daughter? Great! He hadn't expected the ignorant Edwards boy out in Wyoming would make good on that part of the assignment.

He owned a million-dollar "cottage" at Fox Lake, an exclusive golf club and condo complex surrounded by mountains and evergreens and situated thirty-five miles southwest of Laramie.

Not that far as the crow flies from the log cabin snuggled deep in the mountains of the Snowy Range, up past Centennial. (But *The Man* knew nothing about that, yet, because Butch didn't know, when he'd called Milwaukee from Cheyenne.)

His fancy summer place was near enough to Laramie, Jerica Davidson's university home. *The Man* didn't want to get too close to the action, whatever was going down. He'd bet his last diamond tie tack, though, that whatever the Edwards boys were up to, it had something to do with the President's daughter having gone missing.

He ordered his pilot to check his Learjet. They would take off as soon as the pilot gave the thumbs up. *The Man* wanted a good seat in the bleachers, just not on the fifty-yard line

CHAPTER 26

▼

THE CHASE

Along with the rest of the world, two of Wyoming's television stations, KTWO out of Casper and KGWN, Cheyenne, broadcast the news of the missing lass. Almost as an afterthought, the state stations mentioned a UW campus demonstration, to take place later that day. Something about tree huggers, or maybe rats, toads, or mosquitoes.

*   *   *   *

CNN's Marci came alone to meet Alison at the Beanery café in West Laramie. Ali recommended chalupas and for herself ordered a single rejeno with a green tossed salad. She hadn't had time to be selective when she left Cheyenne in her rush to sit with the First Couple, so she still wore the goofy looking, floppy platinum wig. Pretty Marci, with bangs and pageboy, said it becomed Mrs. M, but Ali knew better. They spoke quickly, but in some detail about Jerica. Alison could see no harm in sharing her daughter's news about Jerica's somewhat unsavory companions this summer. Joan the professor wasn't as suspicious as her mom, but she did worry.

Marci wanted a fast tour of the campus town. Like Carl Crosby, she needed some background. They took Ali's car, a sporty, red, Pontiac Grand Prix. Laramie was stuffed with people, like her green pepper and rice casserole, she said, bringing a grin to the reporter's face.

As they zipped around campus and town, spotting a platoon of motorcycle riders headed for a rally, a field full of RVs from the senior citizens' hostel, shoppers after back-to-school items, and plenty of tourists and gawkers, Alison thought she'd come apart at the seams. Somebody was following them! When she slowed, so did they. When she turned a corner, they did, too. From her rearview mirror, she spied a couple of men with dark faces and black hair.

Reminded her of the President's Aide, *Mario Pesci!*

But he was supposed to be on the up and up. According to the First Family and also her Aunt Nasturtium. If not Mark Prescott, who? Muslims?

Alison was less worried about herself than she was over Marci. The young woman was under her care. She must save the reporter at all costs!

Hardly responding to Marci's questions, Alison darted hither and yon. She hoped she could keep her wits, because the green Ford was still back there.

At last Marci captured her attention. Some remark about Jerica.

"Think about it, Alison. If she'd been kidnapped, wouldn't the President or somebody have heard already? Wouldn't there be a ransom note? Some demands should have been made, by now. Say, an exchange caper. Release some political prisoners somewhere, and the gang will give up Jerica."

Taking her eyes off the street ahead to stare at Marci, Ali nearly hit the back of a garbage truck. She slammed on the brakes before addressing the reporter. "You think Jerica's involved with some dirty mischief? On her own volition?"

"Face it, Mrs. Morrisey. It's a distinct possibility that Jerica's run off of her own free will. As I said, no demands, no note, no nothing. She ran away because she wanted to. That's what I think. What do you think?"

Alison didn't have time to think. Quickly deciding on a strategy to get her tail out in the open, she zoomed past the garbage truck and stepped on the gas

"Where are we going?"

Alison pointed to the right, to the Territorial Prison, now a historical park with western entertainment and periodic showcases. Out here on Snowy Range Road the speed limit was forty-five. The green Ford hung back. If she had any sense, she supposed she should return Marci to her motel and get herself into the President's suite. But then she'd only worry that the next time she poked her head out the door somebody would shoot it off. Might as well face her fears immediately. See what happened.

At the junction with the ramp to Interstate-80 she had to make a decision; get on the highway or head on west toward Centennial? Alison chose the latter, mainly because the light was green ahead and, to the right, a big truck lumbered slowly.

"What th'hell?" Marci insisted this time that Alison explain her actions.

"Couple of guys following us; me, rather. They've been back there since before we left campus."

Marci started to turn around, but Ali's hand on her arm gave pause.

"No, don't look, unless you've got a compact with a mirror. This may sound paranoid, Marci, but back at the White House last week when I squelched an assassination attempt on the wife of a foreign government officer, the President's security people warned me about fanatic Muslims. Supposedly, they have long memories, and don't easily forgive. I've been warned to watch my back."

They passed through West Laramie to reach the turnoff for the airport. Ahead was Sheep Mountain, home of the wild big-horn sheep; also Centennial, the mountains and forest, the snow-capped peaks, and the ski slopes. (Plus a secluded log cabin, that currently housed a young woman, now famous around the world.)

The dark green Ford drew closer. No cars intervened; no other cars, period. "What do you think they want to do, Mrs. M?" Now there was a note of panic in Marci's voice, all sign of ridicule gone.

"Kill me," Ali said with seeming calm. "You, too, since you're with me."

"Oh, my God."

"If that's a prayer, Marci, fine. We need it." She didn't say what it was if it weren't. No time. "Open the glove compartment, Marci. Can you shoot?"

"What do you want me to do with this?" The reporter stared at the 9.9 ounce Beretta, an 8-load, semi-automatic handgun.

"Shoot 'em." Alison accelerated—seventy, eighty miles an hour. The Ford too put on a burst of speed, nearly bumping bumpers with her bright red Grand Prix. "Lean out your open window, Marci, and get off a couple of shots. Aim for their tires first, but if you miss, point the shooter straight at the windshield."

"Oh, my God." Marci tried, but her hands shook. The first two bullets went wild.

"Only eight bullets, so take good aim next time."

There was no next time.

Alison careened around curves, swooped up and down hills, training her eyes ahead with only an occasional glance in the rearview mirror. When they started shooting, she'd need to duck. She hoped Marci wouldn't panic.

The dark-skinned driver banged her car hard. She stepped on the gas. Bump, bump. Bump, accelerate; bump. At least they weren't shooting, not even in response to Marci's two shots. Alison made a sudden decision. Her beautiful car? Th'hell with it.

When the green Ford speeded up she slammed on the brakes, catching them in the radiator and smashing it. Water and steam gushed. The Ford stopped dead. The dark-complected men in the slicked back, black hair, wearing black suits and black ties on white shirts got out. In her rearview mirror, Alison saw them staring at their car and scratching their heads.

It took her no more than a quarter mile to slow her pretty red Pontiac, now with its bumper dented in and its trunk lid sprung, to whirl back around in the middle of the road. Again she stomped hard on the gas.

Without looking at her passenger, Alison held out her hand, palm up. "Give me the gun. Quick, Marci."

"What are you going to do?"

"Shoot 'em."

She didn't mean it, of course. She did intend to scare the hell out of them, though. Ambidextrous, Alison switched the Beretta to her left hand and, as they passed the stranded thugs, she got off two more shots. Just the pair, but they hit the targets. She blew both tires on the road side.

The thugs would have a tough time getting to Laramie without calling for a tow.

"My God, where'd you learn to shoot like that?"

"This is Wyoming, dear. As our former Senator, Alan Simpson, once said, *In Wyoming, gun control means how steady you can hold your gun.* Maybe every native can't shoot, but the double cousins certainly can. Our great-great-grandmother Rose made sure of that."

Back in town and near the Beanery, Alison pulled up and stopped. She needed coffee. Yet neither woman moved. Ali shook all over.

"How could you do that? Where did you get the strength, the courage?"

Shuddering, perspiration flowing from every pore, Ali whispered, "One never knows what one can do until put to the test, Marci. I had to save us both. You, especially, since you're my guest. You were just along for the ride. They were after me."

Marci wiped her brow with a Kleenex tissue. "Reminds me of those guys on the hijacked plane that crashed in Pennsylvania," said the reporter. "They gave their lives to protect the President and the White House. I know you would have done the same. You thought President Davidson was the assassination target at that state dinner when you threw yourself in harm's way."

Alison shook her head. "Hardly a good comparison." No time to protest further. As for Magda, Ali didn't want to go into all that—how she'd accidentally defrayed the assassin's knife, or why she'd come to fall atop Magda Oblasky at all.

Ali wasn't at all sure of the answer herself. Some things one does unconsciously, she concluded.

Privately, she wished Randy could have seen her in action. Maybe he wouldn't forever call her his discombobulated little dingbat. On second thought, he would no doubt haul her home, chain her to the stove, or to the computer to process his nonexistent correspondence.

She sighed, ungluing her hands from the steering wheel by peeling them away as if from glue. One by one, she stretched and massaged her fingers.

The two women returned to the same café and ordered coffee.

*   *   *   *

Back on the road the two men, brothers, stared at their disabled car and conferred. They didn't like it one bit, this assignment. Educated in the States, they spoke good English, could pass for Americans, their superiors said. Which is why the fanatic Muslims had taken their parents, siblings, and other kin hostage until the dirty deed was done.

"Their revenge, not ours," the elder brother complained to the younger.

"Yeah, but we got to do it. Who knows the torture our family may be subjected to. Even as we speak."

"I know, I know. But I don't have to like it."

They weren't accustomed to guns, either. A quick training session in the Iraqi desert and they were sent on their way. Which didn't make them comfortable with the idea of carrying around shooters or becoming shooters themselves.

"Can't postpone the job too long."

I know."

CHAPTER 27

▼

ALISON'S HUSBAND

Randolph Morissey had arrived home to an empty house. After talking to his wife on the phone, he sat down to pout.

Silence. No wife, no Clara. No aromatic odors of bread, cookies, or pies baking. Why didn't Alison come home?

Deep fatigue and worries over both his physical and his financial health sent the retired geologist to his study. Trembling, he switched on the computer and used his password. Unshaven, unkempt, his eyes could barely focus on the numbers scrolling down the screen.

All his investments, wiped out; the Russian and the Brazilian rain forest funds he'd been speculating with so wildly. Gone, every last cent. He still couldn't believe it. As if leaving town would have made everything come right in his absence.

Leaning back in his faded green cracked-leather swivel chair, Randy removed his glasses and rubbed his eyes. Then he unlocked the bottom drawer to draw out his private medical reports. Sweat breaking out, his hands shook.

He was not a well man, he'd acknowledged that some time ago. He hadn't wanted any local doctors knowing anything about his condition, so he had left the state. Six weeks, maybe a couple of months, no more. That's all he had left. Nowhere near enough time to recoup the Morissey finances.

A line came to him: *He whom the gods would destroy, they first make sentimental.* Randy's romantic notions of protecting his wife, of enhancing the fortune she'd turned over to him to guard, and that he'd expected to make grow like an experimental pumpkin into mammoth size, was gone. Rotted, wasted, shriveled to nothing.

Instead of guarding, enhancing, he'd lost it all. Before leaving home to hide out in the mountains by himself, Randy had done one more thing. He'd taken out a half-million-dollar life insurance policy. That, too, was in jeopardy.

The insurance claims people would surely investigate his death. He must destroy the doctors' reports; leave behind no evidence that he'd anticipated dying when he took out the policy. Then, and only then, would he put his final plan into action. He must protect Alison at all costs.

Turning off the computer and relocking the drawer with the medical records intact, Randy rose, wobbled, lost focus, and sat back down again. He needed to think, to make specific plans.

On the way to the kitchen and toast—surely he could find bread, butter, and the toaster—he caught a glimpse of himself in the mirror. In its antique gold frame, the mirror was a keepsake; passed down to Ali from her great-great-grand-mother Rose.

He didn't appreciate his reflection scowling back at him. Thinning gray hair across a balding pate, jowls, wrinkled pale skin, shoulders slumped above his now skinny frame. Not much left of the vigorous and physically fit geologist who'd clambered over hot deserts in foreign countries in search of oil.

In the kitchen Randy noticed the answering machine light blinking. Perhaps Ali had called back to say she'd be right home. Or somebody else with news. Instead, the recorded voice was that of a stranger. The woman identified herself as Magda Oblasty, of Kyrgyzstan. Hmph. That woman from one of those little "stan" countries; *stan*, meaning *land*. Land of the Kyrgyz.

Randy listened repeatedly to the message. After three times, it still made no sense. Something about Magda's husband; kidnapped, held hostage with thirteen others, including four Japanese and a senior Kygyzstan military officer. Amidst tearful sobs, Magda said her husband's captors demanded exchange for several militants from Tajikistan. Her husband was part of the group seized by Tajik militants who'd invaded Kyrgyzstan. Magda, however, wasn't at all clear about their objectives.

Furthermore, the silly woman insisted in her message that her "performance at the White House" had something to do with her husband's inclusion among the hostages. "Performance? At the White House?" Randy muttered aloud. What had the silly goose done, jumped up on the table to start singing? Surely she wouldn't do a striptease. She was a dingbat, but that was a bit much. Out of contact with his wife and the world, Randy had no idea what had transpired while he was gone.

One more rerun of the tape. Now he caught Magda's plea. "You must help me, Mrs. Morissey. You must help get my husband free." Next, in a whisper, came the warning. "Only, be careful. They may want to kill you, too."

What in the world? Why would some strange Muslims half-way around the globe want to harm his wife?

What was all this about? Why should Ali care?

Second thoughts. Now he remembered. Mrs. Oblasty was the woman who had demanded Alison dance attendance on her at the White House dinner, which was why Ali had taken off with the President in Air Force One. Randy wondered, but only briefly, how that venture had come out.

When Ali got home and heard Magda's message, Randy would order his wife to steer clear this time. She didn't need to get involved in every dang fool thing, especially not a hostage take-over in some strange and no doubt dangerous land.

Without her guardian, namely the husband who knew what was good for her, no telling what would happen to his pretty little girl. Suddenly Randy grasped the truth. Poor little discombobulated Alison would have to learn all by herself how to cope, how to get by without him. He wasn't long for this world.

CHAPTER 28

▼

THE "BROAD" AND THE DEMONSTRATION

The Man's hit man wasn't plural, and she wasn't male. She'd got into this business by default. Her lover had got himself hit and she was left alone. She'd bummed around with him for two decades before he was taken out. With the offer to take over for him, she'd shrugged. Why not. No family, no friends; no skills, no job experience.

Sexually abused as a child, and then abandoned, she had neither known love nor felt it for others. As for her *sweetheart*, their relationship was sardonic, sarcastic, cynical, and hardly affectionate, except for their coupling in bed and then they usually played rough. Although she used the *sweetheart* term in her head, she'd never verbalized the endearment.

He called her *The Broad*. She was. Broad in the beam; husky, short, with wiry gray hair; not at all the image of a hit woman. Perfect cover. As for self-identification, she continued thinking *The Broad*. That's what she'd been called; that's what she was.

She didn't weep over kiddies, puppies, or kittens in trouble. She didn't go for love songs, romance novels, or soap operas, and hated family dramas. Give her action movies: Schwartzenager, Segal, Stallone, Charles Bronson. She was big on horror—Steven King, chainsaw massacres, people getting their heads split open with an ax. *The Broad* didn't analyze it, or feel glee. She just grit her teeth and smirked.

The Man's instructions, coming down the pipeline, had sent her to Wyoming. She was told that Ellery and Lily could have teamed up with Butch, Bud, and Callie. The six-figure hit: take out the whole bunch. Seemed like small potatoes for so many people. Maybe she should re-negotiate.

She did a background check on Bud and Callie. Not much information on either one. Bud Andrews: carrot-top; owned a battered green Ford pickup; age nineteen; hailed from across the tracks; son of a railroad worker and a waitress, both dead from a car accident with a drunken driver. Bud had gotten a financial-need scholarship to study accounting. Couldn't cut it in English; flunked. Dropped out. Joined up with Butch Edwards. End of story.

Callie Jenkins: dirty, dishwater blond hair (dirty, period); age twenty-one; drove a blue Dodge Intrepid; got an academic scholarship; key fact—before getting hooked on drugs, she was a Chi Omega sorority sister and roommate to Jerica, President Davidson's daughter.

The dossiers on the Edwards brothers and Lily came from Milwaukee.

Butch and the other four, plus Jerica, had all gone missing; suddenly, simultaneously. *The Broad* figured it had something to do with the upcoming campus demonstration on tree hugging. She'd been told, back in Milwaukee, to look for that sort of thing; spot her victims, take it from there.

With the discovery that the missing Davidson girl could have joined the gang, this caper was taking on a whole new intent. Pretty serious. Especially if she was supposed to target Jerica, too. She ought to get a million. Or two.

It figured. Her contacts thought a woman would come cheap. She decided to case the environment. Decide later whether to come through for *The Man,* or demand more up-front money before proceeding.

Meanwhile, a key player, though on the sidelines, seemed to be one Alison Morissey; mother to the professor that Bud and Callie both hated. This Mrs. M. was also known as the *Surrogate Mom* (whatever that meant) to the President of these United States. Which meant she was no doubt close to the Davidsons and right smack in the middle of all the commotion over their missing daughter. What a pain in the ass, all this extra trouble. You bet she needed more dough.

Ahh, but wait a minute. Think again. If she couldn't locate the Edwards boys or discover the hideout of their gang—which was, possibly, where they were holding Jerica—she could follow somebody who might know. Or eventually would. What with all these people searching for Jerica—all the military and manpower and money expended, some news ought to break soon. And when it did, Mrs. Morissey would be among the first to know. Count on it. Yup, it would be easier to stalk one little woman than an army of FBI and Secret Service.

*   *   *   *

Standing beneath the trees on the fringe of what was purported to be a campus demonstration on behalf of environmentalism, specifically saving trees, Alison nudged the Secretary of State, while casually gesturing across the way. "Look over there, Nasty. That guy wearing the *Butch Cassidy* tee shirt. Do you know him?"

Nasty squinted and reached for the glasses dangling on her bosom. "No, why?"

"I don't like his looks."

"There you go, again, Ali. First you pick on my grandmother's godson, Mark Prescott, telling the President he could be an assassin. And all because you didn't like his Mediterranean looks. If I recall, you thought he was a Muslim ecoterrorist. Now you're discriminating against this guy because he's scruffy? Talk about racial profiling!"

Properly contrite, Alison hung her head. Still, she wasn't absolutely convinced that Mark was who he said he was; namely, *legit!* Because, only yesterday in the President's suite, he had mumbled to her that this might be a good time to call in *The Brotherhood*. She could readily believe that *Mario Pesci* had not cut the umbilical cord to his Mafia connections.

As for this *Butch Cassidy* fellow sauntering about, he no more looked like a university student than she resembled a lioness. Granted, people of every age enrolled in college nowadays. But, didn't they all have some sort of college "look" about them? No, she supposed not. She'd better watch herself. She didn't want to be accused (again!) of discriminating, or even characterizing.

Led by a small disorganized campus group, the demonstration didn't look like it would amount to much; not so far. Just a bunch of motley looking college kids shouting and waving home-made, tree-hugging placards.

At that moment a young chap jumped up on the makeshift wooden platform set on sawhorses. He grabbed the bullhorn to complain about Texas A&M and their bonfire disaster back in '99. "They murdered trees! Innocent trees, mind you, just to haul seven thousand logs up in a pile and set fire to it."

Nasty whispered to Ali, "You notice he didn't add that eleven Texas Aggies paid with their lives, and twenty-eight more were badly injured. Looks like trees are the focus here, never mind people."

On the fringe of the small crowd now came dozens of senior citizens, those visiting campus with the hostel. Then a bunch of bikers arrived, from among those passing through town; plus a number of business people who had emerged from the student union on break from their management seminar (where Joan was among the earlier consultants). Then came Cowboy football players, still wearing their padded-shoulder uniforms. And members of the UW marching band, who'd expected to use the central park for marching practice. Instead, they joined the brass band *from nowhere* (nobody, then or later, could identify the first band). Off key and out of sync, the band blared.

Naturally the media showed up; quicker than you could blink, drawn like an army of ants after sugar or a flock of pigeons after breadcrumbs or a bunch of kiddos after Koolade. At the forefront of the press marched CNN's Marci, with Phil, the photographer.

No new news of Jerica, and little new action, beyond all that was launched two days earlier; namely, the whirly-birds whirling overhead, and the cop cars prowling the streets, and the sheriff's deputies thundering over county roads, and the FBI listening in on every phone call coming into the Davidsons' suite at the Park Inn, and Robert with Caroline and Jose and Juanita going nuts, and Julia making tearful pleas and Dom making snarling demands on television for the return of their daughter, and Carl Crosby writing statements and long speeches, and Rose Washington Lincoln's ears growing tired from pressing the phone to her head, and Mark Prescott pacing and scowling and stepping behind the potted palm to place secret phone calls on his cellular telephone. Other than all that— nothing.

So the media didn't have much new news, beyond reporting the same old news. Researchers had dredged up every possible photo and anecdote about the First Miss, and the pundits endlessly hypothesized, but field reporters like Marci were at a loss. So the press, too, showed up on campus for the purpose of observing how people hugged trees, and to catch the odd interview.

Joan also appeared in the park, plus a few other professors, having returned early to campus to work on research projects or fall-semester course syllabi, Joan told her Mom. "Looks like all the shouting and that brass band playing pulled them to their windows and out the doors. Like bees to honey."

Next among the family to appear came double cousin Jeff Vicente and his son, John. Jeff never did get off to Casper, he said. John's eyes were red from crying. He missed Jerica terribly, he confessed.

Nasties One and Two had returned from San Miguel de Allende the minute they heard the news, they said. Aunty Nasturtium was mama to both Nasty Two and her brother, Jeff.

Now John tugged at Alison. "I need to talk. Privately." The two slipped away, unaware that a woman with a broad bottom stealthily followed them.

Beneath a pair of tall evergreens, John said, "What do you think, Alison?"

"About what?"

"Everything."

She paused a few moments. Making a sudden decision, Alison drew a deep breath, and plunged into the fray. She'd been doing a lot of thinking, but had shared her views with nobody, not even Lisa. Not until now.

"I think you should cosy up to them, John. Join those tree huggers and animal-rights people. See if you can identify the inner core."

"What are you talking about? I don't understand."

"I believe there's a connection. Jerica loves animals; Julia heads the national conservation group. Jerica went missing, just as you and she had only just begun to renew your friendship; developing some romantic feelings for one another? Why would she leave you, us, at such a time? What could have been so urgent, so appealing, that she'd desert you—and everybody else, including her parents—with no explanation. Except for some great or worthy purpose. Like this group of demonstrators; on behalf of their cause."

"You mean, uh, you think Jerica is part of all this? I haven't seen her. And surely I'd have noticed if she were here."

"Of course she wouldn't make a public appearance, John. Not with all this commotion she's already caused by disappearing."

"Where's this leading, Alison?"

"Join them, John. Make a big splash. You don't have to take command or challenge their leaders. Be very sincere, though. Act so genuine that the protesters will accept you without question. Entice them to take you to their bosom as one of their own."

Pausing only briefly John said, "I'll do it!" Then he and Alison moved deeper into the trees to huddle and continue whispering.

Their palaver finished, John extracted a twenty-dollar bill from his wallet and dashed off. Alison stayed behind, within the shadows of the cluster of evergreens. With Randy's binoculars at her eyes, she could see people up close; close enough to read lips. She saw John proffer the bill to a pretty young thing wearing scruffy shorts, thongs, and a tee shirt sporting a *Proud to be a Tree Hugger* slogan. The girl promptly pocketed his contribution, passing to John a placard with the same inscription.

Then Alison observed John boldly approach a spokesman armed with megaphone, apparently a group leader. Ahah, this was the guy with *Butch Cassidy* splashed in cursive across the back of his tee shirt. So much for Nasty Three accusing her of discriminating against the fellow for looking scruffy.

*   *   *   *

When Alison had stepped into the trees to meet with John, *The Broad* followed. Ali nor John noticed their shadow, for she was good at what she did.

When John Vicente raced after the *Butch Cassidy* tee shirt, *The Broad* didn't know whether to follow him or stick with Mrs. Morissey. She chose the young man.

*   *   *   *

Suddenly a huge explosion rocked the earth, rattling windows in nearby buildings and breaking windows in cars parked too close. People ducked.

Or screamed.

Or grabbed each other, friend or stranger didn't matter.

Or fell to the ground with arms over their heads.

Alison did none of these things. Randy's binoculars swinging on its rope about her neck, she ran toward, not away from the explosion.

Behind her, in the same direction, ran three more people; one woman and two men; black-haired men who looked like they could have been Muslims. Or Mafia.

CHAPTER 29

▼

THE
"BROTHERHOOD"

CNN'S Marci and her photographer Phil neither ducked nor quivered. They didn't even look at each other. Like Siamese twins, they raced for the bomb site: Merica Hall. Marci was first to discover the dead bodies. And one live one— Secret Service operative, Caroline Wasson from North Carolina. Marci had met Caroline in the Presidential suite. Alison arrived on the heels of Marci in time to hear Caroline's last words.

Lying dazed on the sidewalk, Caroline looked into Marci's eyes. "It's Jerica. We were following her." Then the Secret Service woman expired.

But Marci had it on tape. And Phil had it on camera. The photographer extracted and stuck the precious videocam cassette into his backpack and stuffed the camera into his cycle's saddlebag. He started and revved his Harley-Davidson and Marci jumped on behind. A quick wave at Ali and the pair disappeared.

Moments later, after running red lights and weaving between vehicles in and out of traffic, the CNN pair arrived at their van in the Park Inn side lot, where many other media trucks were stationed, every one of which were labeled. ABC, CBS, NBC, Fox News, the Casper and Cheyenne TV stations; plus representatives from the big newspapers—*The Denver Post, The L.A. and New York Times, The Wall Street Journal,* among others. The stations' vans, like CNN's, were topped with rotating dishes pointing to communication satellites out in space; or south to Denver, or north and east within Wyoming.

Others among the working press and official authorities had their own agendas: call the President, the Governor, the cops, the fire station, family, friends, strangers. Was the First Couple safe? Alert the Secret Service, the FBI. Incoming calls, on every official and press phone demanded to know what was happening, who was responsible.

Calls to CNN, the FBI at the Holiday Inn, and the Secret Service at the Park purportedly had come from the ecoterrorists who claimed the blame.

Not many more minutes passed and the news circled the planet:

"The First Miss blows up the University of Wyoming campus!"

"The President's daughter defies DAD of the country to run off with a bunch of terrorist crazies." The sound bites rolled out like pea green vomit in *The Exorcist.*

"Ecoterrorists take the credit, claiming they have many cells across the country, including in Milwaukee, where an historic courthouse barely escaped destruction." Newsprint and anchors alike sought to outdo one another.

Out at Fox Lake *The Man*, wearing a polo shirt by Ralph Lauren and drenched in fragrance by Aspen played golf. His caddy, sitting bored in the golf cart with the radio on, got the news and ran to tell the Big Man. *The Man* hit his ball into a water hazard and cussed. Hiding a sneer at the news, he bent over his expensive golf bag by Gucci to get another ball; orange, this time.

In Cheyenne where Dollie Domenico's Honeylips perched on a genuine leather saddle atop a bar stool, Morton the Maniacal saw Marci on CNN say she'd interviewed a Secret Service woman who said she'd spotted Miss Davidson from across campus. Caroline Wasson had run with Robert and Jose after Jerica, calling her by name, when the First Miss disappeared inside Merica Hall. Right before it blew up.

"Fancy that," said Dollie.

"Wow!" exclaimed Harry the Hurtful. "You know I got to meet her, don't you, sweeticums? Right before my wife and I left the Morissey house."

"Yeah, your 'wife.' How dare you say such a hurtful thing to me, your real and only true wife."

South of Tucson in the adult resort (read: retirement) community of Green Valley, Charles Castle saw the news on the TV set positioned over the bar in the Mexican saloon where he regularly sloshed himself with Cabezo, Mexican beer. He sighed, thinking of Ellery and Eden and Lily, who'd tied him up in their RV while Todd, bless his soul, had let him go in time to be saved. Charles missed Bonnie so much. He wished with all his soul they could have gotten away together. What'd he care about the President's daughter? (It didn't occur to Charles that the Edwards boys could be responsible for "making another tree-hugging statement" via this bombing, too. Even if it had, he wasn't about to call anybody to report.) Anonymity, Charles Castle craved it after what he and Bonnie had been through.

∗   ∗   ∗   ∗

Colonel Schwartzkopf landed his Super Cobra helicopter in the open, bumpy field a half-block past Park Inn and Motel 8. He liked the Apache and Blackhawk better, but this was not a combat mission. The Colonel hopped out to head for the Presidential suite to get his next assignment, if any.

Alison too quickly returned to the Park Inn to be with the Davidsons. Rose Washington Lincoln manned the phone. Carl Crosby scribbled furiously; the President needed to make a statement soon. Julia was sedated and Dom was with her. Mark Prescott paced.

"Mario," Alison said, without apologizing for using his real name. "Isn't this situation serious enough to count?"

Pesci paused in mid-step to turn and glower at her. Or did his forehead, dented in by a pony when he was a child, Aunty Nasturtium had said, merely look that way because he wasn't smiling? Ali hoped this wasn't another stab at racial profiling.

"Count for what?"

"You remember, Mario. You said if I ever needed you—the Pesci family, I mean—that you'd be 'with me.'"

"'Witchew.' You got to pronounce it right, Alison."

"Well?"

Mark-*Mario* grinned, which automatically wiped away all signs of the vicious snarling manhunter she'd imagined. "You're right, Alison. The whole brotherhood is witchew."

"Not me, Mario. It's DAD who needs you now." DAD, Dominic Alexander Davidson, *DAD of the Country*—a familiar campaign slogan spotted on billboards and bumper stickers

CHAPTER 30

▼

THE FIRST FAMILY

"I can't stand it," said Julia, emerging from her sedative-induced stupor.

On the couch beside Ali, Dom used the remote to switch from channel to channel. "Everybody's carrying the story." To the First Lady, he said, "All over the world, people are being interviewed and giving their opinions. They know nothing, nothing. Yet everyone talks like they've got it straight from the horse's mouth." Dom glanced at Carl across the room, who grinned at DAD's homily.

The doctor approached Mrs. Davidson, needle in hand. The Morisseys' family doctor knew nothing about Randy's ailments, only that he'd missed his last checkup.

"No, not another shot," Julia protested, pulling away. "I've got to stay lucid and conscious. Jerica might call, to tell us this is all a bad dream."

Crosby did not look up this time. He sat at the table writing, pausing intermittently to stare out the window before crossing out whole phrases and writing more.

Pesci reached into his breast pocket to pull out a cellular phone. He excused himself to the President, saying he had calls to make.

FBI agents arrived to adjust their equipment. They jabbered into phones and walkie-talkies. They reminded the First Couple what to do if a ransom was demanded.

The President glanced up to stare, his eyes rimmed red with fatigue and worry. "You've been saying all this for the past seventy-two hours."

More incoming calls. Rose Washington Lincoln said the Governor and Senators Macomber and Perry were standing by; they'd keep themselves available for whatever help they could provide. Congresswoman Patty Pruitt, already there, sat in the next room.

Back at his post in Cheyenne, Detective Fletcher was in contact with the Milwaukee police. Albany County wasn't Walt's jurisdiction and he thought he could do more good using official sources, the nation's cop network.

By this time, Milwaukee police had combed the federal courthouse and outdoor bomb site, including the remains of the Edwards boys' RV looking for clues. It wasn't enough to believe the callers, the ecoterrorists who claimed credit for the Milwaukee explosion. And now for the Wyoming bombing as well. Could be a red herring; could be someone and some other reason entirely for trying to take out the historic old building.

"Got something for you, Fletch," said a Gulf War buddy who never had called Walter *Walt*. "We made the license plate on the RV. Registered to one Eden Edwards, who died in the explosion."

"Hey, that's not much good."

"Yeah, it is, Fletch. Cause Eden has—or had—two brothers, both of whom have gone missing."

When the Milwaukee cops contacted neighbors, he said, they learned of the connection to Judge Sullivan—the lumbering accident to Mr. Edwards' back, the bankruptcy suit. "And the Edwards boys' conversations—overheard—threats, actually, against Judge Sullivan."

"So the claim of the ecoterrorists for the bombing was all BS. They took advantage of the opportunity." Walt growled his frustration.

"Maybe. Maybe not." (Back in Milwaukee, Walt's counterpart was apparently saving up for the punch line.) "Get this, Fletch. Little brother Eddy went to Wyoming. This was back before our bomb went off. So maybe that's where the other brother, Ellery, went too. Maybe the Edwards boys are your culprits."

"Ah, a possible connection. Anybody else get away? From the RV, I mean. That you could identify."

"Dead woman, older. Dead man, a young fellow. Those were the bodies we found. Oh, and Eden Edwards. No Ellery, though. There could have been another woman; young. We found the remains of what looked like a blond wig. And Gus, the bailiff, said it was a blonde who threw the bomb and then shot the judge."

"Bout time you shared that bit." The detective chortled. "You sure can keep a guy in suspense, dragging out your report like that."

Walt turned over the watch to the apple-cheeked baby-faced rookie Bobby Gilbert and left for Laramie. At the door the detective stopped. "Hey, Bobby, gimme that file on the car you had checked. You know, the blue Dodge Intrepid you had the boys go over."

"You want the evidence we found? The tablespoon of fertilizer, the loose wires we couldn't figure out what could be used for?"

"Uh, no. Better preserve that stuff. How about fingerprints?"

Bobby said that information too was all in the file.

CHAPTER 31

▼

AFTERWARDS

The bombing of Merica Hall and the sighting of Jerica at the site was the reason given for centralizing the search. No longer was it sprinkled all over like pepper on an omelet but now focused specifically on Laramie. Also, Jose had spotted Jerica's roommate Callie and Bud coming out of a West Laramie bar.

Bud's Bar (no relation to the gang's Bud) was a small saloon sporting five booths, three tables, and a dozen stools. A football hangout, the bar featured football pools, for the UW Cowboys and the Denver Broncos, especially. Slogans speckled with dust and smoke hung lopsidedly above the bar, one reading: *We sell fishing equipment by the bottle, case, keg, jug, or barrel* and another two stuck together as one, proclaiming: *Do you want to talk to the man in charge? Or to the woman who knows what's going on?.... I'm 51% sweetheart, 49% bitch; don't push it.*

Earlier, their ideas bubbling like vomit from the two Secret Service crews, they had suggested the kidnappers could have carted Jerica away to Billings and on north, or to Rock Springs and beyond, to the west coast, or to Denver and south.

"They could be in Mexico or Canada by now," Caroline had said.

"New York or San Francisco," Robert had amended.

"Or perhaps on the moon," said Alison dryly.

Except that now Robert and Caroline were dead. And Jose lay in the hospital suffering from third-degree burns and a concussion that kept him unconscious. There was nobody among the teams left to interview, because Juanita wasn't available. She was glued to the Park Inn conferring with the President and her supervisors in the Secret Service.

Why Merica? people wanted to know. Why not some more historically significant or currently important building? Merica Hall was an old white-frame building situated between Old Main and Hoyt Hall. Hardly the place anybody would choose to blow up. CNN's Marci sent Phil searching for background.

Both Hoyt and Merica were once girls dormitories and both were named for UW Presidents, Joan said. "Merica served from 1907 to 1912, had a Ph.D. in sociology, and taught economics as well. He was known as a builder—of lives, of academic programs, and of bricks and mortar. Later, in post-WWII, Merica Hall became the School of Pharmacy."

So why destroy Merica?

At the Park Inn, Rose Washington Lincoln said she'd alert somebody if any more suspicious calls came in. There had already been a lot of crank calls, but the FBI handled those. Rose was tired. The President's secretary asked for and got a replacement, a youngster hardly old enough to shave.

Crosby scribbled on. Mark Prescott disappeared.

The Davidsons retired to their suite with the heavy forest green drapes that darkened the room. Alison pulled over herself one of cousin-in-law Isabelle's crocheted poncho-style shawls, the purple one, and curled up on the comfy couch to snooze.

When she awakened, Ali overheard Julia and Carl conferring. The First Lady gestured wildly as she stood over the speechwriter seated at the table. "I don't see why the police or the FBI don't check Callie's phone records. My daughter's, I mean. Jerica paid all the bills in their apartment."

"That's a wonderful idea, Mrs. D," Carl said. "Check out both local and long distance calls made from that phone. Both before and since Jerica's disappearance."

"And before and after the explosion that destroyed Merica Hall."

Carl reached for the phone to call the FBI. Julia sat on the other end of Alison's couch and buried her head in her hands, the tears regathering.

Ali looked at both Carl and Julia like they were crazy. "That might sound like a good idea, but it's impossible."

"What?" said Julia, raising her head.

"Huh?" said Crosby, his hand hovering over the telephone.

"Long distance calls, sure. But not local. The phone company keeps no records whatsoever of the numbers that are called, unless they are going to bill for it, as in a long-distance call."

"Are you sure?" Carl asked.

"The only time records are kept of *free, local numbers* dialed, is when it is suspected ahead of time that illegal activity is being conducted from a certain phone. The police must have sound reasons. Civil rights, privacy laws. These arrangements must be made in advance to track the dialing of future local numbers from any given phone line."

"How do you know all this?" Julia murmured.

Alison didn't bother to describe her involvement with Fletcher on several recent cases. No point; no time. "Records of numbers dialed for long distance calls, cellular calls, and others that are charged per-call are maintained to document and sustain billing inquiries, but that's the only reason for keeping such data. Good grief. Billions of local calls are dialed each day. Maintaining records when there is no reason to do so would be a needless expense. Why would any business bear the cost of storing data on five billion calls a day when there is no off-setting revenue to cover that cost?"

"So how can we get the numbers Callie might have called?" Julia asked.

Alison thought this whole exercise silly. But she replied, anyhow. "There's Caller ID, you know. Surely the police, FBI, deputies, Secret Service, somebody, has checked Jerica and Callie's phone to see if it has that service. If so, it's a common police investigative technique to check whatever incoming calls have been received. Punch 'redial' to identify the last <u>out</u>-going phone call. However, most Caller ID devices record the last twenty-five to fifty <u>in</u>-coming phone numbers. That's how you can check. Presumably, it's already been done."

"I didn't know that," said Julia.

When Rose Washington Lincoln answered the phone, it was for Alison.

"Jeff, here, Ali. I don't seem able to find John. You seen my son?"

CHAPTER 32

▼

THE BODIES, THE QUESTIONS

"The world will little note nor long remember what happened here, but I will. The First Lady and I will never forget the courage and bravery of these young people, these Secret Service people who gave their lives in the fulfillment of their duty—to protect and seek to find our daughter Jerica."

CNN's Marci recorded and Phil filmed. People round the world might not remember long, but they would briefly note the photo op and DAD's compassion.

"*The world will little note nor long remember?*" At the Park Inn, Alison raised an eyebrow at Dom's speechwriter.

Carl grinned. "Seemed appropriate for the moment," he said modestly, his thermometer switching on as the blood rushed up from neck to face. "After all, Dom does look like President Lincoln; might as well cop a few—mind you, just a few—of Abe's famous words."

"Rather like John F. Kennedy did in appropriating and modifying his famous phrase from Oliver Wendell Holmes, Jr." Alison referred to the phrase President Kennedy made famous in his inauguration speech: *ask not what your country can do for you; ask what you can do for your country.*

"Kennedy's remark was also a paraphrase from similar statements made by both Warren Harding and Le Baron Russell Briggs."

Their debate quickly forgotten, the pair watched the rest of Marci's report over CNN. The pretty brunette with the pageboy had done her homework and lined up some good sources to stand in the wings ready to be interviewed.

Caroline had no family that could be located. Her body would be flown on an Air Force plane back to Washington for burial and recognition in Arlington Cemetary. Robert, too, but his parents had arrived in Laramie to accompany their son's corpse, and to be greeted personally and thanked by the President. These Secret Service people had gone way beyond the call of duty. Like soldiers on the battlefield, Dom said into the camera. They'd given their precious blood, their very lives, in service to their country.

Alison thought it a bit melodramatic, but a sideways glance at Carl showed a glowing boy, proud as punch, pleased with himself and the speech he'd written. The President's delivery, in his deep bass voice, together with his sorrowful expression, lent dignity to Crosby's words. Alison only wished Carl hadn't made Dom sound quite so soppy. Some people, members of the opposition party determined to dig up dirt, might think her good friend, the most powerful man in the world, was less than sincere.

Alison wished Julia could be by her husband's side, but the First Lady was again sedated. As she was when Don visited Jose in the hospital when the President was once more trailed by the press.

✳   ✳   ✳   ✳

Out at his seventeen-room "cottage" at Fox Lake southwest of Laramie, *The Man* mused over Marci's report on CNN. He, like others, wondered: Why Merica Hall? He knew he'd said "Hoyt," because an assistant professor with his office there was the son of a major timbering competitor.

Edwards had readily agreed to Hoyt, because the Wyoming ecoterrorist cell leader said Hoyt Hall was the office home of that professor who had flunked Butch's two gang members. Butch was supposed to have set the explosives to go off when he was sure both those two professors would be in the building.

What was so significant about that old white-frame Merica Hall that the Edwards brothers should switch targets at the last minute?

He aligned his orange golf ball for a nice putt across the oriental carpet at one end of the fifty-two-foot long living room. Deep in thought, he gazed out the big picture windows overlooking the golf course on one side and, out of another, a view of Fox Lake with Medicine Bow National Forest as backdrop.

First, the Edwards boys had gone after Judge Sullivan in the Milwaukee courthouse; got him, too, though that didn't matter to their boss. Then they were bent on taking out Joan Vicente. *The Man* paused to stare at the big sixty-inch television screen. Neither professor was mentioned among the dead. A dozen people were injured, no more. Summer, no students; afternoon, some of the office workers could have been on break.

The only deaths reported were Robert and Caroline. But Caroline was still alive when found by the CNN reporter who got the Secret Service woman's statement on film.

He realigned his ball, then paused again at another thought. What had happened to the hit men? He suspected it was plural; not one, but two men. They were supposed to take out Ellery and Lily. On the phone, Butch had said his girl, Callie, and his brother's girl, Lily, could pass for doubles because they looked so much alike. Even their body odors were similar, according to Butch.

He propped his club against the wall to go behind the bar and mix a stiff scotch. He was alone here. Alone everywhere, since his wife had left him, and two separate hookers had tried to rob him of wallet and credit cards. He didn't trust anybody; not women, no longer. Though of course a wealthy suave man like himself had plenty of beautiful acquaintances along with a host of yes-men among his corporate underlings. Still, he had no confidantes; never had had. Sure couldn't trust a wife, or any woman.

As Schopenhauer wrote: *For woman, rightly called by the ancients, sexus sequior, is by no means fit to be the object of our honor and veneration, or to hold her head higher than man and be on equal terms with him.*

The Man could appreciate the Muslim fanatics. Too bad that while attacking America, the Taliban hadn't taken out his timbering competitors.

He pondered several scenarios. Instead of killing the Edwards boys and Lily (Callie, too; that would be okay), what if the hit men had teamed up with his own ecoterrorist bumblers? And got caught up with hugging trees?

No, too preposterous; made no sense. No money in it. He sure wouldn't deliver the other half of the hefty payment he'd promised, not until and unless they delivered: took out the first two, if not all four. Same price, either way. Ellery and Lily, sure; but perhaps Butch and Callie, too.

Back to his original question: Why Merica instead of Hoyt Hall?

Perched on a bar stool, he jerked, knocking over his glass. Unaware, he decided it was time to get off the side bench high in the bleachers. Get himself on the fifty-yard line.

The Man left for Laramie.

What he wanted to know was what the Edwards boys were doing for money. He'd cut off their supply. They would need to pick up another cache.

CHAPTER 33

▼

RUMORS AND SPECULATIONS

A gang held up First Bank in Rock Springs. Got away with seventy-five hundred dollars, no more. Nobody caught. Except on camera.

Jerica Davidson! The First Miss caught on film robbing a bank!

No doubt about it, her unmasked image had come clear from the bank's camera. There she was, standing in the middle of the lobby, wielding a submachine gun; a masked man behind her yelling at customers and tellers to "Get down! Close your eyes and duck your heads or I'll shoot 'em off!"

It was the Patty Hearst story all over again. CNN's Marci was too young to recall, but old-timer media professionals were not. With a backup for research and her own access of the Internet, Marci soon had the Hearst account.

Patty Hearst, abducted by, or volunteer member, of the SLA, the Symbionese Liberation Army, ecoterrorists, sounding like the old Communists with their stated creed: *Down with oppression, cause a revolution, overthrow the government, down with the establishment.*

All the money and all the power of the Hearst family had not been able to protect, free, or acquit the poor little rich girl. Once broadcast over the airways, her verbal confession and commitment to the SLA were taken for fact. With her face and figure viewed on the bank's camera when the SLA robbed it, poor Patty was a goner. What seemed to be true must surely be so.

Wasn't this the same or a similar scenario? CNN's Marci had it on tape: the dying Secret Service woman as eye witness. Caroline spotted Jerica Davidson in Merica Hall just before it blew. That didn't make her an ecoterrorist. Could have been coincidence, the believers all across the land and around the globe argued.

But now she'd robbed a bank. This time everybody, not just a dead Secret Service gal, had seen the First Miss. Jerica was right there in front of the camera. Right before their eyes she had robbed a bank.

"A thief! They're calling my baby a robber, an ecoterrorist!" Julia sobbed.

The doctor approached with another needle, a nurse with water and pill.

Alison objected. "Mrs. Davidson is stronger than you think. Let her be."

Dom agreed. Julia didn't care. Valium, darkened room, bed, oblivion. She couldn't take it any more—the reports in papers and on the tube. Speculations, polls, person-on-the-street interviews. Though some vacillated, many others allowed themselves to be brainwashed. What they heard, what they saw; couldn't refute the press, people said. Ecoterrorism. Banks robbed for money to support their cause and themselves, while they regrouped. The nation could anticipate the continuation of attacks, the television and reading audiences were told, while the ecoterrorists sought conversions and gathered more believers to the bosom of their misguided values.

"We can't trust anybody anymore, Ali," Julia said. "The whole world is against us. You've got to do something. You and The Clan." Then Julia fell back onto her pile of pillows. She sank into the blessed oblivion of a troubled, drug-induced sleep.

Laramie's cafes, all sixty-seven of them including a dozen fast-food places plus twenty-five or so bars pulsated with diners and their speculations. When the twelve thousand university students returned, forty or so percent of whom would be looking for part-time work—primarily in the service industry as grill cooks, servers, bartenders—the problem of getting served would be lessened. But this was August. Add the seniors, RV buffs, bikers and tourists, and the town was bulging like a man bursting with gas in an antacid commercial.

Employers and food and drink managers said they were losing their bloody minds. High-schoolers and stay-at-home moms seeking part-time, temporary work had no trouble getting hired; with no experience, no references.

The Park Inn—its rooms and suites, restaurants and bars, pool and perimeter—was closed to the public and the press. But the paparazzi arrived anyhow; posing as employees, clambering over fences, hiding in the shrubbery, prying and poking, snoopinig and snapping photos. The First Couple's tragedy and dilemma over trying to hide from the press; their experience could have been likened to the fame surrounding Princess Di or Jackie Kennedy Onassis.

Tabloid reporters waylaid employees, friends, officials, and bystanders with their mike-in-the-face and flash-in-the-eyes obsession and intrusion with their hackneyed questions: "How did you feel when you heard…(saw, learned, discovered)?" "What do you think is the truth?" "What should the FBI and Secret Service do?" "What should they have done?" "What would you have done in their place?"

Then came the biggies, the key questions:

"Is it possible, do you think, that Jerica could actually be held as an innocent captive?" Their choice of words made this option sound impossible.

Why was it, Ali wondered, that guilt was so much more titillating than innocence?

Finally, the ultimate question. "Should the President resign?"

*   *   *   *

Over the ensuing days and nights, Alison periodically returned to Joan's townhouse for a shower, change of clothes, and a restless few hours of troubled sleep. Except at the bottom of her mind, she had all but forgotten Randy. He hadn't called her again. That one time only, to demand she come home to bake cookies.

A week had passed, a week of devastating news broadcasts, of meetings and private sessions, of pleas and Presidential statements. Of FBI and Secret Service and city police and county deputies and now the CIA all scurrying around like ants ejected from their ant hills, and Peter and Brad and their fellow Air Force and Air National Guard pilots buzzing round like hornets kicked from their nests.

John and Ali—before they parted and before Merica Hall blew up—had agreed to meet at the Old Corral, a restaurant-bar-hotel complex out west in Centennial. Double-cousin Jeff's son had her cellular number and Ali carried the phone with her at all times. No word. No calls, no clues. She and Lisa had driven the sixty-mile round trip out to the wee mountain village a half-dozen times, already. No signs, no news. Nothing.

Meanwhile, the President's advisors and the Secretary of Defense and the Secretary of State, among others, arrived at the Park Inn. The business of the country must be pursued. Top-level meetings and red-phone teleconferences convened over the Kyrgyzstan hostage situation, and whether the U.S. would stand with NATO in going in with Air Force fighters and battleships (no ques-

tion yet of ground troops). Other pressing political and economic issues intervened, along with various natural disasters to call forth the President's
compassion.

Carl Crosby scribbled furiously, following Dom's notes and verbal guidelines.
The President regularly appeared on television to placate the people, to indicate
that he was still clearly in charge. The Vice-President showed up in person at various sites around the country to commiserate—on the site of hurricane and tor-
nado devastation, of freeway bridge and highway collapses, of mass murders, and
one yellow bus toppled off a viaduct with thirty-two children injured, but no
child killed, thank God.

Alison, with or without her daughter, power walked every morning early, four
miles minimum, more when she could spare the time. Her spirits so mangled, she
had to keep her body in shape, exercise it, feed it properly. She couldn't stick
glued to couch and television, the Davidsons' suite and handholding. Exercise, to
relieve muscles and clear mental cobwebs.

When she thought of Randy, Alison worried about his continuing silence, and
why he refused to return the calls she periodically left on their voice mail.

No word from or about John. Lisa, Peter, and John's dad, Jeff, knew what Alison had suggested John do: take a precarious path that could lead who knew
where, with who knew whom. Jeff could have been very angry with his double
cousin, but he knew his son, John: level-headed, sometimes pigheaded; the young
physicist was not easily influenced by the opinions and ideas of others. Ali may
have suggested that he try to join the ecoterrorists, but he would have gone on his
own had he thought of it first; the decision was John's, not Alison's.

Retired, Peter had no commitments. Yet there was nothing that he could follow up on; he, like Walt Fletcher, or anybody official, had nowhere to turn. For
there were still no demands from the would-be kidnappers, no confessions, no
word that Jerica was being held hostage. Most of the world concluded, as was the
case with Patty Hearst and the SLA, that Jerica had willingly joined and was, by
now, a full-fledged ecoterrorist.

The clan, like the Davidsons, refused to believe these rumors.

"What are you going to do, Alison?" Jeff asked. "Return to Cheyenne?"

"I just can't. I'm waiting to hear from John."

"Thank God," Jeff said. "Where will you be, then? Joan's?"

"Later. Right now I'm off to Centennial again."

Then she changed her mind. "Peter, Lisa, wait. I've another idea."

Carl and Julia's phone scheme for collecting clues to Jerica's whereabouts had prompted Alison to re-think and plan anew. She wanted so badly to talk to Walt Fletcher first, but she simply could not wait to locate him.

"Let's go to Rock Springs. Peter, you can fly Lisa and me, right?" The clan owned a Cessna. Alison said she wanted to interview the bank personnel.

"Surely that's been done," Peter hedged.

"The bank personnel might not have told everything; pressure from the cops making them nervous. To a little lady, fellow citizen, it might be different. Maybe somebody will recall things they forgot, or that didn't register at first."

The Schwartzkopfs bowed out, but their son-in-law, Brad Gifford, complied. He flew Alison out and back in a single day.

Which was how and when Alison learned of *the stench!*

"You wouldn't believe how awful that robber woman smelled, Mrs. Morissey," said a young redhead who'd once stayed over night at the Morissey house. Friend of somebody, Ali vaguely recalled; John Vicente, perhaps, from his undergrad days at the U. "But she got killed," the redhead concluded.

"What?" Recalled to their current conversation, Ali gasped. "Who? The stinker?"

"Right."

*   *   *   *

The Broad from Chicago didn't know what to do, spit or go blind. Although she'd followed the JFK-look-alike, thinking he could lead her to the Edwards boys, she'd lost him in Centennial. Made her mad, made her feel like an amateur. Meanwhile, all the media, FBI, CIA, Secret Service, tourists, Alison Morissey and family, all prowling podunk Laramie, Wyoming. Very confusing.

She called her Chicago contact, who called his Milwaukee contact, who finally revealed *The Man's* cellphone number. But nobody knew his location.

By that time *The Man* had taken a third-floor room decorated daintily in the purple-trimmed, lavender-painted, Victorian bread-and-breakfast across from campus. He didn't like it, wasn't comfortable with all those ruffles and ribbons, but it was the last room in town; vacated only an hour earlier and unexpectedly, or he wouldn't have got that. Getting a decent meal or prompt service wasn't easy either, so he went off to the Old Corral in Centennial for lunch. He sat on a heavy wooden chair at a heavy wooden table in front of the fireplace, where a few logs burning slowly and lowly welcomed diners in that high cool village.

The Broad was pretending to browse in the gift shop, under the same roof, in the same Old Corral establishment, when she reached *The Man* on his cellphone. Her smoker's voice deep and gravelly, she sounded like a man, which was what he had expected. No cause to change his opinion.

"You sound so far away," she said. "Like you're on the moon."

"Yeah, well, what do you want?" He hunched over the phone, cupping it in his hand to avoid being overheard.

He needn't have bothered. The only diner sitting near him was Alison Morissey. And she was hearing impaired. Ali didn't know him, and he didn't know her, so it didn't occur to her to lipread. Her own cellphone kept its peace.

In the bar between the gift shop and the dining room sat a couple of swarthy skinned, slicked-back black-haired men with black beady eyes. They had positioned themselves where they could watch Mrs. Morissey. All she did was eat a salad, so all they did was sip their beers. Coors, Lite. They hated their assassination assignment; kept postponing it with the excuse of flu and toothache.

Alison lingered over lunch, woolgathering. She hadn't been home for a week, and Clara wasn't there anyhow. (She was away visiting an old school chum.) Although the Morisseys had voice mail and she continued to leave messages for Randy, he didn't pick up. Furious with her, he must be pouting.

She nibbled her salad and sipped ice water and told herself to focus.

There were good reasons why all the players in this deadly scenario remained oblivious of one another. *The Man* and Alison in the same place at the same time was the single coincidence. When *The Broad* had lost John's trail, she returned to unobtrusively gluing herself to Mrs. M, because she thought that eventually the nosy busy-body would lead her to the ecoterrorists.

As for *The Man*, he was there because, in his opinion, the Laramie cafes were too crowded and the service too slow.

The Arabs whose kin were being held hostage half a world away, were assigned to follow Mrs. Morissey. This was the woman, they were told, who had foiled the revolutionaries' proposed assassination of Mrs. Oblasty. The dark-skinned men couldn't sit around in Centennial forever. The respite from all the tourist and media babble was nice but the action, surely, remained focused back in Laramie. Their target, Mrs. Morissey, would surely return to town shortly.

After *The Man* left the dining room and *The Broad* left the gift shop and the swarthy men left the bar, Alison's phone rang. She grabbed it and, under camouflage of her long blond wig, whispered into the instrument. "John? Or is this Randy?"

Had it been her husband, he would have bellowed; screaming at her with demands, like where was she and his fresh-baked bread and home-baked cookies and pies? No bellow, no screaming.

"Can't talk long," John whispered. "Can you meet me in Centennial? Two-three days from now. Noon. Okay?"

"Where? At the clan's cabin?"

"Right. See ya. I gotta go...."

The connection was already broken. What did John mean, "two-three days"? Which one? Oh dear, now she'd have to return twice more to be sure. Only, next time, she would have a definite meeting place.

CHAPTER 34

▼

A MYSTERIOUS DEATH

Alison soon forgot everything and everybody else: Jerica, Dom, Julia, John; plus, what, if anything, she could do about Magda Oblasty.

Because the light of her life, her floorlamp—*bright on the top, skinny in the middle*—had just burnt out.

Randy was dead! Why he died where he did was a mystery. Enroute from Laramie to Centennial, he'd collided in his black Oldsmobile Cutlass with a big truck; killed himself, but nobody else.

What would make him think she'd left for Centennial?

Could Randy have somehow glommed onto a clue or clues that nobody else had? About Jerica's whereabouts? Made no sense. Couldn't be. Still, she should check it out. With Walt Fletcher's help, perhaps.

Not now, though. Later. Sometime. Now there were all the decisions and arrangements to make, details that Clara nor daughter and granddaughter, nor the Schwartzkopfs could do for her. The memorial service, the scattering of her beloved's remains on the clan's Centennial property—the small acreage with log cabin built by her great-great-grandmother Rose over a century earlier.

Alison was numb with grief.

CHAPTER 35

▼

MOURNING LOSSES

CIA agents frantically checked their computers, the Internet, and their counter-parts around the world—Scotland Yard, Interpol, the Mossad. The security advisors imagined international ecoterrorists, as in Carlos the Jackal, the Palistinian Liberation Organization, or perhaps one or several fanatics trained by al Qaida.

FBI agents suspected Americans, from white racists, anti-abortion and pro-life demonstrators, environmentalists, pseudo-military survivalists, anti-world trade protestors to AIDS activitists, gay and lesbian proponents, or inflamed cult crazies modeled after the Unibomber or the Oklahoma City bombing. Or could be international terrorists posing as Americans or slipping over our borders like those responsible for the World Trade Center and Pentagon terrorism attacks.

In addition to the Secretary of State and Secretary of Defense having arrived in town to meet with the President, others showed up, including Dom's chief economic advisor and the Secretary General of the United Nations. Also, an under-secretary from the U.S. Treasury Department and representatives from its sub-agency, ATF, the Bureau of Alcohol, Tobacco and Firearms.

One old University of Wyoming campus building destroyed and one western Wyoming bank robbed might not seem like much. But with the link to the federal courthouse in Milwaukee, the FBI there too began thinking global instead of local. They weren't taking any chances. The Wyoming and Wisconsin "incidents" might be but the tip of the sword; buried to the hilt in the sand, representing a well-planned organized chaos about ready to crash again onto American shores.

Left to the city cops and county deputies were the local worries. Let those people focus on the ordinary, said the CIA, FBI, ATF, and Secret Service crews rushing about, bumping into each other, swearing with the crash of their computers, and ordering from room service everything from Cokes and Pepsies to Coors and the hard stuff, food and snacks; plus Bufferin and Alka-Seltzer.

While the media hyped the notion of Jerica as ecoterrorist and bank robber, the moral majority persevered with their prayer circles and prayer meetings. Nobody was going to tell them what to think. With no evidence to the contrary, they would go right on assuming that young Jerica was one of their own, a believer like her parents. The President's stepdad was, after all, a Baptist minister.

*   *   *   *

Alison scheduled her husband's memorial service at St. Mark's on Central Avenue in Cheyenne, because Randy was Episcopalian. The President and First Lady didn't show. Alison didn't expect them to. With all their security personnel, there wouldn't have been space for anybody else, including the clan.

Representing the Davidsons, however, came Mark Prescott, Carl Crosby, Rose Washington Lincoln, and Jerica's remaining Secret Service woman, Juanita Jorgensen. This foursome sat across the aisle from Alison—in what would come to be called, in the media, the "government section."

*   *   *   *

The Man did not attend Randy's memorial service. Why would he? The Morisseys meant nothing to him. He didn't return to his Fox Lake cottage nor to his Milwaukee office. Not yet. Something ought to break soon and he anticipated being there for the finale. Since the bank heist, he figured the cops must be closing in by now. Unless the shmucks out here were too dumb to analyze and follow up clues. He checked out of the ruffly room in the bed and breakfast across from campus to take up residence at the Old Corral out in Centennial. Maybe he'd hike in the mountains. Get some exercise.

The Broad didn't follow Mrs. Morissey to St. Marks, either. She remained in town looking for clues to the whereabouts of the Edwards boys and, when taking breaks from that, she enjoyed chug-a-lugging beer in a back booth at Bud's bar in

West Laramie; down by the tracks, where freight trains lumbered and rumbled by every fifteen minutes.

*   *   *   *

In the back row of the Episcopal Church and scrunching down low were two swarthy men in black suits and white on white ties, their black patent leather shoes polished to a fine sheen. Although they kept their heads bowed, both men, brothers, glared from beneath bushy eyebrows around at the assemblage. Looked like everybody in Wyoming's capitol city had turned out. Morissey must have been a popular guy.

He wasn't. Randy had few friends and no kin. Besides the Vicente-Auld family in attendance, plenty of Alison's friends, acquaintances, hangers-on, and looky-Lous showed up, the latter of whom mostly wanted a peek at the tiny black-draped, black-veiled widow. Wearing a red wig. Ali couldn't find the salt-and-pepper version of her own lost hair and didn't think the long wavy blond model was appropriate. No matter, the wide-brimmed black hat and veil should hide the color. And her tears.

She had loved Randy so much. Not all his eccentricities, heavens no, but she'd adapted herself to those. Most of the time. Given the chance, she'd have gone right on baking cookies and bread and making excuses for him.

Absurd. To be thinking such thoughts at a time like this. But what was she supposed to be thinking? She couldn't feel much. Not yet. The deep mourning would come later, she suspected. The healing, too, she hoped.

*   *   *   *

That her grief gave Alison something else in common with Dom and Julia did not surface right then. Nor that a lot of other people were also suffering:

Charles Castle down in Green Valley over the loss of his Bonnie.

Lily, over Todd's death back in Milwaukee.

The Edwards boys over their dead dad and middle brother, Eden. And, also, since the bank heist, the Jenkins, up in Medicine Bow, mourned their daughter. Callie had taken a hit in the neck from an alert bank guard's .22; killed on the spot. No chance to confess.

The Schmidt family mourned Robert's death, resulting from the Merica Hall bomb. Jose's parents, Mr. and Mrs. Lopez, sat side by side holding hands at Ivinson Hospital in Laramie, where their Secret Service son still hovered, comatose, between life and death.

Juanita visited Jose every day. Otherwise, she spent her time conferring with her supervisors, and with the FBI, the National Security people and, sometimes, with the President. Also, with Alison. Juanita felt so down in the dumps, suffering from guilt; at having lost Jerica, at not finding her yet. Alison's sensible words, delivered tenderly, had not helped the distraught Secret Service woman.

Lots of people in Wisconsin and Wyoming were also hurting, although perhaps to a lesser degree, for they were related to the injured—the innocents who'd been in the wrong place at the wrong time: on the sidewalk outside the U.S. Federal Courthouse in Milwaukee; in or near Merica Hall on the UW campus; in the Rock Springs bank.

*　　*　　*　　*

Flanked by her daughter on one side and granddaughter on the other, Alison sat quietly in the church. Next to Joan sat Big Jack and, on Nickee's side, sat her grandfather, Jason Jacquot. Nicole had lost Granddaddy Randy; she clung to Jason now.

Joan and Nicole shared small packages of Kleenex with Alison.

Behind them sat the Schwartzkopfs and Giffords, with the BB twins and Nickee's son, Stevie. The children didn't quite understand the purpose of the service, but they were used to sitting quietly in church, sucking on peppermint Lifesavers, hugging their Beanie Babies, or scribbling in small notebooks.

Next came the Nasties, with Morton the "properly" Mournful. Counted among this set of double cousins were Tom and Jeff Vicente, brothers to Nasty Two, uncles to Wyoming's Secretary of State. Jeff's son, John, was conspicuous by his absence.

Jeff wasn't mourning anybody. He hadn't liked Randy and thought cousin Ali was better off without the blustering banty rooster. Or she would be, once she got used to the idea of widowhood. Jeff no longer grieved for the loss of his son. Not since John had made contact with Ali. Whatever he was up to, John would soon surface. A true Vicente, the lad was resourceful and clever. He'd be all right. Not that Jeff wasn't impatient to see his son reach closure to his impromptu escapade.

Across the aisle sat the state capitol and Washington D.C. crowd, including the Governor with Dr. Wilma Sanford and her son. Also Senators Macomber and Perry, with Congresswoman Patty Pruitt.

Alison's brothers came, too: Dale from Victoria, Texas, and Russell, from Tucson. And Lisa's brothers, Abe and Linc, named for their father, Abraham Lincoln Vicente, from Casper and Cody, Wyoming.

Despite their Irish-Welsh Auld-Deighton lineage, no wake was scheduled immediately preceding or following the memorial service. The scattering-of-ashes ritual would come first. Later, the clan would gather at Alison's, where Clara and her niece had prepared a number of casseroles, salads, and desserts. Not that their efforts were needed, since food contributions had been pouring in steadily since the news came over television, newspaper, and word of mouth of Randy's death by car-truck collision west of Laramie.

Behind the clan sat Walt Fletcher. While waiting for the ushers to complete the long process of finding seats for the people streaming in and lining the back and side walls, the detective mentally recapped and summarized. Recalling Alison's experience in Rock Springs, he realized she had never met Callie, Jerica's roommate at the Chi Omega house. Neither had Walt, but he'd had the young woman's blue Dodge Intrepid in his grasp no more than a few days prior to the bank heist.

The female bank robber had worn a mask. With her death, neither the hospital nor the police personnel had found any identification; nothing. No fingerprints on record, no priors. They had drawn a blank.

Okay, so the teller's partial description sounded like Callie, but her mom and dad said No. The stench surely couldn't have been Callie's. Walt didn't remember any offensive odors emanating from the car they'd searched that Butch Edwards was driving when picked up. Another stinky woman?

The connection, to Walt, seemed clear. Had to be this gang, including Jerica, who'd robbed the bank. Damn! The President's daughter spotted on camera. She had to be a willing participant. Or, could she have been drugged? Or hypnotized? What about brainwashed?

No way around these things, which is what the Secret Service, CIA, and FBI all claimed. In fact, according to Alison's information, gleaned from lipreading in the Presidential suite, people from these agencies refused to believe it could be anything other than the Patty Hearst story all over again.

Like Ali, and the nation's loyal and patriotic believers, Walt didn't want to believe in Jerica Davidson's guilt. He closed his eyes, the better to think.

Ah, yes. From the Rock Springs bank teller, Alison had caught that extra bit of news that nobody else seemed to have. The stench. What did it mean?

Opening his eyes to check whether the service was about to begin, Walt glanced across the aisle and up the few rows that separated him from Alison. How did she do that? get people to talk. This wouldn't be the first time. Somehow she could get complete strangers to relax, open up, reveal more than they even knew they knew, or share more intimate details about themselves and their lives than they would have imagined possible.

Walt thought of what Charles Kuralt once said about Studs Terkel: *When he listens, people talk.* That phrase aptly described Alison Morissey.

He reminded himself to ask Bobby: Had he, or the lab boys who scrutinized Callie Jenkins' car smelled anything bad? Perhaps they'd aired out the car before Walt got to it. Better check. The "stench" could be significant.

Behind the representatives of state and federal government and behind Walt Fletcher, Martha Washington and Betsy Ross pouted, while their sons, Matthew, Mark, Luke, and John, sat quitely and respectfully.

"The least the ushers could have done was find us a place on the side with the *doubles!*" Martha moaned.

"Like always, we're shoved off somewhere with the nobodies," Betsy said. (Had the Governor and Congressional representatives and the President's aides heard her, they surely would have laughed—to be referred to as "nobodies.")

Hepzibah and Isabelle were not offended to be seated on this side. Old Hepzibah, out of deference to the dead, did not knit, but her gnarled fingers fretted with her frilly handkerchief as substitute to her habit. Without her wool, she hardly knew what to do. Isabelle patted her mother-in-law, when she wasn't glancing sneak-peeks over her shoulder. Her husband, Rudolph, he of the bulbous red nose, had sent a telegram. Isabelle expected him to arrive at any moment. "Oh God, Mama, will Rudolph expect to speak?"

"Hush, child. Don't blaspheme in the Lord's own house. Everybody and his mouse will no doubt want to eulogize. Why not our Rudolph?"

In point of fact, there were few people assigned to or who had requested to speak. When the minister had asked Alison who to expect or call upon, she'd merely shook her head and shrugged. Colonel Peter, who probably knew Randy as well as anybody (except Ali) reluctantly agreed. He and Lisa labored long over the statement that should be genuine and sound sincere.

Beside the Secretary of State sat Harry the Huffy, acting inappropriately gleeful with the seating arrangement. He puffed out his chest and tried not to look too perky. At last one of the Vicente snobs, namely Alison, had got her come-uppance. Not at Harold's hand, but no matter. Somebody had to pay for what had happened to him!

The bank president had caught Harold Morton snooping in the vault, housing safety deposit boxes, trying to get access to Mrs. Morissey's private box. He should have had a series of plausible excuses ready in case his presence was discovered, but in his eagerness to play (like a mouse, when the cat's away) during the president's absence, Harold had forgotten that critical issue. He didn't get demoted, back to the hateful teller's cage. He didn't get fired, either. His boss said he couldn't do that to his old friend, the Secretary of State. But Harold lost his plush private office. He was stuck out in the lobby now, at a desk in front of the big plate glass window where every nobody passer-by could see him sitting there—like a foreign fish in a fancy aquarium. Doing nothing. No customer accounts assigned to him.

"Just try to look busy," his boss said with a sigh of disgust.

Which was why Harold had bought the little laser beam attached to a small implement looking like a pen. His new hobby—flash the piercing bright light in the eyes of pedestrians and drivers who dared glance his way. Annoy them, like he was annoyed. Create itsy-bitsy, teensy-tiny havoc. With nobody the wiser.

The service was beautiful, with the organ music playing, the choir singing, the candles lit and glowing, the whimpering and sighing, the funereal atmosphere and Godly phrases. Neither Alison nor Joan wept. Alison would do that later; Joan, perhaps never. Her father had died before the two of them could make their peace.

Mid-way through Peter Schwartzkopf's eulogy, Joan quivered, wavered, and leaned sideways like the Tower of Pisa. Her former husband, Big Jack, sat steady as stone. Like Mount Rushmore's George Washington, Thomas Jefferson, Abraham Lincoln, and Teddy Roosevelt carved from that high natural cliff. Jack leaned close to encircle the shoulders of his long-lost love.

Martha Washington and Betsy Ross nudged each other and smirked. "The fires of love may be banked, but don't tell me they aren't still smoldering," Martha whispered. "Look at Big Jack and Joan—how close they are."

"Ironic," Betsy said. "For two decades, Randy sputters at Joan, trying to get her and Jack back together. Only after Morissey disappears into the forest and then into the jaws of death do we see his dream come true."

"Hush!" squeaked Isabelle, scowling over her shoulder.

Suddenly the side door burst open and up to the pulpit strode a rumpled, disheveled man with long flowing gray hair and beard to match. His big red bulbous nose glowed like Rudolph the Reindeer. The Reverend Rudolph Vicente pushed aside the clergyman and, with big Bible open in one hand, he raised the other in a fist.

"I call for all you sinners to repent!" Rudolph shouted, as Isabelle cringed and Hepzibah stared straight ahead, stony faced and unblinking. "Down on your knees, oh ye sinners. Confess your sins and come unto the Savior. Thus sayeth the Lord your God."

Alison lurched.

Joan and Nicole squeezed hard on the hands of mommy, grandma, Big Jack, and grandpa Jacquot.

Martha Washington and Betsy Ross smirked.

The Governor, Senators, and Congresswoman stared.

Mark Preston (nee Mario Pesci), Rose Washington Lincoln, and Juanita Jorgensen looked from the hell-fire preacher to Mrs. Morissey and back. Carl Crosby didn't look or say anything; he scribbled furiously on a half-rumpled piece of paper, using the back of a hymnbook for support.

The detective neither smiled nor frowned. He knew the Reverend.

Harry the Honorless giggled.

Wilma cried. Her son, Mark, handed her a Kleenex and then turned to wink at Matthew, Mark, Luke, and John.

On the back two rows, across the aisle from one another, sat four black-haired men, all dressed in black; two with white-on-white ties and the other two in black ties on blue shirts. They glared. At nobody in particular.

The double cousins, one and all, gasped.

Colonel Peter and Jeff Vicente rose as one and with no fuss and no muss, calmly reached the pulpit to escort their just-plain-first-cousin-in-law back out the side door from whence he'd heralded.

"Good grief," Ali muttered.

CHAPTER 36

▼

SCATTERING THE REMAINS

The swarthy pair had not yet tried to make another hit on Mrs. Morissey. In fact, they hadn't even followed her for a whole week. The driver had come down with the flu and the passenger with an impacted wisdom tooth. Miserable and mangy, they had holed up in their motel room at the Camelot off Snowy Range Road near the Interstate, calling out for pizza or heating Campbell's Chicken Noodle soup on a hotplate. Home remedies, passed down in their families to their mamas and on to them, was all they had to "doctor" and nurse themselves back to health. Meanwhile, every day they fielded incoming phone calls from Kyrgyzstan to "Get on with it. Or else!"

"I wish something would happen to cancel our assignment," said Flu to Toothache. "Like NATO or the U.S. President declaring war in Eurasia."

Alison still had a tail, though—*The Broad*. Expert at surveillance, the square woman with the short, wiry gray hair and the broad beam frequently changed rental cars, keeping her distance in several of the Chevies she preferred. She didn't go to Cheyenne while Mrs. Morissey was making arrangements for her dead darling. She wouldn't be joining any funeral cortege.

She had trailed Alison to Centennial every day the past week before the woman's husband was killed, hoping that Mrs. M would lead her to her targets. The little lady had appeared disappointed with every trip, which told *The Broad* that what was supposed to happen wasn't happening. Body language suggested somebody was failing to show. Missed connections or purposeful postponement, she supposed. *The Broad* figured that whoever was supposed to meet Mrs. Morissey had something to do with Jerica, and thus with the gang. And thus with the Edwards boys and Lily, her own targets

Which meant—what? That they were hiding in or near Centennial? She saw Morissey's death and the memorial service only from her own perspective—she'd get a couple of days off; before Alison again resumed her vigil of trying to meet somebody out there. She could browse or lounge around town. She chose Bud's Bar down by the tracks as her away-from-home refuge. Couldn't sit in the motel day and night.

Which was where *The Broad* heard about that day's campus conference on conservation and environmentalism. There was nothing significant linking Bud's Bar with tree and furry-creature huggers. With thousands more people in town for this mountain-west gathering, the conferees were probably crowding every bar.

Barely half-interested (and that much only because of her connection to the ecoterrorist Edwards boys), she eavesdropped. Seemed these people were serious, not pseudo-interested out to piggy-back their own revenge on a cause that had long since gone global.

The conventioneers came and went, replaced by more of the same. Somebody suggested that ranchers who felt threatened by the Endangered Species Act would have less to worry about if more money were spent on wildlife protection. Somebody from the Wyoming Game and Fish Department said that recent attempts to list several animals as threatened or endangered meant that soon, "Every square inch of Wyoming will have an endangered species on it."

Listening to the talk made *The Broad's* head spin. Save the trees, protect the critters, keep the waters and air clean. She lit up another cigarette and puffed and exhaled and ignored the scowls from the environmentalists in the small crowded bar. Then she decided to follow them, because, from what she'd overheard, they could be hooking up with her lead, Mrs. Morissey.

*   *   *   *

Many of the people at the church stayed in Cheyenne, including the large contingency hanging around outside. With no hearse, casket, or pallbearers, there wasn't much to see except the exit of the rich and powerful, whose limousines and Mercedes and Rolls and chauffeurs and body guards awaited.

Dollie Domenico caught a glimpse of Harry her Honeylips on the arm (not the reverse) of the Secretary of State. He winked and smirked at the bartender and she stuck out her tongue at him.

If Nasty Three noticed, she was not obviously aware.

Lisa noticed. So did Nasty Two. But since Morton the Miserly was now Nasty's son-in-law, this was one rumor the Family Gossip would not spread.

CNN's Marci and Phillip and a host of other media reps arrived in time to interview bystanders—including Dollie Domenico, who demurred; she'd have enough of Harry Honeylips' wrath on her head for her childish tongue gesture, without having to explain any quotes she gave the press.

This service was, after all, for the dead husband of the President's *Surrogate Mom.* Worthy of a few lines and shots, perhaps at the tail end of stories featuring the President's ongoing tragedy.

Few reporters, other than Marci, knew that Randolph Morissey was not the President's surrogate or foster father. Or that Randy had resisted his wife's semi-adoption of the younger Dominic. Dom's own stepdad, the North Dakota Baptist minister, kept a low profile regarding his famous son.

The President changed his mind. "I want to go, Julia. To the service out past Centennial, at least. Where Ali intends to scatter Randy's remains."

Julia agreed. They left the Park Inn in their big black stretch limousine that Rose Washington Lincoln had earlier located and commandeered and made sure was serviced and secure, ready to take the President and entourage anywhere he wanted or needed to go, at a moment's notice. Already the four small American flags were affixed to the four fenders and they fluttered merrily in the breeze.

They were not alone. Besides Mark Prescott, Rose Washington Lincoln, and Carl Crosby in the limo with the First Couple, the motorcade included Secret Service people mounted on their motorcycles fore and aft. Following this group came the cars filled with government officials and foreign dignitaries and, naturally, all manner of press people, some of whom were caught unawares and nearly missed the parade. Not Marci and Phil, however.. With Marci steering their motorcycle and Phil clutching her from behind, they joined the group leaving the Cheyenne church.

The President's entire entourage sped from the Park Inn onto Interstate 80 and around Laramie to exit on Snowy Range Road. The President said they would pick up the funeral cortege as it came by.

When the environmentalists, conservation people, and tree-and-critter hugger folk heard about the President's motorcade designed to hook up with a funeral cortege coming through town from Cheyenne, a lot of them decided to tag along, too. From Bud's Bar and dozens of other saloons, taverns, lounges, and cafes, the word spread, followed by, "See ya out on Snowy Range Road," or "Catch up with you behind the President and entourage."

Few if anybody knew what was going on, but it sounded like fun.

Back in Cheyenne, the two teams of black-haired, beady-eyed men had left the sanctuary while the two big tall clan men ejected the wild-eyed, loud-mouthed, pulpit-pounding, Bible-beating fellow with the long gray beard and shoulder-length mane of matching hair.

The two black-haired teams didn't know each other and one team didn't care. Yet both sets had emerged from the church simultaneously. Straight into the arms and videocam lenses of the media. While the first pair automatically covered their faces, ducking their heads into suit lapels, the other couple of swarthy-skinned men dodged and raced for their car, a forest green Ford.

Thus it was that the Ford managed to pull in two cars behind the big black stretch limo that carried Alison—and Nicole, Stevie, Joan, Big Jack, Jason Jacquot, Detective Walt Fletcher, and the Schwartzkopfs, Peter and Lisa. Fletcher was there not only because he was Ali's good friend, but also for protection. His own idea.

The other pair of slick-backed black-haired men were delayed and ended up farther back in line driving their late-model, navy-blue Buick Regal. The Buick fell in behind the Giffords, all the double-cousin "boys," and the Nasties, including Harry the Horrid, but ahead of the just-plain-first cousins, including Martha Washington, Betsy Ross, Matthew, Mark, Luke, and John; and Hepzibah and Isabelle, with the still-ranting preacher, Rudoph.

Preceding the cortege on motorcycles and in police cars came a full rank of Wyoming state highway patrol and a few Cheyenne cops, with rookie Bobby Gilbert in the lead. All of these people were joined by a half-dozen Albany County deputies in sheriff department vehicles.

The Cheyenne funeral cortege heading for Centennial, presumably to view Alison scatter Randy's remains, streamed into and through Laramie, exiting off the Interstate on busy Grand Avenue to proceed slowly past the university, through town, and over the viaduct that crosses nine railroad tracks at that point. They took the curving road over the Laramie River and past the Territorial Prison and Park, then back under the same Interstate and out onto Snowy Range Road.

Which was where they picked up the President's motorcade. And the eco-people. And *The Broad*.

It was like a parade. Solemn, sure; a sight to behold, nonetheless.

"A tempest in a teapot," Lisa mumbled. "Oh, pardon me, Sweetie," she corrected herself, with a pat-pat to Alison's wrist.

"No offense taken, Lisa," Ali replied gently. "I couldn't agree more. Who'd have thought it would come to this. All we're going to do is scatter Randy's remains. What's to see?" She felt like boo-hooing, but caught herself by turning to Joan.

"What happened with your search of the Patty Hearst story, dear?"

"You don't want to hear that right now, surely."

"Why not? Take our minds off all this."

So the professor described the articles and books she'd read. How the petite college coed, daughter of the powerful Hearst family, of newspaper and Hearst Mansion fame, had come to be abducted from the apartment she shared with her live-in sweetheart. How she'd been held captive in a closet for fifty-seven days, blindfolded with hands tied; how she'd only been allowed three baths in all that time. The Symbionese Liberation Army terrorists "preached" their revolutionary (read: communistic) propaganda day and night. Patty wasn't brainwashed, it seemed, as some people back then had proposed (and as now other people imagined might have happened to Jerica). It was pure survival instinct that led her to dictate a taped message to the world claiming she'd willingly joined the SLA and, later, in assisting with bank and other robberies. Result? The Hearsts, with all their money and all their powerful friends, could not save the poor lass. After running with the SLA for eighteen months, Patty was caught, tried, and imprisoned.

"Oh, God, no," Alison wailed. "What an awful, terrible story. What if nobody finds Jerica before it's too late? Before her gang pulls off another few capers and meanwhile convinces the world through their claims that she's a willing volunteer?"

"Told you, Mom, that you didn't want to hear the Hearst story."

In Centennial—as in Laramie and before that, Cheyenne—peopled lined the streets to leer and cheer. *The Man* joined the crowd in front of the Old Corral to gawk. The driver of the forest green Ford asked what th'hell they were doing here. "Sticking out like a sore thumb," said his brother from the passenger seat.

"Like a kid bundled up to make a snowman in August," said the driver.

Then he remembered. "Remember our assignment. We gotta take out that Morissey woman, the poor widow lady."

"I know," said the passenger. "Got to do it today, too, or our family will start dying, one by one. Our time's run out."

"Yeah," said the driver. "We better expect the worst. We'll be killed."

"Better us than our whole family tortured, raped, and wiped out."

"I guess," said the driver, slamming on his brakes, for he had nearly hit the Giffords' car in front of them.

"If we're supposed to be guarding Mrs. Morissey," said the passenger in the navy-blue Buick from near the tail end of the parade, "We're sure stuck in the wrong place, way back here."

"Maybe I should pass these pokey cars and move up the line," said the driver.

"Not yet. Cause too much notice," said the Buick's passenger. "The cops would pull us over. Then where'd we be?"

"We shouldn't have joined the motorcade on our cycle," CNN's Marci said to Phillip. "Doesn't look proper. Or we'll be mistaken for Secret Service or cops."

"Speak for yourself. We can zoom on around everybody any time. Now?"

"No, not yet, Phil. Wait and see what happens. If anything."

"I'm glad we're here for the grand finale," Crosby said to Lincoln.

"What do you mean?" Rose said to Carl. The President's secretary glanced sharply at Dom's speechwriter. "You expect we'll run into Jerica up in the mountains?"

"Naw, I just meant scattering the remains."

"This is stupid," Martha Washington said to Betsy Ross. "You know we shouldn't have come. They'll push us to the back and we won't get to see nuthin'."

The Man made a sudden decision. In front of the Old Corral in Centennial, he jumped into his car and set off after the President's limousine and police escort, wedging his way into line ahead of the dozens of other cars wagging the tail. Bystanders, he figured, not realizing there was a nature-lovers conference in Laramie that had attracted the very types of people he had thought to incite over the murdering of trees. They could easily halt or slow down his competition, if not him and his timbering corporation. Of all that, however, he remained oblivious.

Nasty Two stared at her son-in-law. "Really, Harry, did you have to dump a whole bottle of cologne on yourself? What is that stuff?"

"'Brute'," he puffed proudly. "But don't call me Harry. Name's Harold."

"*Dios mio! Que familia!*" Nasturtium One muttered.

"Huh? Speak up, Grandma," the Secretary of State said, ignoring Harry and rolling down the window to release the stench.

In the lead car, Alison momentarily forgot about both Randy's remains and her own grief. It suddenly occurred to her that John was up here in the wilderness somewhere. Since they'd last talked—over the phone when she was lunching at the Old Corral—so much had happened. Randy was killed. Also, prior to the memorial service, Peter with Lisa and Jeff had come up here to check the condition of the Vicente cabin.

Before all that, the bank heist and the video revealing Jerica's participation with the ecoterrorists. Right there on camera, for all to see; Jerica wielding a gun, an automatic submachine, waving it at tellers and bank customers. Alison's own flight with Brad to Rock Springs in the family's Cessna.

Yet John continued to deny that Jerica was involved. In their brief phone contact, he swore to her innocence. Alison, like John, had not for one moment wavered in her loyalty to the Davidsons, even to the daughter she hardly knew, despite her repeated overtures that spring and summer to get close to the girl.

John's word was insufficient. She had to find some clue, a thread that when pulled would unravel this tangle.

Alison scowled, looking sharply out of both sides of the limousine.

"What is it, Mom?" Joan demanded.

"How about a Valium, Gam?" suggested Nicole.

The Schwartzkopfs leaned forward, Lisa recommending a brief nap.

"I don't think so," said Walt Fletcher, accurately reading his old friend. "She's thinking. What is it, Ali?"

Alison ignored everybody but the Colonel. "Peter, when you, Lisa, and Jeff were up at the clan's cabin, did any of you scout the area?"

Peter and Lisa both looked puzzled. "We cleaned," Lisa said. "Jeff 'scouted,' as you called it. Anything in particular you wanted him to look for?"

"Suspicious activity. Strangers, around where they shouldn't be."

"She's hallucinating," Joan said of her mom, as if Alison were no longer present

"She misses Granddad," Nicole proposed.

"I'm not on another planet, girls," said Alison, with a laugh that quickly turned to hysterical giggle. She'd remembered something else. "The Rock Springs bank teller said the blonde stank."

"Huh?" said Joan.

"What in the world?" said Lisa.

"What's that got to do with anything?" said Nicole. To the others she said, "Told you she's hallucinating."

"Shut up, everybody," said Walt. "Go ahead, Ali."

"Jerica never stank in her life. Oh, well, perhaps as a baby with messy diapers."

"Muth-errrr!"

"Gam?"

To Fletcher, Alison said, "I believe the Rock Springs bank robber with the submachine gun was made up to look like Jerica."

He snapped his fingers in sudden awareness. "Of course. A double."

CHAPTER 37

▼

UNRAVELING THE THREAD

Alison had found the thread. And pulled it.

Which didn't do her much good while stuck in the forefront of the funeral cortege. By then they had pulled off the main road for the long climb up the gravel road to the Vicente cabin. Time to collect her wits, think about Randy and the service to come before scattering his remains.

At the end of the long procession, *The Broad* abruptly decided she wasn't about to go crawling at five miles an hour up into the mountains and forest. She pulled past the motorcade to continue, in second gear, on up the steep (but paved) incline. Pulling into a roadside picnic area, she parked, reached for her backpack, and locked the rental car, this one a white Cherokee Jeep. She had everything she needed, and intended to hike through the forest, take a shortcut and catch up with the bunch up ahead.

Back along the line, the navy-blue Buick Regal suddenly pulled out of position to pass everybody.

CNN's Marci pulled out to follow the Buick. "I got a hunch, Phil," she said over her shoulder. "Got your camera? I'll bet we're in for some action."

The lead limousine carrying Alison banged its undercarriage over some big rocks; busted the oil pan. The chauffeur abruptly stopped.

Alison hopped out, Fletcher right behind her.

From his rear-view mirror mounted on the left-front of his motorcycle, Cheyenne rookie Bobby Gilbert spotted the stopped limo. Raising his hand, the whole bunch of cops pulled over.

But not before the pair in the forest green Ford jumped out of their car to stealthily approach Mrs. M from behind.

Sensing though not hearing something wrong, Alison dived, literally throwing herself into the ditch at the side of the road.

Guns out, the Ford's occupants ran after her.

"Duck!" Fletcher yelled to his companions tumbling out of the lead car, just as the men from the Buick opened fire.

Down went the Ford's occupants. Shot dead, or nearly.

Down went everybody else who'd popped out of their cars up and down the line. Save for the President. Juanita Jorgensen held tight to one arm each of the First Couple. She wasn't about to lose another Davidson.

Phil caught it on camera. Armed with portable mike, Marci was ready. She crept up to the moaning man writhing on the ground.

Bobby Gilbert and his fellow officers pulled their guns, their batons, their handcuffs, and, in one young woman's case, the Miranda card.

Back beyond the President, half the cycle-mounted Secret Service people circled the Davidsons' car, facing outwards, while the other half hesitantly stepped forward, trying to decide whether to leave Dom's side to check up front.

Behind the President's entourage, the three-and-a-half dozen cars full of environmentalists and tourists had already pulled over. Their passengers opened their doors, poking heads out windows, yelling and shouting questions.

Mark Prescott (nee, Mario Pesci) whispered to the Cheyenne detective, who barked at Bobby, who yelled at the Buick's occupants, "Halt, in the name of the Law!"

Alison crawled out of the roadside ditch. When she threw herself to the ground, she'd landed on a soft bed of pine needles. So she wasn't hurt. When the shooting ceased, she scooted right back out again. To crawl over to the injured guys to check for life. She discovered one man dead. Hearing the other one groaning, she scooted over to check. Blood bubbled from his lips as he tried to rise and failed. He motioned to Alison to lean down close.

She bent over to catch what might be his last words.

"I'm so sorry, Mrs. Morissey. We didn't really want to kill you."

"I wondered about that. You had plenty of chances."

He sputtered and tugged on the lapel of her lightweight black linen jacket. "No time, no time. Please, Ma'am, tell the Muslims to *let my people go.*" Then he died.

Alison couldn't imagine what he meant by that, but she aimed to find out.

It took awhile to sort out, and hardly anybody would know what had actually transpired, but it did become clear to a select few that the men in the navy-blue Buick were acting on behalf of the President (Mario Pesci, actually) to guard Dom's *Surrogate Mother.* Which is why they were prepared and able to take out the Eurasian assassins assigned to hit Alison.

To the Cheyenne and Laramie cops, to the Albany and Laramie County deputies, and to the President's Secret Service brigade, Detective Walt Fletcher, without implicating Mario and his *brotherhood,* said the shooters were legit. The Buick team were supposed to be on the alert for the Ford pair. They did and they had.

Problem solved.

This one.

The Albany deputies took charge of the bodies. This was their county.

With hardly anybody's curiosity satisfied, everybody hopped back into cars and atop cycles. The procession proceeded. As if there had been no interruption.

Except that Alison had lost her black hat and veil.

When they reached the Vicente cabin and everybody had again clambered out, old Aunty Nasturtium demanded of Alison, "What in the world are you doing with red hair?"

"We're the redheads, not you," Nasty Two reprimanded.

"Good grief," said Nasty Three.

"My word, how inappropriate," muttered Morton.

Seemingly no worse for her harrowing near-miss experience, Alison took charge. She clutched the urn holding Randy's remains. First, she directed Mark to play his guitar to lead them in singing Randy's favorite hymns: *Nearer My God to Thee* and *When we Meet Again in that Sweet Bye and Bye.* Alison even let cousin Rudolph offer the benediction.

Which he did. Except that, droning on and on with his supplications and entreaties, he acted as if he didn't know he was ever supposed to quit.

Nicole and Beth, as usual, timed his performance. They'd even taken bets; under twenty minutes, Beth would win and Nickee would have to write the series of ads and design the commercials for their budding Cheyenne travel agency; over twenty minutes and Nicole would win.

Nickee won.

They might have high-fived each other, but, just then, out from behind the Vicente-Auld family cabin ran a dirty bedraggled blonde yelling "Help me, help me!"

▼

THE CABIN IN THE FOREST

With the environmentalists circling the sincere mourners, the family and the President and his entourage continued to sing. Mark Sanford launched into a series of songs by John Denver, the quintessential nature lover. The quartet of Matthew, Mark, Luke, and John sang in harmony, clearly enunciating the words.

Except for those near Alison, few people saw or heard the President's daughter. Juanita, first to reach Jerica, clasped the shivering blonde to bosom like a lost twin.

"I'm so sorry, Juanita," Jerica sobbed on the shoulder of her Secret Service protector. "You were so right. I needed protection. I was s-so b-bad."

"There, there, Sweety. I still love you."

Behind Jerica stood John Vicente, wringing his hands nervously.

Repentance and make-up time with Juanita over, Jerica clutched John's big hand in one of hers to run toward the First Couple and Alison.

Marci and Phillip got everything on film and sound.

"Oh, Daddy, Mummy, I want you to meet John Vicente, Alison Morissey's cousin. Uh, *double* cousin. John saved my life!" Jerica turned to hug Alison. "Oh, thank you, Mrs. M for sending him to me."

When pressed, she whispered—for her parents' and Alison's ears, only. "He saved me from torture, from rape, and surely from certain death. He pretended to be rough and tough and got the gang to assign him to be my keeper. He kept Bud and Butch off me, and Lily from scratching my eyes out."

Obviously Jerica had much more to say, but by then the media had surrounded the Secret Service, who pressed close, Juanita foremost among them. Reporters from the Fox cable news and from ABC, CBS and NBC intruded with their microphones and camera lenses and newspaper people with their poised pens and notebooks.

The CIA and the ATF, the local city cops and county deputies together managed to shove aside the media. When two FBI agents stepped up with handcuffs to reach for Jerica, Walt joined Alison and Juanita in providing a bulwark.

"No, you don't," Fletcher bellowed. He was off his patch but didn't care.

"Step back, all of you," the President growled in his deep, authoritarian voice. "This is my daughter and we'll deal with questions and statements only after she's had a bath, sustenance, and rest."

Under Fletcher's orders, Bobby Gilbert turned to lead a pack of Albany County deputies back toward and around the Vicente cabin. From whence Jerica had come. Her captors must be nearby, Walt whispered to Alison.

They were. But even dumb Bud wasn't likely to run out in the open to try recapturing Jerica. Bud, Butch, Ellery, and Lily cowered among the trees, trying to creep back to their own cabin, a football-field length farther into the forest above the log cabin built so long ago by great-great-grandmother Rose DuMaurier.

In his earlier scouting—the task that Alison had assigned to him—John's dad, Jeff, had remembered this other cabin and had surveyed and reconnoitered. At the time, however, nobody was home, so he hadn't learned much.

Suddenly there was a burst of fire, followed by wails of sobs and screaming. Coming from the other cabin. Sudden silence. All in seconds.

It's not humanly possible to do everything at once and it wasn't for Ali, either. Everything—meaning yell, run, warn people, grab her gun, aim, and shoot.

But that's nearly what happened.

Alison drew a small, pearl-handled .22 Smith & Wesson from her beaded handbag; nudged Juanita beside her; ran, crouched, and got off a few rounds.

So did Juanita.

A fraction of a minute passed, and Walt pulled the trigger. Right on target. Down went *The Broad*. Before she could shoot her Russian Kalashnikov rifle. This time it was aimed squarely at Jerica.

CHAPTER 39

▼

POSTMORTEM

The First Couple, Alison, and pertinent others gathered in the Presidential Suite at the Park Inn. Randy forgotten for the moment by everybody, it seemed, except for his wife, Alison leaned her head on her hand. She hardly felt like sipping the hot tea Julia Davidson ordered. The group had assembled, Walt Fletcher reminded everybody, for the postmortem.

Jerica had not agreed to crawl out of the Morisseys' bathroom. When she resisted, Callie had whispered that she had a new drink she'd concocted, passing it through the window. "Non-alcoholic," she promised.

Fletcher clarified, for anybody not already in the know: GHB (*liquid ecstasy*) and Rohypnol (*roofie, Roche*) are drugs associated with date rape cases, the detective said. "These two drugs—colorless, odorless, and tasteless—are easily slipped into the drinks of unknowing victims. Because both GHB and Rohypnol cause sedation and produce amnesia, they often prevent a sexual assault victim from identifying and successfully prosecuting the perpetrator."

Apparently Callie had laced her experimental fruity drink with the stuff.

The gang had also used it to keep Jerica sedated long after her capture. And yes, it was Jerica's look-alike, as Alison had concluded while enroute to the cabin, who had played the part of the First Miss in the Rock Springs bank heist. Except that Lily stank. Callie often did, too, but not after she smelled the new arrival from Milwaukee.

It was John Vicente, with his knowledge of chemistry, who kept them from keeping Jerica drugged. He feared for her sanity and her life. Ecstasy, which goes by several names including "X," "Adam" and "MDMA," is both a stimulant and a hallucinogen, Walt said further. People use Ecstasy for energy to keep on dancing and to improve their mood. "However, this drug increases the heart rate and body temperature, sometimes to the point of heart and kidney failure. It also appears to diminish the sense of thirst, and Ecstasy users have died from acute dehydration. Brain-imaging studies have shown that frequent Ecstasy use may damage brain cells that produce serotonin, a natural chemical that is partly responsible for memory and mood."

The happy chemical. Ali chortled, thinking how happy the double cousins often were, even in the face of diversity. "The Clan must be blessed with lots of serotonin."

Through all this account, John and Jerica clung to one another.

"Like two ova in a fallopian tube," Lisa whispered to Alison with a giggle. It was their favorite phrase for describing their own close soul-mate relationship.

"Why bomb Merica Hall, though?" Alison demanded.

Which was what CNN's Marci and the whole world wanted to know.

"That's an easy question to answer," Jerica said, finally able to grin, though unwilling to release John's hand. "Bud was a dodo. He didn't know Hoyt Hall from a hole in the ground. Thought he was in Hoyt when he set the explosive in Merica."

Thanks to *The Broad,* the rest of the ecoterrorists were dead: the Edwards boys', Ellery and Butch; plus Bud and Lily. (Callie had already died, shot in the lobby of the Rock Springs bank.) It was Walt Fletcher's bullet that took out the hit woman. So there was nobody left to interrogate. End of story.

Except for *The Man.* His presence and identity and role behind the scenes continuing unknown, he returned to Milwaukee to find some other way to fight his competition and gain a monopoly in the timbering industry.

With the results of the CIA investigation, the Davidsons and Alison learned more details about her would-be assassins. Originally from Saudi Arabia, these Arabs and all their family had relocated in Kygyzstan. Better climate and job opportunities. Father, brothers, uncles, and cousins all worked in the hydro-electric industry. Life was good.

Until the Muslim fundamentalists captured thirteen members of the family to hold as hostages until the *Job was Done* on Alison Morissey. The brothers in the forest green Ford were determined to do it, though they hated it. Mrs. Morissey was targeted, as suspected, because she had foiled the fundamentalist terrorists' attempt on Magda's life.

When all this was revealed together with Alison's account of the Arab's dying words, "Tell them to *let my people go*," Dom came unwound.

"That's it. I've had enough. While Jerica's been missing, I've nevertheless been very busy—conferring, consulting and debating with my counterparts throughout the world. Also, our people have been gathering intelligence and building a coalition around the planet. No more discussion. It's time to act. We're going to war in Eurasia. First we aim to free the hostages and the beleaguered women, including Magda's husband and the families of these men here, too. Then, along with the United Nations, we'll feed the hungry and help the knowledgeable establish a stable government."

And the press went wild.

CHAPTER 40

▼

DOUBLE COUSINS

Harold Morton sat on one of six saddle-topped stools at the long long bar in the saloon in downtown Cheyenne.

"Dollie," he crowed. "Can you believe who I'm going to be double cousin to? Uh, as soon as they get married."

Had his wife been present, the Secretary of State could have told Harry that the new relationship would only be "double-cousin-once-removed-in-law," but she wasn't there. Nasty Three knew nothing about Dollie Domenico.

"Double cousin to the President's daughter. To everybody!" he said.

Dollie looked up from swabbing the bar with a dirty damp rag. She stared at him in disbelief and horror. "That's what all this was about? You dumped me so you could be a *double cousin?*"

*   *   *   *

"Can you forgive Callie for aiming to kill you?" Alison asked Joan later, at Randy's wake. She didn't want her daughter burdened with a hate package.

"*We may pity, though not pardon thee,*" Joan said. "Shakespeare's *Comedy of Errors*. Enough said? Don't worry about me, Mom."

Alison turned to address the happy couple. "So, when's the wedding?"

"Next spring, when John gets his degree," Jerica said, grinning.

The double cousins cheered.

0-595-28215-6